OUTSIDE

Also by Shalini Boland:

HIDDEN
Marchwood Vampire Series #1

THICKER THAN BLOOD
Marchwood Vampire Series #2

A SHIRTFUL OF FROGS
A ww2 timeslip adventure

Coming January 2013:

THE CLEARING
Outside Series #2

OUTSIDE

a post-apocalyptic novel

Book One
The Outside Series

Shalini Boland

Published by Adrenalin Books

ISBN 978-0-9569985-1-4

For Amara

PROLOGUE

The woman swung the huge armoured vehicle out through the iron gates and turned left onto the poor excuse for a dirt track that ran parallel to the Perimeter. She remembered when Britain was open and free with real roads, pavements even, before all the trouble started.

As she turned, the full glare of the dying evening sun blinded her and she flicked on the windscreen filter. She heard a muffled thud, looked to her left and saw a dark figure lying by the side of the fence. She didn't stop, but glanced in her wing mirror and made brief eye contact with him as he lifted his head.

'A man,' she breathed out. She'd been holding her breath for quite a time and sucked in another lungful of air. She felt a lip-biting pang of concern, realising she must have hit him. But everybody knew you didn't stop for anything outside the Perimeter. *I'm sure he'll be okay.* She reasoned, convinced and then banished her conscience.

'Won't be long now,' she said to herself, looking ahead at the vast tract of wilderness.

CHAPTER ONE

RILEY

Pa is a black marketeer. Nobody and everybody knows this. Pa pays people not to rock the boat. He pays the guards, he pays the neighbours and he even pays his friends. He pays off just about everyone – a litre of whisky here and a bag of sugar there, and in return we live a life of ease and comfort. Pa believes in the carrot approach just as much as the punishing stick. As long as he doesn't draw too much attention to himself from the wrong quarters, we're safe and free.

Pa can get his hands on just about anything from before. If you've got a craving for a pot noodle he can probably magic one up from somewhere. But it'll cost you all you've got and more besides. Pa isn't swayed by threats or tears. He'll hold fast and stare you down and if you can't pay you might get a bullet in your head, or worse.

This morning, my parents are standing together in the doorway of the sitting room. Behind me, the sun floods in through the windows and they edge closer to avoid squinting into the too-bright light.

Their faces are ghost white and Ma's nose and eyes are pink and swollen. She shivers and her teeth chatter as though she's chilled and it isn't the warm July morning it appears to be.

'Riley, can you sit down?' Pa asks.

'Okay,' I say. They're acting weird. It's freaking me out. My legs are heavy wood and I'm not sure I can make the three feet required to reach the sofa.

'Okay,' I repeat. But I don't move. I just keep looking from one to the other and they stare back almost as if they're afraid of me.

'Riley, sit down,' Pa says.

I walk to the sofa and sit in one corner with my hands on my lap. The leather is cool against my legs in the warmth of the room. Fear has travelled up from my stomach to my throat and I can't swallow. I feel sick.

'Riley,' Pa says, running his hands slowly through his hair.

'No!' Ma loses it. She sobs and stumbles towards me. Sits and buries her head in my chestnut curls, rocking me backwards and forwards, moaning and muttering. I can't breathe she's holding me so tight.

'Sweetheart, let go, you're crushing her. Go and lie down upstairs if you want. I'll tell her.' Pa's voice is soft and broken. It doesn't sound a bit like him.

She lets go of me, cups my face in her hands and kisses my face all over. 'No, It's alright, I'm alright,' she says not taking her eyes from my face. 'I'm not leaving my baby.' She leans back, trembling. I press my hands back into my lap and she wraps her arms around herself, still shivering and rocking.

Our house has always been a light and happy place. I don't understand what's going on. My face and pyjama top are wet from Ma's sticky tears. I let my mind wander for a minute, away from the awful strangeness of what's going on and I hear the low background hum of the generators overlaid by the familiar whirr and thrum of a copter hovering overhead.

Has Pa done something wrong? Are we in danger? Do we have to leave the Perimeter? All the most awful things I can think of crowd my brain. And then ... Skye! Why isn't she here? My little sister is usually up before me. I hesitate, not wanting to pose the question. Maybe she's too young for this conversation and they've sent her out of earshot. She won't like that; she'll kick up a real fuss. But then I would have heard them arguing and everything has been quiet this morning; abnormally quiet up until now.

An unwanted thought creeps into my head and I push it out.

'Where's Skye?' My voice sounds high pitched and distant, like my ears need to pop.

Pa comes close and crouches down in front of me. He takes both my hands in his and looks into my eyes.

'Something's happened.' He breaks off. 'We're waiting for ... We're not sure ...'

And then something really horrible happens. My powerful, strong, wonderful Pa starts crying. Proper messy crying where his face twists and his voice is broken. Pa *never* cries.

'Pa ...'

I'm not a typical daddy's girl. I love the bones of him, but I feel easiest around Ma. We always talk make-up, fashion, gossipy stuff and laugh a lot together. Skye belongs to Pa and

Pa definitely belongs to Skye. They're a team. I never feel excluded exactly, but I don't have the same natural connection they do.

'Riley,' he says. 'I don't know how to say this.' He looks over at Ma who's staring at him in horror. 'Skye is ... Skye is. Oh Riley, she ... she's dead.'

I stare down at the patterns on the carpet. I've never noticed just how vivid the individual colours are. The over-all effect is of a soft warmth, but I focus on a particular strand of red that seems almost luminous, as if it's going to jump out of the weave and hit me in the face.

I wake up in my parents' bed. A moment of peace and then everything rushes towards me in a crash of disbelief and pain ... Skye.

Ma lies next to me on top of the quilt, humming in a scary way while she strokes the hair off my face. I must have blacked out, fainted or something after they told me Skye was...

'Ma.' I speak gently, as if talking to a young child, but she carries on humming. 'Ma!' I pull away from her and wrench her hands from my hair. 'What happened to Skye? Where is she? She can't be ...'

'Sh, sh baby,' she croons to me and kisses my forehead.

'Ma, you're scaring me. Are you okay?' I can hear the tremor in my voice.

'Everything will be alright', she says in a strange new childish way. 'Just sleep and it will be okay.'

I throw myself out of bed, run out of the bedroom and almost fall down the stairs to find my father. He's standing in the lounge talking to some of the guards, including Roger Brennan, the Head of Perimeter Security.

Even though we don't really speak to any of them, we know all the guards by name. They've guarded the Talbot Woods Perimeter for the past sixteen- and-a-half years since the fences first went up, just before I was born.

This spring a new guard started - Liam. This thrilled us as we rarely get to see new people. On his first day, his watch stopped and Skye and I sneaked him a new battery out of Pa's supplies. Since then, we've been friends of a sort. We've never properly chatted, but he's about nineteen or twenty and always has a wink and a flirty comment for us which makes us blush and think he's wonderful.

The only other people we see are those who live in the Perimeter and of course the delivery drivers, trades people and the army. Occasionally we get a glimpse through the wire fence at a rare passer-by.

I wait downstairs in a blur of grief and anxiety until the guards finally excuse themselves and leave Pa sitting on the sofa. I desperately need to speak to him to make sense of what he told me. I stupidly start to hope there's some sort of reasonable explanation and Skye will come running in to ask us what we're making such a fuss about.

Pa stands up and holds his arms out to me. I stumble into them and breathe in his comforting smell of diesel oil and cologne. We sit next to each other on the sofa, his arm around me. He kisses my hair and strokes my cheek with his fist.

'You alright?' he asks gruffly.

'No,' I reply.

'No,' he echoes.

'What happened?' I ask in a quiet voice. 'How can she be gone? It's Skye. She's my sister. She can't not be here anymore.'

'I don't know. Luc found her this morning.'

'Luc?'

My sister thinks ... thought seventeen-year-old Luc Donovan was the cat's pyjamas. This summer especially, he's all she talked about. *Luc's so good looking, Luc's so amazing.* She adored him. I always pretend to be disinterested when he's around and I'm sure he thinks I'm a stuck up cow. Pa interrupts my thoughts.

'Luc found her next door, in their poolhouse. It was an accident. She ... she fell through the glass door ...'

'What? That doesn't sound right. How can you fall through a door?'

'I don't know, Riley. But I'm bloody well going to find out. The guards have got Luc in there. I'm going down to get some answers.'

'Skye ...' I say. 'It can't be true.'

Pa stands up. 'I'll be back in a minute. I'm just going to check on your mother.' He walks quickly from the room and I know he's crying again. He doesn't want me to see.

What Pa told me doesn't make any sense. I have to speak to

someone, to find out what happened. Nothing feels real. I haven't even cried. I open our front door and walk down the block paved driveway. Liam, the new guard, is standing outside our house. I hesitate, wanting to know every terrible detail but at the same time I can't bear to find out.

'Liam!' I call out.

He looks across at me with awkward pity and I can tell he'd rather be anywhere else than here with me, Skye's sister.

'Riley, I'm sorry about Skye,' he calls over, not making any move to come towards me. 'I can't be talking to you about this though.'

'But she's my sister. I've got more right to know than you have.' It comes out angrier than I meant.

Liam chews his lip and strides towards me. He takes hold of my arm and leads me back up the drive and around the side of the house. There's a heat haze shimmering up off the ground ... or is it my vision blurring? He takes off his guard's hat and twirls it around nervously in his hands. A grade one buzz cut shows off a nasty scar on his forehead where you can see the stitch marks, but handsome features offset this bullet-proof exterior. I'm pretty sure he's the coolest person I know.

'Okay, I'll tell you what I know,' he says. 'But I don't want to and it's not nice.'

CHAPTER TWO

RILEY

I tense, bracing myself for what Liam is about to tell me.

'There was a struggle of some kind,' he starts.

'A struggle? I thought it was an accident.'

'No. Not an accident.'

I try to process this information. If it wasn't an accident then it must have been ... something else. Something worse.

'A piece of glass from the door went into her throat which is what ... what killed her. So at first it looked like a terrible accident. The thing is, she was also partly strangled. There was some bruising which points towards ...'

His words merge. This is beyond normality. I think I might throw up at this graphic onslaught. Teetering on the edge of hysteria, a scream forms without a voice. My knees go soft.

'Whoaaa, Riley, are you okay?' Liam drops his hat and puts his arm around me. He sets me down on the ground. I lean back against the side wall and he crouches in front of me. 'I'm sorry, I shouldn't've said anything. I'm an idiot.'

'No, Liam,' I croak. 'You're brave to tell me this. Please tell me the rest. I need to know.' No matter how hard it is to hear this horror story I make myself listen to the rest.

'We're holding Luc as the only possible suspect.' He studies my face for a reaction. 'I know it's crazy, Luc's no more a killer than you, but he found her and there are no other suspects.'

'Luc?' I let his words sink in. I can't believe it. No way can Luc be involved in this, he just can't be. 'I knew they were questioning him but he can't be a suspect. What about Eddie and Rita? They won't let you hold him.'

'Actually, Luc's parents employ us, but security is paid for by *everyone* here. We've told the Donovans we won't contact the army till we're sure of what happened.'

'Right.'

'Riley, I feel bad telling you all this, but don't worry about Luc. You just need to think about yourself and your family.'

I nod.

'I've got to go but I don't want to leave you like this. Are you gonna be okay? Shall I help you back inside?'

I shake my head.

'Look,' he continues, his brow creased. 'Please don't tell your father I've told you any of this. He told me not to say anything and I think he was right. I shouldn't have told you, I've made you even more upset.'

'Liam.' I shake my head again. I can barely speak. 'I won't say anything. Go, before you get into trouble. Thanks for telling me. I know that must've been hard.'

'I'm sorry, Riley. I'll see you soon.' He touches my arm, retrieves his hat from the ground and walks away.

I stay sitting on the ground, letting my mind shrink and expand, trying to keep the bloodied images from clawing their way back inside my head. Skye is gone.

I shakily stand up and stagger towards the house. Putting my hand to my throat, I feel pain, like someone is strangling me, choking off the air. How can Luc have anything to do with this horror? It must have been accidental. Luc is always so sensitive to Skye and her feelings. He obviously knows she had a crush on him; well it was plain for everyone to see. But he treated her affectionately like a little sister. Our families have been close since before we were born. I've got to see Luc to hear what he has to say.

The doorbell rings accompanied by rapping on the front door.

'Mr Culpepper, Sir.' The voice belongs to Roger Brennan, Head of Perimeter Security. I open the door and let him in. 'I need to see your parents,' he says.

'Okay,' I mumble.

Ma's still asleep upstairs. Pa gave her something strong to calm her down. I don't want to think about it, I just have to get through each second at a time. I'm in a nightmare that won't be over for a long time yet.

Mr Brennan follows me into the kitchen where Pa's been sitting in silent grief for what seems like hours. Pa stares up at him.

'Okay, Riley,' he says, dismissing me from the room with his eyes.

'No, Pa. I want to stay.'

Mr Brennan looks from me to Pa. Pa slumps his shoulders

and nods in resignation. I sit next to him, drawing my knees up to my chin. He turns to the guard and gestures to another chair. Roger Brennan takes his hat off and sits down.

'There's been a development. We've released Lucas and we've discovered a possible murderer.'

I dig my nails into the tip of my thumb until it hurts. Pa doesn't react.

'We haven't apprehended him yet,' he continues, waiting for us to digest this news.

'Possible murderer,' Pa says the words slowly. 'What does that mean exactly?' Tears start to roll down his cheeks.

'I'm so sorry, Sir.' Roger Brennan suddenly drops his bluff guards' manner. He bows his head for a moment. 'I know this must be hard for you. Shall I go on?'

'Please.'

Mr Brennan squares his shoulders back. 'His name's Ron Chambers. He's an electrician.'

Pa's head snaps up. 'Chambers?'

'Yes, Sir.'

'Didn't he work next door at Eddie's? I'm sure he said he had a man named Chambers working there.'

'Yes, he worked at the Donovan's for a few weeks. It seems he cut a hole in the perimeter fence in their garden.'

'What?' Shadows cross Pa's face. 'How?'

'The hole's hidden from view by the undergrowth and you'd never know it was there unless you looked for it. He must have made it while he worked there and then ... I don't know ...

Maybe he crawled back in late last night, or maybe earlier this morning. We're not sure of the timescales.'

It shocks me to hear how an outsider gained such easy access to our Perimeter. But even more shocking is seeing Pa like this. It scares me, makes the ground shift beneath me.

'I'm gonna kill him,' Pa whispers through clenched teeth, tears still sliding down his cheeks.

'Mr Culpepper, Sir, I can only imagine the horror you're going through, but please know we're doing everything we can.'

'The only thing you need to do is put a bullet in him.'

'A team has gone to apprehend him. Once he's questioned and found guilty, we'll get the army in for the execution or we'll do it ourselves. We won't let him get away with it.'

But he does get away with it.

This afternoon, eight of our Perimeter Guards went to Ron Chambers' apartment at the Charminster Compound. They arrested him and brought him back to the Guards' House, here at Talbot Woods. But he refused to talk.

Pa went down there and tried to gain access to his cell, but Brennan wouldn't let him in. I heard later what happened.

'You're not going to stop me from ripping his head off,' Pa said, furious the guards were keeping him from exercising justice. Pa usually got his own way and it must have driven him crazy to know my sister's murderer sat only a few feet away.

'Sir,' Roger Brennan said. 'Mr Donovan told me to ask you to wait. Told me to tell you you'll get your chance.'

'Wait for what? There's nothing to wait for. I need to finish this now!' Pa was enraged, but the guards held firm.

'Not just yet, Sir. I know how you feel.'

'Bollocks do you know how I feel!'

Roger Brennan spoke calmly. 'The case is too high-profile. If you kill one of Charminster Compound's tradesmen you'll land yourself in a whole heap of trouble.'

'So?'

'Do you want to start a perimeter war? Where would that leave you and your family?'

'My family ...' Pa couldn't finish his sentence. He tried again. 'I won't kill him yet. Just let me in that cell. Just give me five minutes alone with the ...'

'All in good time, Sir. I'm sorry but I have my orders.'

It turns out they should have let Pa in there to do his worst, as later that night Ron Chambers escaped.

How he got out of a locked cell in a highly guarded perimeter is a mystery. Ma's Armoured Vehicle disappeared at the same time and they're assuming Chambers must have stolen it.

Liam was knocked unconscious during the escape but was otherwise unharmed. Pa and Roger Brennan both suspect inside help, and blame is hopping from shoulder to shoulder. It doesn't change anything. It still looks like an almighty cock-up.

No one seems to have a clue who's responsible and why they would want to help the killer of my fourteen–year-old sister.

CHAPTER THREE

Eleanor

Abigail Robbins was princess bitch of the county. Originally from a snooty suburb in North London, she came late to our school, a mainly middle class Gloucestershire comprehensive. When she arrived, we were part way through the summer term of year eight.

The warm morning had been laid up with a dose of double History and everyone sweltered in the airless classroom while Mr Croft droned on and on about the War of the Roses. I was desperately trying to stay awake when the door creaked open and a girl walked in, jolting us all out of our semi-comatose state. She looked like something out of 90210 – perfectly groomed and perfectly cool. Nothing like us imperfect mortals. I heard the collective inward sighs of fifteen adolescent boys.

'I'm Abi Robbins,' she said to Mr Croft, while gazing down at her immaculately shaped nails.

'Yes? Are you lost?'

'No, I'm Abi Robbins. I'm in your class.' She spoke to him slowly as if he was the stupidest man on the planet.

Mr Croft ran his finger down a list in front of him. 'Ah, yes. You're new. You're a bit late.'

She didn't reply, just raised her eyebrows heavenward to

imply he was an idiot. Everyone sniggered and Mr Croft glanced up to see Abigail look innocently and expectantly at him.

'Ah, yes, very good. Yes, if you could find yourself a seat we're talking about the rival houses of Lancaster and York.' His voice faded into the background.

Abigail glanced around the room until her eyes locked with mine. She gave me a conspiratorial smile and shimmied across the room to an empty desk behind me.

When the bell rang for break, she sought me out and linked arms. 'Hi, I'm Abi.' She dazzled a smiled at me.

'I'm Eleanor,' I replied, looking sideways at her. She had almost white blonde hair and was every magazine's version of how a girl should look.

'Hey, Ellie.' She nudged me playfully with her elbow. 'So what d'you normally do in this dump then?'

'Umm ...' I hesitated, taken aback by her familiarity and confidence. 'Those are my friends over there on the wall.' I pointed through the doors to a small group of girls I'd known since we were five.

She stopped walking and turned to observe me. 'You're quite pretty you know,' she said. 'But you should straighten your hair. It's a bit wild.' She laughed.

'Oh, d'you think so?' I twisted a curl self-consciously around my finger. 'Takes ages though, straightening it.'

'But it would *so* be worth it. I could do it for you.'

'Yeah? That'd be great. So, d'you want to come and meet my friends then?' I asked, aware of their eyes on me and Abi.

'Don't take this the wrong way,' she said. 'But you could do so much better than hanging round with *them*. They're probably nice and everything, but they look a bit ... mmm ... sad?'

It was an education, being Abigail's friend. Outrageous, witty and beautiful, she could also be hard work, you might even say, exhausting. She had a gaggle of sycophants and anyone who didn't do the prerequisite amount of forelock-tugging would be on the receiving end of some pretty harsh treatment.

I didn't agree with much of her behaviour, but I didn't disagree with her either and she never questioned my refusal to join in. In some ways I think she admired the way I resisted the group mentality and she never tried any of her bully-girl tactics on me. She knew I would never have stood for it.

From the ages of thirteen we did everything together: girly shopping trips, joint birthday bashes, pyjama parties and endless discussions about music, clothes and, of course, boys. I was fairly confident, but compared to Abi I was a dormouse.

Despite her popularity at school, her perfect stick-thin figure and platinum beauty, I sensed an unhappiness in her. I also had a vague awareness that she was jealous of me. But Abi was the prettier of the two of us and always went out with the best-looking boys, so why should she feel jealous?

I didn't mind. I knew I was attractive enough in my own way, with my dark curls and violet eyes. 'Elizabeth Taylor eyes,' Grandaddy always called them, and I never ran short of admirers. But I was naïve and flattered by her attention. I didn't sense the danger.

CHAPTER FOUR

RILEY

The days loom ahead like tall grey mountains I have to climb. I wake each morning with the same agonising realisation and it takes every ounce of willpower to drag myself out of bed. Ma's mountains must be even taller than mine because she rarely makes it out of bed at all.

On the morning of Skye's funeral I feel a mixture of terror and relief. This is the day I've been dreading, but it'll soon be over. I shower, dress and go downstairs. Pa says little, walking around with red-rimmed eyes and a translucent pallor to his normally healthy bronzed skin.

'Where's Ma?' I ask.

'Where d'you think?'

'She can't still be in bed. It's today. She has to ...'

'I know,' he interrupts. 'We have to wake her up, get her dressed.'

'God.' The thought of dealing with Ma makes the funeral seem like a walk in the park. I force myself back up the stairs and into my parents' bedroom. She's lying curled up under the covers.

'Hi, Ma. Are you okay? You have to get up.'

'I mean, how could I not have known?' she says, without

opening her eyes. 'How could I not have known my fourteen-year-old daughter wasn't upstairs asleep in bed where she should have been? What kind of mother am I?' Her eyes snap open.

'Come on, Ma, you have to get up.' I swoosh back the curtains and open the window, letting a warm summer breeze dilute the stale bedroom air.

'Never mind she was only with Lucas Donovan!' she continues. 'He's a hormonal boy and she's a young girl.'

'It's not your fault, Ma,' I say uselessly, knowing my words won't stop her from berating herself over and over. She keeps ignoring my attempts to reassure her. 'Come on, you really have to get ready. I've put your clothes on the chair.'

'Come on,' Pa echoes, walking into the room. 'We can't let Skye down today. We have to be strong.'

But she goes on and on, repeating the same things. Blaming herself, making Pa and me want to scream. We coax her out of bed and between us manage to get her dressed.

To my relief, Grandma and Grandpa finally arrive by helicopter. Grandma pays extra special attention to me and, although she hugs Ma close and kisses and strokes her hair, I can tell that she's also cross with her for leaving me to fend for myself in my grief. Grandma's appalled at the state Ma is in; by that I mean her drinking. They conduct all their conversations in rising whispers but I can hear them perfectly well.

It's wonderful to have such gentle attention lavished upon me after the barrenness of the past few days and, in amongst my sorrow, I feel safer and calmer. I'm dreading my beloved Grandparents going back home.

Grandpa chides Grandma for being too hard on Ma.

'She's just lost her baby you know,' he reminds.

'Oh darling, I know. I'm so sorry,' cries Grandma and holds Ma close. Ma cries some more and clings onto her parents like they're Skye come back from the dead. Grandpa just stands solidly there, looking very old and very sad.

The funeral service takes place beneath the fruit trees at the bottom of our garden. Close to three hundred people come to mourn and the whole day is slow-moving and surreal. I don't remember much of the service. Only that there were people talking about me as if I wasn't there, which I don't suppose I was really.

In bed I finally weep for Skye. I cry and cry until sleep dries my tears.

The days drag on like stubborn weeds that refuse to be pulled and everything seems fuzzy and disjointed. Even our Collie-cross, Woolly, lies dejected at the back door, with his black nose resting on his paws and his eyes cast downwards.

A few days after the funeral, I answer the front door to see Luc standing there with a carrier bag in his hand and a nervous expression on his face.

'Hi, Riley. How you doing? Stupid question. Can I come in?'

'Course.'

He follows me into the kitchen and sits at the breakfast bar while I make us a cup of tea. We don't say much but it feels comfortable and natural. I put our mugs on the counter top and he passes me the carrier bag.

'What's that?'

'They were Skye's DVDs. She lent them to me a while back. I thought you'd ...'

'S'okay, you keep them,' I say.

'No, no,' he starts to protest and holds them out for me to take.

'Please ... I can't ... I don't want them.'

He realises I mean it and dumps the bag on the floor by his feet.

Luc and I have known each other since forever. Whenever he was at a loose end he would always make time for my little sister. She would bug the hell out of him and he always gave in and paid her some attention. Ma thought Luc was an angel.

He and Skye were constantly laughing and mucking about together but I was never included in their games, or rather, I chose to exclude myself and then found it too hard and undignified to let myself back in. The stupid thing was, I knew they would have had me in their little gang in a heartbeat. But I always felt too nervous. I thought I wouldn't be enough fun, I'd be dull and boring and I wouldn't know how to act around him.

We sit in awkward silence for a minute and then do that hideously embarrassing thing of talking at the same time, apologising and then asking the other person to carry on.

'God, how lame are we,' I say and we smile at each other.

Skye's name hangs in the air between us like a great big

invisible banner. I don't want to say it aloud in case I start to cry, but then I guess Luc doesn't want to bring up the subject either. He's too wary of upsetting me. Eventually the need to find out more overcomes my reticence.

'D'you think you could tell me what happened? When you last saw her.'

Luc looks at me, working out whether or not I'll be able to handle what he has to say. I steel myself and it takes all my strength not to let any tears fall. I know he won't say anything if he sees me getting upset.

'You know she came round the night before ... before she ...'

'Before she died,' I say, shocking myself at the baldness of the words. Luc's eyes bore into mine, assessing the damage, but I stare back, dry-eyed. He judges it safe to go on.

'It was about two in the morning. She could've just rung the doorbell but, typical Skye, she threw some stones at the window to wake me up. She's a nightmare sometimes!' Luc smiles, then sucks in his breath and looks down when he realises he's just used the present tense. I touch his arm to reassure him and prompt him to continue. We both take a sip of tea.

'She always liked to be a bit of a rebel and kind of show off in front of me. But I didn't mind. I think waking me up at two in the morning was her way of telling me she wasn't a little kid anymore, that she was cool. Do you know what I mean?'

I do know what he means. It's just the sort of thing Skye would do. Anything fun and off limits had instant appeal for her. Visiting Luc at two in the morning fell into both these categories.

'She woke me up from a really deep sleep and I wasn't in the mood. I got a bit annoyed. But then she guilt-tripped me with her cute face and sad eyes.'

'I know what that's like.' We flash knowing grins at each other.

'She said she was bored. Bored! At two in the morning! So she persuaded me to come down for a swim. We swam and mucked around for about half an hour. But then it got a bit weird and awkward and it looked like ... it looked like she was going to kiss me.' Luc's face flushes and he raises his eyes to me, embarrassed.

'Well, she did have the most massive crush on you, so I'm not really surprised. What did you do?' I asked.

Skye was so unlike me in that respect. If she wanted something, she just went for it without overthinking things. I'll always envy her that. Life was simple for her. She wore her heart on her sleeve and didn't embarrass easily.

'Well, it kind of dawned on me she wanted something more to happen between us.' Luc looks at me, awkward at having to tell me this. 'To be honest, it scared me. She's only fourteen, she's way too young and anyway I'm not interested in Skye like that. I really like her, she's a laugh and sweet and everything but she's ... she was more like a mate, like a little sister I suppose. I really didn't want to hurt her feelings.'

I listen to it all with a lump in my throat. I can picture Skye getting excited at the thought of telling Luc how she felt.

Believing he would have felt the same way about her. My heart thumps. It's hard to listen to this but I need to know.

'So I panicked,' Luc continues, 'and before she could make any sort of move on me, I told her I was really tired and going to bed and I'd see her the next day.'

He pauses and I can see how hard it is for Luc to talk about this. The memory itself must hurt enough, but telling *me*, Skye's sister, must be doubly bad.

'She looked a bit upset and said 'okay', in a way that meant it obviously wasn't okay. But I was more worried that she was going to tell me she liked me and then I'd have the whole nightmare of trying to let her down gently. I was being a coward.'

'No you weren't. You just didn't want to hurt her feelings. Anyone would have felt the same.' I try to comfort Luc but at the same time I think of Skye and her disappointment, of the fact she'd died with Luc's unspoken rejection in her ears.

'I don't know,' he says, 'and I can't change anything now. I did what I did. I went back to bed. I just left her sitting there on the edge of the pool with her legs dangling in the water. I thought she'd get dried off, get dressed and go home. That was the last time I saw her ... alive.'

Luc drags the back of his hand across his eyes and blinks, not looking at me. He jumps up and paces around his stool before sitting back down. He doesn't elaborate on how he found her body the next day and I don't ask.

'Riley, I am so sorry. You do know this will haunt me for the rest of my life. If I could go back to that night, I would never have left her there.' He's on the edge of tears, but he continues. 'I don't know which is worse – that Chambers could've been lying in wait the whole time we were outside, or that I left her alone while he broke in. You've got to believe me, I *wish* I hadn't left her alone. I know it was just a crush and I could've easily let her down gently instead of running away.'

He's going round in circles now, blaming himself. I do my best to try to reassure him that he couldn't have known and that of course it isn't his fault. But all these conflicting thoughts zigzag across my brain.

Part of me *does* blame Luc. Part of me is actually furious with Luc and furious with Skye. Why on earth did she have to go round there at two in the morning? I wish that Skye had been a little older and I wish that Luc had been attracted to her, because if he had let Skye kiss him, then maybe she would still be alive today.

CHAPTER FIVE

RILEY

It's high summer and the days are long, shimmering and surreal. Pa throws himself into his work. He divides his time between the beach hut areas, where he negotiates hard for his goods, his underground storehouses and Hook Island. He has hundreds of employees on his payroll - from pirates and drug-dealers to little kids running harmless errands.

He's always been a workaholic, but this feels different. He's harder, tougher. A brittle veneer covers his features and you wouldn't want to break through it, for fear that what lies underneath wouldn't survive the exposure and would simply evaporate.

Ma, on the other hand, is disintegrating. She's got no armour; her pain is on show for everyone to see. She blames herself for not keeping a closer eye on us girls and says it's all her fault. Pa keeps getting cross with her and then he relents and comforts her. But mainly he just stays away from home.

Tonight, as I lie in bed unable to sleep, I hear them arguing about the empty bottles. Ma has drunk the place desert-dry. Their bedroom is down the hall from mine and, after opening my bedroom door a fraction, I hear snatches of their voices.

'It's impossible,' Pa says. 'No one could possibly have put

that much alcohol away. You should be dead.' He doesn't sound angry, just incredulous.

'I wish I *was* dead,' she slurs. Then she laughs.

'Stop it. You're really worrying me. You need help.'

I hear her say something else, but I can't make out the words.

'No!' Pa shouts. 'Absolutely not!'

My heart speeds up and a hot flush sweeps across my scalp. Please God, I think, stop them arguing. Please let them be normal. But my prayers aren't answered.

'If you think I'm getting you anymore alcohol, you're mad!' Pa continues. 'What? So you can drink yourself to death. What about Riley? Have you forgotten you've got another daughter?'

I close my bedroom door in fright as a crashing noise rushes down the hall towards me. Ma must've thrown something. I can hear her angry screams. The bass notes of Pa's voice soothe her shrill hysterics and gradually her screams subside.

I stand with my back to my bedroom door, out of breath as though I've been running hard. I hear it all, listening with horrified fascination. Skye has gone, my father is an emotional void and my mother is a drunken mess. Another smash, another shriek, another shout. I have to get out of here.

I don't want to go out in just my t shirt, so I pull on a pair of denim cut offs, tiptoe into the hall and creep down the stairs. I unchain the front door, unlock it and stumble outside into the warm night air. The panic subsides a little and I breathe in deeply through my nose. My world has sunk into an abyss from which I can't imagine ever escaping. Nothing is solid or sure anymore. Life has become a shifting swamp of monsters and nightmares and I want to wake up.

I find myself in Luc's driveway - I've wandered next door. Knowing his parents are still away, I ring the doorbell and wait. After a minute I see the hall light come on and the outline of a person. Normally I would never ring someone's doorbell in the middle of the night - that was Skye's territory. But there's nothing normal about my life anymore.

'Riley?' Luc says through a yawn. 'You okay?'

I shake my head.

'What is it?'

I shake my head again, suddenly overcome with the urge to cry.

'Come in,' he says, concerned.

I don't explain or apologise, but follow him through to the lounge.

'What's up, Riley?' he asks, sitting on a large armchair. 'Did something happen?'

'No,' I squeak, trying desperately not to cry. I sink onto the sofa and chew my nails.

'Do you want to talk about it?' He tries again.

I shake my head and try to get rid of the lump in my throat.

'I just want to do something normal,' I whisper, knowing how ridiculous that sounds after coming here in the middle of the night.

We sit there for a minute in silence. I try to compose myself, not wanting to break down in front of Luc. I hear the ticking of a clock. It sounds as though it's getting louder, but I must be imagining it.

'Wanna play Uno?' Luc asks, standing up and going over to the sideboard. He opens a drawer and pulls out a pack of cards.

'I love Uno,' I say. 'Me and Skye always used to play.'

One hour later and I've managed to get the earlier events of the night down to a background hum in my head.

'How come you always beat me?' I throw my cards onto the floor in disgust.

'Sheer skill,' he replies.

'Cheating I reckon.'

'No, you're just a bad loser,' he smirks.

'God, you're annoying.' I pick up some of my cards and bend them back in an arc, like Pa had taught me, so they flip across into his face.

'Yeah, Riley, very mature.'

I smile. But despite my new-found light-heartedness, I want to talk to Luc about something more serious, something that's been bugging me for a while. We've gotten easy in each other's company and I don't want to spoil it. I also don't want him to think I've lost the plot even more. But I decide to just say it.

'Luc ...'

'Yeah?'

'I want to find Chambers and make him pay for what he did to Skye.'

'I know.'

'No you don't. I really mean I actually want to leave our Perimeter and track him down. He killed my sister and he's out there; somewhere.'

Finding Chambers has now almost become an obsession with me. If I shoot him in the head, will it lessen my pain? If I torture him and extract a confession, will the sadness leave me?

'I do know, Riley,' he says again. 'I want to make Chambers pay too. I can't believe he escaped.'

'So will you help me?'

'It's not that simple. How would we even find him? He's probably fled the country by now.'

'But if he is in England I have to find him. I want to put a gun to his head and I want to pull the trigger. I don't want ... He can't get away with what he's done.'

'Let me think about it, yeah?' He reaches across and touches my arm. 'We should think about it.'

It's a couple of days later and Luc and I have agreed to meet down by the stream at Coy Pond. Woolly trots by my side and I have to hurry him along as he keeps getting distracted by one glorious smell or another.

Luc's the only person I feel at all comfortable with now, but he's been barred from coming to the house. Ma's got it into her head that he's somehow to blame for Skye's death. It's crazy. She's known him almost since he was born. So now I have to visit him in secret, which isn't hard given Ma's oblivious state.

I see Luc every day. His folks aren't due back for another few weeks and he hates being at his place on his own, where it happened. We've been going for walks or talking and playing cards. As far as I know, he doesn't spend any time with his other friends.

Luc's already waiting when we arrive and Woolly bounds ahead to greet him, causing the ducks and moorhens on the bank to take flight or flap and waddle for cover. Luc slides off the high stone wall and almost runs towards me, his eyes shining. I'm always pleased to see him these days but I wonder what's behind his enthusiasm today. He's normally more laid back and I feel good that he's so happy to see me.

'There's been a sighting of Chambers,' he grins. 'They spotted him two weeks ago heading north out of Warminster in your mum's AV.'

'Who? Who spotted him?'

'Two soldiers stopped him for a routine check, but they let him go. Idiots.'

'What! Why did they let him go?'

'I s'pose they didn't know who he was. But when they got back to their base they saw his picture and ID'd him as Skye's killer. The army's out there now searching the area.'

'That's great, Luc,' I interrupt. 'But that was two weeks ago. He could be anywhere by now.'

'I haven't finished,' he says. 'Yesterday, a guard in the West Country thought he saw him.' Luc takes the rucksack from my hand and swings it on to his back. 'Come on let's walk. I thought you'd be pleased.'

We follow the stream.

'I am pleased,' I say, 'but there's no way they'll find him. A guard *thought* he saw him? It might not even be him. The army isn't really interested. We'd have a much better chance of finding him ourselves. We're involved. They're not.' I hear the negative tone in my voice and see Luc's disappointed face. 'But it's better than nothing,' I add. 'Maybe they will catch him.'

We walk in silence for a bit. I don't know what to say. I think I hurt Luc's feelings with my unenthusiastic response. He walks beside me with an unreadable expression on his face and I trawl my brain cells for something positive to say, something that will sound genuine. I'm not a very good liar. After about five minutes of unwanted silence, Luc stops and puts his hand on my bare arm.

'Look, Riley, I completely understand you want to go and find Chambers yourself. Skye was your sister and she was my friend and it's completely crap he escaped justice, but we don't know where he is and, even if we did, how would we get out of the Perimeter? We've got no transport. What would we do even if we did find him?'

I don't reply.

'He's obviously dangerous and he's not going to come back with us willingly. Not to mention what it's actually like out there. I mean, Riley. It's bad. There's no law. It's nothing like it is in here, in our cosy little Perimeter.'

I listen to all his reasonable objections as we walk, and I scuff my flip flops along the broken path that runs by the side of the stream, knowing in my heart that everything he says makes sense. But I feel disappointed and flat. The finality of Skye's death hits me again, like a full stop when there's still so much more to say. So Luc's next words come as a shock, interrupting my resignation:

'Oh, d'you know what? Sod it. Let's give it a go.' He stops walking and turns to face me.

'What? Really? You mean ...'

'Yeah, let's try and find him, if that's what you really want. We can only try can't we? Then at least we can say ...'

But I don't let him finish his sentence.

'Do you really mean it? You'll help me?' Maybe he's just humouring me. Does he think we can actually do this? But when I look into his eyes, I realise he's one hundred percent serious.

We spend the next five days in a frenzy of activity. It's just over a month since we lost Skye and finally I can do something positive. I really feel hopeful that we might find her killer.

Pa must know I spend all my time with Luc, but if he does know he doesn't say anything. Ma is still half mad with grief and I've tuned her out of my day-to-day existence in order to cope with it. When I'm away from her, I don't let myself think about her and what it means for my family's long-term relationship. If I give it more than a few seconds thought, I start to panic and feel sick, so I focus on Luc and on our secret plan.

We've arranged to leave the Perimeter on September 7th - exactly two months after Skye's death.

CHAPTER SIX

Eleanor

When we were sixteen and studying for our mock 'A' Levels, my school's Sixth Form organised one of those American-style prom nights as an end of year bash. Abi and I loved to laugh at the cheesiness of it all, but at the same time we were excited by its possibilities.

It was to be held in three weeks' time, at the end of June. The theme was Sixties Psychedelia and we'd already notched up several hours experimenting with hair straighteners, false eyelashes and powdery pale pink lipstick.

I didn't have my eye on anybody special to go with, but Abi was besotted with a boy called Samuel who lived in the village. We'd first met him and his best friend, Johnny, in a local pub garden.

Nobody made a big deal of the fact we were all under-age. We weren't getting drunk, just hanging out with our friends, drinking half pints of lager and eating salt and vinegar crisps. Taking time out from tedious end-of-year exam revision, we'd taken over two long trestle tables and were planning our forthcoming prom night and our far-off summer holidays.

On the next table sat two eye-catching blokes, one of whom I recognised as the blond tousled-haired, good-looking-but-knew-it, Samuel Bletchley. My parents vaguely knew his family, but I didn't know him to talk to. His friend was less obviously handsome, but had a cool self-assurance, with broad shoulders and dark cropped hair.

I kept catching his eye and looking away. They were laughing together and I knew they were discussing me and my friends. Abi sat opposite me and I told her about the nice view over to my right.

'Don't look over,' I hissed. Of course she leaned right back in her seat and stared directly across at them. I shouldn't have been surprised as this was typical Abi behaviour. I was mortified and pleased all at once.

Samuel got up and walked over to Abi. He cast his eyes over her and asked if she would mind if he and his friend joined us. Abi smiled and gave him the cliché that it's a free country. So they lifted up their table and joined it onto the end of ours, spilling their pints in the process.

'So, you have to say *yes*, when Johnny asks you to the prom,' Abi said, tossing the magazine down onto my bedroom floor. She lay on her stomach on the bed, with her feet on my pillow.

'Ask me to the prom? He's not going to ask me to the prom.'

'Course he is. Sam's going to ask *me*, so *his* best mate will ask *my* best mate.' She gave me one of her cyanide smiles.

Samuel was a player and I guessed it would take more than sixteen-year-old Abigail Robbins to tame him, but she was determined to give it a go. Johnny came from the south coast but was living with Samuel while he studied at university in Bath. Their families went way back.

'Don't let me down, Ellie. It'll be a laugh anyway,' Abi said.

'I suppose so,' I replied. 'It's not like there's anyone else I really like at the moment.'

'Cool. So that's sorted then.'

Things being what they were, two weeks before the event, Johnny and Samuel asked us if we would like to accompany them to the Prom. Abi was ecstatic. I'd never seen her so completely smitten and it was the first time she'd been flustered by anything or anyone.

My parents weren't happy with Johnny's interest in me and, If I'm honest, nor was I. He was five years older than me and I thought he'd expect more than I wanted to give. He was very rich, very intelligent and had just finished his third year at Uni, studying Chemical Engineering. He was handsome, but not in a heart-stopping way, and he seemed nice, but something harder glinted behind his smile.

The only reason my parents didn't forbid me from seeing him, was because he came round to see them, to charm them and reassure them I would be safe in his company. Also, my wise mother knew that if she imposed a ban, it would only make him more attractive to me.

Samuel worked for his father, who owned Bletchley's, a long-established Prestige Car Showroom on the A38. Consequently, Abi and Samuel arrived at the Prom in style, with Samuel behind the wheel of a jaw-droppingly cool Maybach Exelero.

Johnny's ride was far from shabby. He called round to my house in his own Aston Martin - a silver V8 Vantage. Despite my indifference to cars in general, I couldn't help but be seduced by this low-slung beauty.

The evening exuded glamour and sophistication. We'd persuaded the teacher in charge that holding it in the school sports hall would be just too sad, and so they'd hired out a local nightclub for the event.

The four of us sat upstairs on the balcony above the heaving dance floor. Abi and I wore psychedelic mini dresses and zip up boots. And we had poker-straight sixties-style hair. We knew we looked good, but that still didn't help me to relax, as most of the time I felt completely out of my depth conversation-wise.

Samuel shouted above the noise of the music. 'Yeah man, I was completely wasted and I told her to ...' He held his hand in front of his face and mouthed something to Johnny.'

'Sam,' Johnny shook his head, 'you are one sick little puppy.'

Abigail ran her hands up and down Samuel's thigh, while she kissed his neck and nibbled his ear. He virtually ignored her and carried on bragging to Johnny about this girl and that girl, this car and that car. I wouldn't have put up with it, but Abi didn't seem to care. She looked relaxed and happy, gazing adoringly at him all evening.

I think Johnny sensed they weren't quite hitting my wavelength, and he nudged Sam.

'Hey, Sammy, tone it down a bit. I don't think Eleanor and Abi are interested in your list of conquests.'

'Whatever, mate, whatever.'

By this time, I'd already decided I would much rather have spent the evening having a laugh with my friends, than trying to act grown-up around someone I wasn't even really attracted to. As soon as I realised I didn't actually fancy him, I relaxed. And then Johnny just seemed more of a temporary inconvenience than the scary grown man I'd been trying to impress all night.

Before the end of the evening, Sam and Abi disappeared off somewhere. She'd hinted earlier she might sleep with him that night. She'd said you were duty bound to sleep with someone on Prom Night, stressing this in a fake American accent. She said she liked the clichéd kitschness of it.

She'd already lost her virginity a year earlier and, at the time, I had assumed that would be the end of our friendship. We were at different stages. I didn't feel anywhere near ready or inclined to sleep with any of the boys I knew and felt sure she would ditch me for a worldlier friend, or we'd just drift apart, having so much less in common. But she liked this shift in our relationship and enjoyed being the one to tell me what I was missing.

One thing I will say for Johnny - he acted like an absolute gentleman all night. He didn't try to grope me once. Just leaned in for a goodnight kiss when the taxi reached my house. I felt obliged to kiss him back and was surprised to find I enjoyed it. A lot. He pulled away first, which took me aback.

'Goodnight,' I stammered.

He smiled and touched my cheek briefly. 'Night, I'll call you.'

CHAPTER SEVEN

RILEY

I sit in the kitchen and eat my cereal absent-mindedly, thinking about our plan. I'm nervous and excited as I mentally run through the supplies we're taking with us. Ma comes into the kitchen and it takes me a few seconds to work out why she looks different. She's dressed, made-up and, strangest of all, sober.

'Darling, come here and give me a hug.'

I slide off the stool and walk towards her. She smells clean and fresh. She must have had a bath. Relief overtakes me. I kiss her cheek - the first time in a while that I'm actually happy to do so. We hug, but she doesn't cling to me or cry. She holds the backs of my hands and pushes me away from her so she can study me better.

'You look gorgeous!' she exclaims. 'When did you get so grown up? Is that my lip gloss you're wearing? Never mind, it suits you.'

'Hi, Ma, you look good too. We've been worried about you.'

'You're such a good girl, Riley. Strong, like your father.' She sniffs and blinks rapidly. 'Now, darling, I've got something to tell you.' She pauses.

I'm intrigued and wonder what's caused the turnaround in her behaviour. Surely she must have some good news.

'I'm going to stay with Grandma and Grandpa for a while.' She stares at me, waiting for my reaction.

My first thought is, I can't go. I can't leave Luc. We've got important plans. My second thought is, she used the word 'I' and not 'we'.

'What? You're going by yourself?' I ask.

During the last month, I would have absolutely preferred it if she had been at my Grandparents' place. I hated to see her in such a bad way and would rather she be grief-stricken anywhere else but here. But now, seeing her restored to her old self, I don't want her to go. I want her to take care of me. To stay. I want us to try to heal ourselves together.

I hadn't realised how much I've been missing the company of my mother. I haven't just been grieving for Skye, I've been adrift without the reliable everyday closeness of Ma. At this moment I almost want to forget my mission with Luc and try to get back to being a family of sorts.

'Just for a bit, sweetheart. The helicopter's picking me up this afternoon. Pa has arranged it all.'

'This afternoon? But how long will you be away for?' Hurt pricks at me and the word 'abandoned' pops into my head. I feel sick. Although she's been as good as useless to me over the past few weeks, I don't want her to go. The thought terrifies me. I feel like a little child, out of my depth and overwhelmed. I feel hot tears welling behind my eyes, but I also feel a creeping, burning anger that mothers aren't supposed to behave like this. She should be here for me. I need her. But I'm not going to beg.

I breathe back the tears before they can fall, and I set my mouth into a hard line. The anger lodges like a piece of stale bread in my throat. She speaks again.

'Riley, darling, we've all had an unbelievably dreadful time of it. I've been ill and I know I neglected you when you needed me. I'm still not quite right yet so Grandma and Grandpa are going to help me get better and then I can come home and we can start trying to get back to normal again. It won't be for long. Please, my darling, please be strong for a little while longer.'

She sounds like her old self but I can see in her face that these words are costing a lot of effort. She looks tired and old. Her make-up doesn't enhance her features, it just sort of sits on top of them like a mask. The panic and anger leaves my body and I suddenly feel so tired I want to curl up into a ball and sleep for a year.

'Okay.' I don't look at her when I say it.

'You're such a good girl. I'll be back soon, I promise. Now come and give me another hug.'

That afternoon, Pa comes out into the garden and tries to be happy for my benefit but I can tell he's upset by the way he keeps clenching and unclenching his fists and sticking his chin out in an almost defiant way, like a little boy.

It's a stiflingly warm day and the wind from the copter blades does nothing to relieve my hot exhaustion. It whips my sleek, newly straightened hair all around my face and the noise irritates me. Pa speaks and I only catch a few words above the noise.

'Stupid idiots. They put it down too near the roses. They'll be blown to bits.' But whereas a couple of months ago he would have been purple with rage. Today he just murmurs sadly. The fight seems to have escaped from Pa like air from a shrinking balloon. Before all this, I would have laid bets on him roaring and threatening throughout the Perimeter to get Skye's killer recaptured, calling in favours, leaving no stone unturned. But Pa's a broken man.

He carries Ma's cases across the lawn and helps her up into the plush cabin where two guards are already seated. She blows us kisses through her tears and then, just like that, she is gone.

Pa and I watch the copter lift off into the air and bank north westwards. I want to go back into the house. I don't want to watch it disappear into the empty blue sky. But Pa takes my hand and holds it tight. Makes me stay.

'Just you and me now, Riley,' he says, contemplating the silent garden.

In the months after the terror attacks, there were looters on every corner. Violent gun battles were an everyday occurrence between the police and the criminals who were previously denied the opportunity to be this bad.

Those members of the police force who survived the horror realised they were fighting a losing battle, so they threw away their badges, kept their guns and joined the remaining civilians trying to make a new life for themselves.

Vicious gangs patrolled the streets recruiting new members

by force, and prostitution rings sprang up everywhere. Nobody was safe unless in the company of armed guards or privateers. The army was a presence but there weren't enough troops to keep order everywhere.

Luc's and my own parents set up our own Perimeter quickly and efficiently, guessing that things had gone too far for them to recover any time soon. They went from door to door in our neighbourhood, explaining what they planned to do, giving each householder a chance to contribute or move out. Not a particularly friendly approach but, as Pa said, there was no time for niceties. Only a few people left the area. Most stayed and are now indebted to Pa and Eddie Donovan.

So everyone has had to adapt to this new, harsher life. We barricade ourselves away with other decent people and those who can afford it hire professionals to protect them. The roads are rarely used anymore, but they still carry dangers from raiders, hijackers and other equally unpleasant characters. The army patrols half-heartedly, but its number has dropped as army conditions worsen and the lure of guards' pay becomes more enticing.

Now England is among the most shut-off countries in the world. Closed borders, no transportation - only a select few own motor vehicles, as most people can't get hold of enough fuel to run them.

The military spasmodically maintain one main road between each major settlement but most of the old roads are overgrown and crumbling, so you need some serious transportation. Tanks are best, though any AV will usually be up to the job. People reluctantly walk or, if they're lucky, ride a mountain bike or a horse. Most people stay home though, as you risk your life when you venture into public areas.

There are always food shortages and a non-existent health service. We're so far gone we couldn't get back if we tried. Our taken-for-granted civilisation, hard-won over hundreds of years, has crumbled back into dark-age chaos. Sixteen years is a long time; the difference between one life and another.

And it's onto these roads we are soon to go. We need to be fully prepared for anything we might encounter. Weapons are a top priority. We've managed to get hold of three machine guns, a couple of revolvers, ammunition and two serious-looking hunting knives. The rest of our packing list looks like this:

4 lighters
2 large boxes of matches
2 torches
6 candles
4 blankets
A length of rope
A ball of twine
Spare clothing
Water purifying tablets
Basic medical supply kit
48 litres drinking water
Food

100 gold coins

350 silver bits

2000 cigarettes to trade

1 crate whisky to trade

30 bars Swiss chocolate (way past its sell-by-date) to trade and to eat

It's been surprisingly easy to plan our journey and hide the supplies. I'm ashamed to say I stole most of it from Pa's underground stores. But I've told him what I did in my note, so none of his workers will get into trouble for the theft.

It's our good fortune and Pa's shady activities that's given us such easy access to supplies. We're definitely among the luckiest in the world when it comes to standards of living and we've got some pretty strong currency in the form of Pa's illicit goods.

We plan to borrow Luc's mother's all-terrain AV which is state-of-the-art and custom-built for maximum comfort and security. It's fitted with full-coverage exterior shock-plates, transparent armour multi-layered glass with blackout mode and run-on-flat tyres. It's also got a hidden compartment beneath the passenger-side footwell, large enough to take a gun and some emergency provisions.

Three days to go and the tension is unbearable.

CHAPTER EIGHT

RILEY

The AV's engine sounds obscenely loud in the quiet of the morning. I'm sure any minute now we'll hear raised voices and see Pa running up the Donovans' driveway in confusion and rage. But apart from the engine noise, I hear nothing.

Chilly and damp, I've got that half-asleep, grubby, early morning feeling. My eyes itch and the skin on my face feels raw and prickly. I wish the heater would hurry up and kick in. I forced myself to eat some breakfast before leaving the house and I can feel it now, sitting in my throat and chest – hard, undigested lumps of cereal.

But we're finally doing this and despite my nerves I'm excited that today has finally arrived.

Luc crunches the gears and the AV glides down the driveway and out onto the tarmac road. There isn't a soul around. A skinny brown fox trots along the pavement and makes a left into Mrs Hannigan's garden. A faint light glows on the blue black horizon behind the avenue of trees but the stars are still glimmering, bright and winking in the not-quite-morning sky. Dawn has all but broken and the translucent moon is fading.

We turn off our familiar road and onto Elgin Avenue. Luc turns to me and grins his cheeky grin.

'Okay, Riley, time to duck down.'

I crouch on the floor in front of my recently vacated passenger seat and pull a blanket over my head. It's very spacious really, not like a regular car. Luc grabs the holdall from the back and places it on the passenger seat, so it part rests on top of my crouched body. This way, no one will be able to see me if they peer into the vehicle.

'You okay?' he asks with a smile in his voice.

'Mmm hm.'

I feel the AV turn and guess we must now be on Glenferness and heading for the gates. I feel us go slowly over the bridge.

'You sure you're alright?' he asks again.

'Yep, I'm fine. Good luck.'

'Thanks,' he replies. 'You'd better not speak anymore until we're clear of the gates.'

'Okay.'

'Okay,' he repeats quietly.

The vehicle slows and I guess we've reached the Perimeter gates. We come to a steady stop and I hear the electric window go down and the engine switch off. The birds are making an almighty racket. Not being a very morning person, I'm never awake to hear the dawn chorus, but they're giving us a rousing send-off today.

'Morning.' Luc greets one of the guards.

'Alright, mate.' I recognise Liam's voice. 'I'm on with Duke this morning. He's just brewing up.' Then he lowers his voice. 'You sure about this?'

'Yeah, we're all set.'

We let Liam in on our plan a couple of days ago. We needed him to pretend to receive a message from Luc's parents, asking for their son to join them in Southampton. We also thought he should know what we're really doing and where we're headed, just in case we meet trouble along the way.

Our plan is to head for the Century Barracks in Warminster where Chambers was last sighted. Once we get there, we'll gather as much information as we can and try to track him across to the West Country. My grandparents live over in those parts, so we'll end our journey with them rather than turning back to Bournemouth.

Ma's at my grandparents' house and I realised I'd much rather face her tears than face Pa's anger when we finally end our journey. I've never been to their house before but Luc's done a lot of travelling with his parents and knows the way. So our plan is to end up at their place once we find Ron Chambers.

We know anything is liable to change once we get moving. New information could come to light at any time or we might run into any amount of unforeseen danger. So Liam has agreed to alert our parents and the guards to our plan if we don't reach my grandparents' house by the end of the month.

He was against the idea at first, fearing for our safety and for his position. But Luc swore to guarantee his job. I also think he feels guilty that he was one of the guards on duty at the time of Chambers' escape, and so he's agreed to keep our secret.

'Okay, I'll get the gates,' Liam says. 'Good luck.' Then he

shouts, 'Mr Duke! It's Luc. Shall I open the gates?'

'Hold on!' Something clatters loudly to the floor and I hear the out-of-breath guard come marching out. 'Morning, Lucas, you're up nice and early.' Charlie Duke's rich Dorset accent fills the morning air and I picture his ruddy face.

He's never ever said more than two words at a time to me, (I think all the guards are too wary of Pa to speak to us) although he always seems cheerful, with blue eyes that disappear into his face when he smiles. He looks how I would imagine a farmer to be - thickset with apple red cheeks and huge square hands.

'Hi, Mr Duke,' replies Luc. 'I want to try to reach Southampton before nightfall, so I'm leaving earlier than scheduled.'

'No problem. I just wanted to warn you there was a bit of rioting outside Ringwood last night. Maybe you should postpone your trip for a couple of days till it blows over.'

'I'll be fine,' Luc says. 'I'll stay clear of Ringwood.'

'I don't think your parents would be too happy with you travelling into that sort of hazard. I'm surprised they haven't assigned a guard to go with you anyway. No offence, I know you're quite capable, but it's always better to travel outside with at least two people in case ...'

Luc interrupts. 'Thanks, but I'll be safe in the AV and I'm armed. They wouldn't have let me do the journey if they were worried.'

'Right you are, Lucas. Well, safe trip now. Send my best to your parents. I'll get the gates.'

'Thanks, Mr Duke. See you, Liam.'

The engine starts and the window whirrs up. After some creaking which lasts about twenty seconds, followed by a loud thunk, we start moving and I feel the transition from smooth road surface to rough, uneven ground.

The AV's got good suspension, but crouched down here on the floor I wonder how we'll be able to stand it – our bones being jolted and our teeth rattling in our heads. Hopefully it'll be less bumpy once I can sit down properly. Luc said we'd only have to cross rough terrain until we reach the main road. I shift my position.

'Just stay hidden for a bit longer,' says Luc. 'I can still see them in my rear view and I don't want to switch to blackout in case Duke gets suspicious.'

'It's okay, I wasn't coming out yet,' I mumble. 'Just trying to get comfy. It's bumpy.'

'I know. I'll slow down a bit.'

'No, it's okay. I'm alright. Maybe just move the bag off my head.'

'Are you sure? I thought a bag-on-the-head was quite a good look for you.'

'Ha ha.' I feel its weight disappear. 'Ah, that's better.' He whips the blanket off next.

'You don't need that now either.' He smiles down at me.

My face must be bright red, my hair plastered all round it in unattractive clumps. My knees are clicking and my left foot's got cramp. God, only several minutes into our journey and I'm already completely inadequate. I've got major butterflies but despite that, our adventure still seems quite abstract and distant. Not enough to make me feel fully afraid yet. I hope it'll stay that way and I'll face whatever's out here with calm dignity and poise and not panic like an idiot.

I peer up at Luc while he concentrates on driving. He seems calm and unfazed. No way on earth could I have done this without him; I don't have the balls or the connections. I may have come up with the idea, but Luc's making it happen.

Thinking of Skye gives me a shot of courage. No matter how scared I feel about everything, I know I have to do this for her. She was my little sister and she deserves justice.

CHAPTER NINE

Eleanor

I met Connor through my brother Tom, a bit of a peace-and-lentils hippy. Always on a march or a sit-in, Tom was the youngest of my three elder brothers and we were really close. He was a long-haired, unshaven darling and I loved him to bits. He always brought waifs and strays home, to the secret delight of Mum, who loved having a houseful of interesting people and the annoyance of Dad, who preferred the quiet life.

But even Dad liked Connor, who was unobtrusive, polite and infinitely helpful. Mum always joked she'd like to trade one of her lazy sons for hard-working Connor.

I'd been seeing Johnny for about a month, when Tom brought Connor home to stay for a few weeks and it was love at first sight. I got crazy butterflies every time he came near. His lazy gentle voice with its soft northern inflection made me swoon and he smelt like heaven.

'You know you're always welcome to our guest bedroom, Connor,' Mum said.

'Thanks, Mrs Russell. But I'm okay sleeping in my bus. I guess it's like my home. If I could park on your drive though?'

'Of course you can. That's no trouble.'

He'd restored the two-tone red and cream VW camper van

himself, and Dad thought it was amazing. He kept hinting to Mum that he'd like to do a restoration job on a vintage car, but mum wasn't having any of it.

'I don't think so.' She spread out her hands in mock-horror. 'We've got enough restoration jobs to do on this vintage house, before we progress on to cars.'

Dad reluctantly agreed, but could often be found on the driveway, mooning after the beautifully restored camper van.

It was a semi-warm late July Sunday afternoon. One of those days where it's scorching hot until the sun goes behind a cloud and then you feel like you need your thermal underwear. Connor had been with us for a week now, and we'd just demolished one of Mum's huge roast dinners. It was a rare occasion where we all happened to be home at the same time - Mum, Dad, Oliver, David, Tom and me - a big family affair with Connor as the guest of honour.

Tom was a strict vegetarian, but Connor had no problem helping us to devour the two huge roast chickens. I regretted the second helping of apple pie and custard I'd thought was such a good idea at the time and decided to get some air in the garden while everyone else watched boring Sunday afternoon sports on TV. I walked around for a bit and then flopped on the rug with my book.

Moments later, Connor appeared and lay down beside me. My heart rate doubled at his close proximity.

'What've you got planned for the rest of the day?' he asked, rolling onto his back and staring up the sky.

'Not a lot. Going out later for a drink at The Crown.'

'Am I invited?'

'I um, I can't tonight,' I stammered. I was supposed to be going there with Johnny to meet Abi and Sam, and how would it look if I showed up with Connor.

I had never dared to hope Connor would be interested in me. I had no option now, but to end things with Johnny. He just didn't compare with this god lying next to me.

'How about Monday?' I said without thinking.

'Great,' he replied and got up. He went back into the house, leaving me lying there in a fizz of emotion.

That night, I got ready for my night out with Johnny. I was dreading it, knowing I'd have to finish things with him. I hoped I wouldn't bottle out, but the image of Connor kept floating around in my brain, so I gritted my teeth and prepared myself for an awful evening. I didn't want to make myself look too nice, but at the same time, I didn't want Johnny to think I hadn't even bothered. I ended up settling on a long summer dress that had never really suited me.

We were supposed to be going to the pub to meet Abi and Samuel and I planned to speak to him on our way back home. But when Johnny came to pick me up, he told me he had two tickets for a photography exhibition at the Arnolfini in Bristol. Ordinarily I would have loved to have gone, but when he told me, my heart sank. I knew I had a long evening ahead of me.

Sure enough, when we got there, I couldn't focus on anything. I just kept thinking about what I should say and how

I should say it.

We had a pizza afterwards and I could barely eat. I just wanted the night to be over. Johnny kept asking me what was wrong. I felt like such a cow. I realised I should probably have told him before we went out and spared us both the misery and the expense. He hadn't even let me pay for anything, which made me feel doubly bad.

Finally we walked back to the car park, Johnny with his arm around me. The silence in the car pulsated with awkwardness. About halfway home, Johnny finally spoke.

'What is it, Ellie? You've been quiet all evening. Are you feeling okay? Have I done something wrong?'

'No, no nothing.' I paused. 'Johnny, I'm really sorry but I can't see you anymore.' The words sounded worse out loud than they had in my head.

He didn't answer and I didn't dare look at him. I had my head down and started to feel car sick. We'd only met for about six dates in all, and they'd nearly all been with Abi and Samuel in tow, so I hadn't imagined he would be too upset. Maybe just a bit of hurt pride. But even so, it still wasn't a very nice thing to do. Over the past four weeks, we'd kissed a lot but I hadn't felt willing to do much else and he hadn't pushed it, to my intense relief.

After a couple of minutes, Johnny spoke: 'Is there anything I can say or do to make you change your mind?'

Oh no. 'Johnny, I really like you, but I've met someone else. Nothing's happened,' I hastily added. 'I wouldn't see someone else behind your back.' That sounded terrible. I racked my brain for something better to say, but I couldn't. I knew I wasn't technically seeing Connor, but I didn't want to complicate things and I knew Johnny would find out sooner or later anyway. I sneaked a glance at him. He looked really gutted and didn't say a word until he dropped me at my house.

'I really liked you, Eleanor. I think we could have been good together.'

I couldn't look him in the eye.

'Let me know if you change your mind.'

I was quite impressed he hadn't asked me who I'd ditched him for and I felt an unexpected tug of disappointment that I wouldn't be seeing him again.

'I'm sorry,' I replied inadequately, and went into the house feeling really down.

Finally, Monday evening rolled around. I'd taken ages to get ready, even though I'd decided to dress down. Connor struck me as a jeans-and-t-shirt kind of boy and I guessed he wouldn't be too into girls who wore tons of makeup. But it still took time to get the no-make-up look just perfect.

Connor took me to a pub on the banks of The River Severn. The warm evening breeze whispered across my skin, heightening my nervousness.

'D'you want to get a table?' he asked. 'I'll get the drinks.'

I made my way across the lawn of the pretty pub garden which sloped down onto the rippling water. It was busy, but I managed to get a table quite close to the river. I stared out across to the hills on the other side, not quite believing that Connor actually wanted to spend time with me. I hoped I wouldn't embarrass myself by talking rubbish.

Ten minutes later, he put the drinks on the table, smiled and sat down opposite me. I couldn't believe how gorgeous he was.

'Abi's not very happy with me,' I said.

'No?'

'No. I was supposed to be going out with her tonight. I feel a bit bad.'

'Oh well, I'm sure she'll cope.'

'I don't think so. You don't know her very well. She'll sulk for a week.' I felt a bit disloyal talking about my friend like this. Connor reached across the table and ran his finger lazily up and down my forearm, making me draw in my breath.

'You shouldn't worry so much about what she thinks.'

'I don't! It's just ... well, you don't know her properly.' I pulled my arms back to my sides, instantly regretting it.

'Okay, okay,' he smiled, holding his hands up in surrender. 'Just an observation. No need to be defensive.'

'I'm not.' Then I smiled back, despite myself. He was so-o good-looking.

I loved his too-pale features which contrasted with almost black hair and dark eyes. His build was slim and lithe and he had the laid-back, easy-grace of an indie rock god. His cool confidence made me nervous, but it was irresistible.

When I'd told Abi how I felt about Connor, she'd turned up

her nose.

'What about Johnny?' she'd said. 'He's the real catch. Connor's just a baby and he's too skinny.'

'He's not skinny! He's athletic. And he's three years older than us.'

'Still a baby in *boy* years. You're mad. Johnny's such a babe - intelligent, rich and completely into you. He's staying on this summer because of you, you know.'

'No he isn't, he's got a work placement down here. I can't help who I'm attracted to can I? And Johnny's sweet, but he's not really my type. Connor's sexy and cool.'

'Well Johnny'll be devastated, and what about us? We were all supposed to go away together next half-term. You're ruining our social life.'

Abi was really annoyed. She knew her grip on Samuel was loosening and now I'd ended it with Johnny she worried Sam would completely lose interest in her. Abi was always used to having the upper hand in her relationships.

The other black mark she had against Connor was that he hadn't been won over by her charms, which she'd turned on to maximum effect. She'd given him the full Abi treatment and it was like watching a master at work. But to my surprise (and intense relief) Connor hadn't bought into her act at all. She actually irritated him and she knew it. This didn't go down well with her at all. It made things tricky though, as it meant she wasn't prepared to listen to me raving about him and so I had to walk a long tightrope between the two of them.

CHAPTER TEN

RILEY

As soon as the Perimeter becomes a distant blur behind us, Luc gives me the all clear to come out from my hiding place. I unfold my body and slide back into the passenger seat. The heater's warm air is now exchanged for a refreshing blast from the air conditioning. It may be September but now the sun's up, it's as hot as midsummer outside.

I take in the unfamiliar scenery - uneven scrubland, deserted shanties and packs of skinny, mangy dogs, lying in shady spots, their pink tongues lolling. The openness of everything unsettles me. I feel like an insignificant gnat about to be swallowed up by the vast landscape and I realise how much confidence and security the Perimeter provides. The genteel fuzzyfelt lawns, immaculate houses and straight roads of our everyday enclosed world that keep me safe.

It's just over four miles from our Talbot Woods Perimeter to the Wessex Way, a sporadically-maintained road that will take us up to Ringwood and then on to Warminster. But we're currently travelling on rough terrain. The Wessex Way used to stretch right into the heart of Bournemouth, but as the years go by, the army is less-and-less inclined to bother with its upkeep. Consequently, the road has shrunk as nature wins the battle.

The AV is well-equipped to deal with the scrub and overgrown woodland, but our progress is still snail-like. Rabbits bound and zigzag across our path with more speed than we're able to muster. I look across at Luc with what must be a doubtful expression on my face, because he laughs.

'Don't worry,' he says. 'We'll pick up some speed once we hit the Wessex Way. It's mind-blowing out here, isn't it?'

'Amazing,' I reply, too wired to really enjoy the surroundings. A million thoughts and worries flash through my mind. 'Do you think the riots are still going on at Ringwood?' I ask.

'I don't know. I've been worrying about that. If I knew a safer route I'd take it but I don't know any other way. We don't have to go directly through the Perimeter, so we should avoid any trouble. And we're safe enough in here. I'm sure it'll be fine as long as we're not there at night.'

We bump along across vast tracts of heather and gorse scrub and negotiate our way around dark stands of conifers. I'm riveted by the dramatic shape of a wind-blown pine - stunted and hunched as if frozen in fear.

Old bomb craters, reclaimed by nature, now blend into their natural surroundings as mossy banked dips and marshy pools. In less than two decades, the landscape has more-or-less reverted back to its natural state, most of it now scrub and overgrown woodland.

All the buildings making up the various Bournemouth conurbations have long since been destroyed; the remaining rubble and debris removed by scavengers either to sell on or re-build elsewhere. Somewhere safer and less desolate. Not a single brick remains.

It's an ancient wilderness with only the odd violent nod towards civilisation - the shell of a burnt-out car, an upturned bus, a frayed rope hanging from a tree with a pile of bleached bones beneath it. I feel exposed and vulnerable, glad for the daylight. I don't want to think about what it will feel like later, in the darkness.

A lone horseman materialises from nowhere. He gallops past, about two hundred yards from our AV. His head's down low and his bay horse is slick with sweat. As he passes, he turns to look at us but Luc activates the blackout mode, so all he'll see is his blurred reflection in our windows. He has a young face. He thunders off in the direction from where we've just come.

'A messenger,' says Luc.

There are no telecommunications these days. We're privileged to have access to the Donovans' radio communication system which links up the guards' houses across the country but this sort of device is rare. Most people rely on the army for news, or the travelling horsemen who earn great sums to deliver mail to loved ones around the country and to pass on important messages.

I think about the dangers these riders face. They're armed, but have nothing like the security we enjoy in our AV. And they're prime targets, for who knows what important information or goods they might be carrying.

After forty minutes or so, the huge walled Charminster Compound looms ahead, sitting incongruously in the barren countryside. The outside wall must measure about twenty five feet high. Topped with razor wire, it's a mish-mash of different bricks, some parts rendered and some parts exposed. It looks like a strange medieval town. A wide deep ditch runs around the outside and a sloping metal ramp at the entrance lies across the ditch, passing under two steel gates that have just swung open.

A convoy of metallic grey armoured buses crawls out of the compound, the sunlight glinting off their roofs. They're the same as those that deliver the workers to the Perimeter and, sure enough, I recognise some of the faces behind the windows. Not all of the buses head in the direction of our Perimeter though and I wonder where the others are going.

'The road we want is a couple of miles past the other side of the compound,' says Luc.

I stare, open-mouthed at the huge circular structure, awed by its size. I never imagined it to be so enormous. I always assumed our Perimeter was much bigger than the Compound. But I see now it's the other way around. I can't conceive of the number of people who must live behind its walls. What do they all do?

'Have you ever been in there?' I ask.

'A few times, but not on business. They use their own guards. Your Pa goes there a lot though.'

I can't imagine Pa doing business there. I always picture him visiting a much smaller, less-intimidating compound where everyone treats him like royalty. But even my impressive Pa would get swallowed up in such a big space.

We carry on, driving around the outside walls towards the road. As we get further away from the main gates, we see hundreds of flimsy cardboard, cloth and corrugated metal huts all around the wall's base - makeshift houses. They seem alright in this weather, but what happens when it rains? What about the winter months? People have cordoned off small rectangles of land to grow produce. Donkeys, ponies, goats and dogs are tethered to wooden posts. Children of all ages run around barefoot and dirty. Chickens scratch about in small wire pens.

Gypsy-looking men and women sit around on the baked mud earth, cooking whole skinned rabbits and unappetising black flatbread over open fires. They've nearly all got shotguns or more primitive weapons on their laps, even the children. Some of the people are horribly maimed with limbs or eyes missing. A lot of the adults have terrible scarring on their faces – a legacy of the bombings before I was born. Hardly anyone pays attention to our blacked-out AV. One or two people glance up with disdain on their faces. No one tries to approach us.

Ron Chambers used to live in this towering compound. I wonder what his house is like. Does he have any friends inside these walls? Suddenly I know it's vital we go and see where he lived. I need to go inside and see if it sheds any light on his whereabouts. I can't believe our plans haven't included a visit to his old place. I know the guards and the army checked it out and found nothing, but now I decide I have to see it for myself.

'Going in there won't help us to find him,' Luc says. 'I promise you the guards will have turned his place inside out. If we go in, someone'll recognise us and we could get sent back to the Perimeter.'

'I'll wear your baseball cap and you can just keep your head down. We'll be fine.'

'There's no point, Riley. He won't have left a map with an X marking his destination.'

'Please. I really think we need to. Somebody might know where he's gone. Aren't you curious?'

I know Luc's being rational and thinking of our safety, but he eventually capitulates and turns the AV around. We drive over the noisy metal ramp up to the now firmly closed main gates.

Our first destination was supposed to be the Century Barracks at Warminster. Luc's parents know the soldiers there and Luc's sure they'll offer us hospitality. We're going to try to find the two soldiers who saw Chambers and get as much information from them as we can. Then we'll head across to the West Country, stopping at perimeters and compounds, asking people if they've seen a man of his description.

Luc's got a copy of the circulated picture of Chambers so we'll show it to people we meet in the hope they recognise him. But Luc and I both agree that he'd probably have cut his hair and shaved his beard by now, which will make finding him that much harder.

I realise Luc's speaking to me again, asking me if he should beep the horn to attract someone's attention. Before I have time to answer, a small metal door opens and a guard carrying a machine gun walks up to Luc's window and knocks on the glass. Luc buzzes his window down. As he does so, we get a blast of uncomfortable heat, unexpected after the cool of the air-conditioning. But worse than the heat is an awful stomach-churning rotting smell. I almost gag. It must come from the compound itself, or from the people who dwell outside in its shadow. Luc doesn't flinch, but palms the guard a couple of silver bits.

'We're here to barter,' Luc tells the guard.

'You'll have to leave the vehicle here, Sir.'

'Can I leave it inside the walls?'

'No.'

'We'll only be about an hour,' says Luc, passing him another couple of bits.

'Wait here.' He goes back inside and one of the gates creaks open. Another guard signals to us to park within the compound in a parking space off to the left.

Although we're now inside the gates, we're still outside the main walls. We've stopped in what appears to be a vast entrance area, a parking lot. I assume the other huge set of gates opens up to the main town. Luc locks the AV and we look around to see where we should go.

'What's that gross smell?' I ask.

'Shh. Most places outside our Perimeter smell like this. It's how people live. In squalor mainly.'

I get that feeling of inadequacy again. There are so many things about this trip I'm not prepared for. I half-wish I hadn't suggested coming in here now. The smell of the place makes me think I've seen enough and the rows and rows of vehicles are a strange sight, making me feel dizzy. But I can't change my mind after making such a fuss to come here in the first place.

We don't see either of the guards, so we thread our way through the cars towards the other set of gates. Most of the parked vehicles are little more than rusted heaps that don't look as if they'll be going anywhere ever again.

Luc holds out his hand and I take it, feeling self-conscious. His skin is cool and firm. As well as the massive gates, there are also several small entrances up ahead with uniformed guards stationed at each one, but strangely all I can think about is the feel of my hand in Luc's.

'I think this is going to be an expensive visit,' he says, drawing half-a- dozen silver bits from his pocket to grease more palms.

Finally we're in.

CHAPTER ELEVEN

RILEY

Once inside, the stench triples in awfulness and the place looks like nothing I've ever seen. The Compound's inner entrance doors open up onto a long street, lined with busy shops and eateries. Above these, precarious-looking flats jut out all higgledy piggledy in various styles. No cars clog the roads, just pedestrians, horses and an imaginative array of non-motorised vehicles: push bikes with home-made trailers, wooden carts, covered wagons and people-powered rickshaws.

In front of the cosmopolitan shop facades, a vibrant street market is in full flow, packed with stall holders and shoppers. I don't think I can recall ever seeing so much activity and so many people together in one place. I feel a little overwhelmed and have to stop to take several deep breaths.

'You okay?' Luc asks, as I tug on his hand for him to stop.

'I just need a few seconds.'

'Here, sit down and put your head between your knees for a minute.' He guides me over to the side of the road, behind a cake stall and squats down, patting the ground next to him. I sit and take a few swigs of water. After a minute or two, I feel slightly less giddy.

I realise Luc has his arm around my shoulders. It feels good.

Reassuring. Eventually, I compose myself and recover enough to stand.

'Take your time.' Luc rubs my arm and smiles into my eyes.

'Sorry,' I say. 'I feel like such a lightweight. But the noise and heat; the smells. So many people. It's amazing, but it's freaked me out a bit.'

'Don't worry, you'll get used to it. I should have warned you what to expect. I didn't even think. You've never been outside before have you?'

'You kind of just assume it will be the same as home. The Perimeter is so peaceful and calm. This is great but it's a bit intimidating, seeing all these people in one place.'

Vendors shout at the top of their voices and buyers haggle over produce with pretended indifference. There are fruit and vegetables in varying stages of freshness, great mountains of autumn-coloured grain, unappetising fly-covered meat, sweets, cakes, biscuits, home-made and second-hand clothing, skittish livestock, toys and crockery. Fire-eaters, jugglers, dancers and fortune tellers jostle for space. Now I'm over my panic attack, I'm hypnotised by it all.

'Is it like this all the time?' I ask Luc.

'Every Saturday, darlin',' an elderly street vendor standing next to me replies. 'Where you from then?'

'Just visiting,' Luc says. He grabs my elbow and propels me forward into the throng.

'I'll mind me own business then shall I?' The vendor goes back to crying his wares.

The main Charminster Road has smaller roads leading off it, which appear to be residential with a mixture of run-down houses and slightly larger apartment blocks. Some of the roads have been converted into small strips of farmland, with narrow paths running in front of the houses to allow access. There are penned animals, garden produce and crops, all patch-worked along into the distance.

Most plots have someone on guard, but it's quite a laid-back affair. A man lounges on a garden chair, chatting to his neighbour, a rifle lying at his feet. The crop-carpeted roads give the overall impression of a quaint rural village and, from what I can see, most of the residents seem to be very cheerful and friendly. I could spend hours wandering the streets, sightseeing. It's a huge and fascinating settlement, but the vastness of the place is going to make finding Chambers' accommodation very difficult.

'We'll have to ask someone where he lived.' I state the obvious.

'Yeah. We need to find someone.'

I get a sudden surge of bravery. 'Excuse me.' I turn to a girl my age who strolls past, biting into a toffee apple. 'Sorry, do you know where I could find Ron Chambers' place?'

'The electrician?'

'That's right,' I reply, not believing she actually knows who I'm talking about.

'Haven't you heard?' she says. 'He's not here anymore. I think he was arrested. Not sure though. He used to live with the other trades on Porchester Road, D'you know it?'

I shake my head.

'It's down there.' She points back down the road. 'Northumberland Mansions. They'll definitely have reallocated his apartment by now though.'

'Thanks very much.' I smile.

'You're welcome.' She gives us a curious stare before turning off down a side street and disappearing.

'Cool, Riley.' Luc punches my arm.

Northumberland Mansions is a large ugly brown block, reserved purely for skilled trades people and their families. It sits on a wide tree-lined road and is probably quite a prestigious place to live. Close enough to the main road and the main gates, but far enough away not to be disturbed by the noise of the street market. Litter covers the pavement though and there's dog shit everywhere.

Luc says I should speak on the intercom, as a girl's voice is less intimidating. We stand in a urine and cabbage-smelling foyer and buzz a few numbers until someone answers. The woman on the other end confirms Chambers has left the compound, but that he used to live in apartment 26B. I duly press the bell for 26B and a man's voice answers.

'Hello,' he says.

'Hi, my name's Riley. Can I speak to you for a few minutes?'

'Who?'

'Riley. I wonder if I could speak to you.'

'Dunno any Riley. You need to go through the committee if

you want an electrician.' The intercom squeals and then goes dead.

'Offer him some cigarettes,' suggests Luc.

I press the bell again and put Luc's offer to him.

'Fifth floor. Come on up.'

We jog up the dim airless flights of stairs until we finally reach the fifth floor and push open an opaque glass door at the top of the stairs. I scrutinise the flat numbers listed on the wall and Luc points to a short, dark corridor on our left. There at the end we see a man peering out from behind his door, with 26B in dull gold lettering on it. He has the chain across and eyes us warily as we approach.

'What do you want then?'

We briefly explain the reason for our visit, saying Chambers is wanted for murder and we're here to see if he's left anything behind that might give us a clue to his whereabouts.

'Who are you then, the Munchkin Army? No offence, but you look a bit young to be playing detective.'

'He killed my sister,' I say quietly, starting to loathe this rude man.

He doesn't reply for a while. Just stares, as if sizing us up.

'Come on, Riley,' says Luc. 'We're obviously wasting our time. We should go.' He turns, as if to make his way back to the staircase.

'Hold on a minute,' says the man. 'Got those smokes you were talking about?'

Luc produces a packet of cigarettes from his rucksack and

holds them out for the man to see.

'Blimey, those look like the real thing? Where'd you get those? Better not ask eh?' He closes the door and I hear the sound of the chain sliding across.

The door opens again, without the chain, and a middle-aged man stands before us wearing a pair of almost indecently threadbare red nylon football shorts and a matching vest. His large white hairy belly protrudes from a gap between the two items of clothing. He pats it.

'Maybe I can start to lose some of this now I'm on the fifth floor with no bloody lift.' Luc passes the cigarettes across and the man steps aside. 'Okay, come through then, but no funny business. I'm watching the pair of you.'

We follow him in and stand awkwardly in his entrance hall. I ask if he'll let us have a quick look around the apartment.

'Got any more of those ciggies?' he asks, eying Luc's rucksack.

Luc raises his eyebrows at me and I reluctantly nod. He produces another packet and hands them to the man.

'You beauty.' He grins at Luc and claps him on the shoulder. 'Mi casa es tu casa' he says cheerily, in bad Italian. 'But I'll come round with you, don't want you rooting through me underwear drawer do I?' He raises his eyes at me, as if to imply I'd enjoy doing such a gross thing.

I shudder.

'Just moved in last week. Bloody lovely place. Clean white walls, wood floors. Can't believe my luck. Didn't find anything out of the ordinary though. Can't believe you're telling me the bloke's a murderer; that's a bit creepy. I'm a sparky, new to the area. Ever need anything electrical doing, just talk to the committee and I'll give you a good deal.'

We follow him around the flat. There's a large lounge, two double bedrooms, an adequate kitchen and a shower room. It's a lovely, airy apartment, simple and clean with high ceilings and, best of all, no horrible smell.

'This is hopeless,' I say. 'We're not going to find anything.'

'You done now?' asks the man, as we follow him back into the hallway. He looks as though he's about to say something, but then he closes his mouth again and gives a tight-lipped smile. 'Well, cheers for the smokes.'

We leave his apartment and make our way back down the five flights of stairs. We're about half way down when we hear an echoing voice.

'Oi, you two!'

I glance up to see the man's round face peering down at us. We turn around and head back up the stairs. When we reach the top, he's got a strange expression on his face and he's chewing his lower lip.

'There was this one thing,' he says.

Luc and I glance at each other and then turn back to look at the man, waiting expectantly.

I feel a surge of hope.

CHAPTER TWELVE

RILEY

I wonder what this man's going to tell us. Could it be something that will lead us to Chambers?

'I found something,' he says.

'What?' Luc says.

'I found it down the side of the sofa.'

I look sideways at Luc. He raises his eyes at the man.

'A lighter. I found a lighter,' the man says.

Something stirs in my memory, but I can't quite remember. 'Can I see it?' I ask.

'Um.' He seems reluctant, but finally concedes and pulls a silver lighter out of his pocket.

I stare at it, puzzled. 'That's Pa's lighter.'

'Your old man's? Yeah right.'

'Check the bottom,' I say confidently. 'And you'll see the initials JRC. My father's initials.' I wait.

He looks at me and frowns. Then he peers at the underside of the lighter and his frown deepens. 'Shoulda kept my mouth shut shouldn't I. That's a nice lighter that is.'

'Thank you,' I say, reaching out for it.

'So.' He smiles at me, showing yellow teeth. 'What's it worth?' He makes no move to hand it over.

'What?' I splutter. Luc puts a warning hand on my arm and I turn to him in annoyed disbelief.

'I'm sure you've got plenty of goodies in that bag of yours,' the man says. 'You can't blame me. I'd be a prat to pass up an opportunity like this. Those smokes will sort me out big time. So don't be tight. A couple more packets and we'll all be happy.'

We do the deal and I finally have Pa's lighter, feeling its warm weight in my hand.

'Cheers,' says the man, as he walks back into his apartment and closes the door without saying goodbye.

What on earth was Pa's lighter doing on Chambers' sofa? It doesn't make any sense. We leave the apartment block and step out onto the street.

'Maybe Chambers was a thief,' Luc muses, as we head back up Porchester Road towards the street market.

'Must have been,' I answer. 'Otherwise, how else do you explain the lighter?' It feels solid and reassuring in my hand, as if I have a piece of Pa. I imagine the lighter feeling pleased to have been returned to its family. Pa doesn't smoke, but a lighter is a handy thing to have. I remember last month, Pa asking me if I'd seen it, but I didn't pay much attention. Funny to think of it all the way over here. I click it, but it just sparks impotently.

We hurry back through the street market, towards the car park. Nobody stops us as we pass through the exit door. I immediately spot the huge AV at the other end of the car park, which is just as well as neither of us had thought to take note of where we'd parked.

Luc's quiet. He seems annoyed.

'Are you cross with me for making us come here?' I ask.

'No, course not,' he replies. 'I'm just annoyed at that bloke. We gave him way too much of our stash. I feel like an idiot.'

'There was nothing else we could do. It's only a few packs of cigarettes and we've got loads more.'

'I suppose. We better get going. We can't be anywhere near Ringwood when night falls.'

'What about if we stay here until tomorrow?' I say. 'See if we can find any more people who knew Chambers. Maybe we'll find out some other stuff about him.'

'We could, but I think we're too close to home and I don't want to risk anyone recognising us. They'd probably be rewarded for taking us back.'

'But who would recognise us?'

'Any of the workers who come to our Perimeter. Some of the guards' families live here too. Anybody really. That's why I didn't want to come here in the first place, but I understand why you wanted to. I just think we're lucky no one's spotted us yet. I don't want to push it.'

'Okay.'

'It gets dark about half seven, eight, so we need to go now. Once we get on the road we'll pick up some speed.

We head out of the compound and onwards to find the road. Luc was right about picking up speed once we hit the Wessex Way. It feels like we're flying. The speedo now reads an impressive thirty five miles per hour, a huge improvement on the measly five to ten we'd gotten used to on the rough ground.

The Wessex Way is a dual carriageway that used to be divided along its length by metal crash barriers. These have long since been removed and now the central reservation is choked with weeds, bushes and trees, so you can't see the other side of the road. This suits us fine as we're not keen to meet any other vehicles anyway. We pass nobody and, about three quarters of an hour later, we come to a huge roundabout.

Luc brakes as we get closer and it's a good thing he does, as three large army trucks rumble straight across our path and away, to our right. They don't stop to give way to us or to check us out, thank goodness.

'They're heading to Ringwood,' Luc says.

'Shall we wait a bit, so they get a good head start?' I ask. 'I don't like the idea of driving right behind them.'

'Definitely. It's only four and it shouldn't take more than an hour to get clear of Ringwood.'

'Good,' I reply.

'I'm going to close my eyes for ten minutes.' He yawns and stretches. 'Keep a look out, Riley and wake me if you see anything.'

He parks up on the grass verge and switches off the engine. My mind wanders over all we've seen this morning and I ponder the sheltered existence I've led.

I try to imagine what Skye would have made of it all, sure she would have felt a lot braver than me in the same situation.

She was always up for anything. I'm overcome with a wash of sadness that she'll never have the opportunity to experience anything like this. I want to tell her all about it and see the look on her face as I describe the Charminster Compound, the horseman, everything.

I study Luc's sleeping face. It's so familiar. I've known him all my life, but he feels different to me now. We're closer than we ever were before.

I suddenly worry in case I've missed something on the road, or that Luc might wake to find me looking at him. That would be too mortifying to contemplate, so I turn away and stare out of the windscreen. Nothing stirs in the hot afternoon and the AV is already starting to feel warm without the air con. I reach into my bag and take out some bottled water. I sip it slowly.

Luc starts the engine, interrupting my thoughts.

'Good sleep?' I ask.

'Mmm, a power nap,' he says, stretching his hand out in front of him like Superman.

'I can't sleep in the daytime, it makes me irritable.'

'Really? I feel great now. I so needed that snooze.'

We cruise around the roundabout and take the last exit, the same one the soldiers' trucks took. We're heading towards Ringwood and I'm keeping my fingers tightly crossed that we don't encounter any trouble from the riots.

The reality of our vulnerability is starting to sink in.

CHAPTER THIRTEEN

Eleanor

The next two weeks were life-altering for me. Connor and I stole every spare moment we could. My family wouldn't have shown him such generous hospitality if they had known exactly how we were spending our time together. We couldn't get enough of each other. While my parents and brothers were out working, we went off in Connor's camper van and, as soon as we found a quiet place to park, we would close the curtains. There, in the illicit gloom, our minds and bodies became the source of endless fascination.

'Ellie, you're amazing.' He kissed my arm, soft butterfly kisses that sent me half-mad and he wasn't afraid to look right into my eyes, unnerving me with his candour. I savoured every single word and every single kiss, memorising it all and storing it away to dissect and revel in later.

He pushed me gently down onto the converted bed. 'I feel like this is my real home - here with you,' he said with a half-smile. 'I know it sounds cheesy, but ... it's how I feel.'

'I know,' I whispered, looking up at him. 'I just wish we could stay here and forget everyone else. I never want to have to go home.'

'So let's pretend there's no outside. This is all there is.' He leant over me so his dark fringe fell into his eyes. He lowered himself down and kissed me until I didn't even know who I was anymore.

The time we spent in each other's company flew past in a momentary flash of brilliant light, but the hours we were apart plodded by like so many centuries of darkness. I lost my appetite for food, but felt like I could live on the love-infused air I gulped down.

Abi couldn't understand any of it, and I felt bad for neglecting her so much. I didn't want to be one of those people who dropped their friends as soon as they got a boyfriend, but I couldn't help it. These feelings were outside my control - a need that made everything and everyone else unimportant.

Even after all this time, I still felt unimaginably nervous in his company. I was always trying to impress him with witty sarcasm, trying to be cooler than I was. I couldn't understand his interest in me. I imagined his type of girlfriend to be an edgy blonde with tattoos and piercings or a svelte raven-haired indie chick. I was a boring middle class brunette to whom nothing exciting ever happened. But he seemed to want to be with me and I couldn't believe it.

One warm evening, we sat together on the top of Smallpox Hill amongst the heather and rabbit holes, gazing out across the sun-faded countryside.

'I like it here,' Connor said. 'It's peaceful. But I miss Ripon.'

'Is that where you're from?'

'Yeah.'

I wanted to ask him how long he would be staying down here, but I didn't want him to think I was being clingy or needy.

'When was the last time you went home?' I asked instead. 'And where is Ripon, anyway? I know it's up north somewhere …'

'Ripon's in North Yorkshire, but I don't go home. Not anymore.' His mouth hardened into a thin line and he started tearing small clumps of grass out of the ground.

'Don't you get on with your parents then?'

'My mum's great. It's my dad …'

'Oh. Sorry.'

'Yeah, well. I like my life now. I just work wherever. And I'm lucky I've got my bus. My grandad left it to me in his Will.'

'What happened with your dad? Tell me to shut up and mind my own business if you like.'

'Nah, you're alright. We never got on. I was never good enough for him. All I ever felt when I was at home, was pressure. Like I was gonna suffocate.' He sent a clod of earth spinning down the hillside and put his hands up in front of his face. I heard him grit his teeth in anger. 'I knew nothing I did would ever make him happy, apart from maybe being a brain surgeon or winning the Nobel Peace Prize or something. So I just thought it would be easier if I did a runner.'

'Connor, I'm so sorry.' I put my arm around his shoulders and he gave me a closed-lipped smile.

'It wasn't easy for Mum though and I feel bad about leaving her. But at least she's not walking on eggshells any more, trying to keep the peace, you know?'

I didn't know. I realised how lucky I was to have my warm, loving family to support me. Connor was on his own.

'But it's not all bad, Ellie. If I hadn't left, I wouldn't have met you.'

His words gave me goose bumps and I smiled at him. In my eyes, he was amazing, with a strength of character I envied. I had never considered I could ever feel like this about another human being. He smiled back at me and pulled me towards him. We kissed a long deep kiss that spread throughout my body. This relationship was turning me into a new person. Someone who was ready for the world. I could do anything I wanted.

Then, one hazy summer day, everything suddenly changed to break the spell.

CHAPTER FOURTEEN

RILEY

Luckily, Luc and I don't see a soul on the Ringwood road. We make it safely around the town in daylight without encountering any riot of any kind. I'm actually starting to feel less worried about the journey. Luc looks tired.

'Do you want me to drive?' I ask.

He flicks his eyes towards me and then back onto the road. He smiles.

'That's okay, Riley. I'll drive today. Maybe you could take a turn tomorrow?' I think he can see a little apprehension in my eyes and has taken pity on me.

We talked so much back home; planning our trip and how we would track down Chambers. But out here on the open road we just speak when necessary or make odd comments about the scenery. Maybe there's too much to think about or maybe we're just tired and a bit spooked by the unfamiliar surroundings.

The road opens up to reveal a great lush green floodplain that must once have been rich summer grazing land, but I can see no sign of cattle or sheep. The road makes the area too exposed to farm and valuable animals would have to be kept hidden out of site.

'That's the River Avon,' Luc says. 'This road completely

flooded last winter.'

I gaze around and see beauty I never imagined could exist in real life. Soft, rolling hills frame each side of us in every colour green imaginable. Dense copses of willows and poplars nod their heads along the river and fields. The clear blue sky is fading to white and the sun bleeds red and gold into the uneven horizon. It's a tranquil rural landscape and it inspires new primitive emotions inside me.

I've never been so scared and so exhilarated in all my life. I'm terrified we won't make it, that something awful I can't even imagine will befall us. But the gentle splendour of the countryside awes me. I can't remember ever feeling so uplifted by nature. It's raw and incredibly freeing to be out here after the constraints of the Perimeter fence.

I suddenly wonder how late it is. 'Should we find somewhere to stop for the night?'

'We've probably got a couple of hours of daylight left,' Luc replies. 'Maybe we should keep going for another hour or so; get a few more miles in.'

'Yeah I don't mind. I suppose we should keep going while we can.'

The engine's steady thrum is lulling me to sleep. We've only ever reached a maximum speed of about thirty five miles an hour and that felt fast. But the road's pitted and scarred surface means we're now bumping along somewhere between five and twenty miles per hour. Not very good for fuel consumption, but luckily the AV's got deep tanks.

I'm drifting in that vague place, somewhere between awake and asleep when I hear my name being whispered.

'Riley, Riley. What's that?'

I come to with a start and look up. It feels like I've dozed for a couple of minutes at most, but when I open my eyes I see that it's twilight already. As my eyes focus, I make out a long dark shape in the road up ahead.

'What's that?' I echo stupidly.

'I don't know. It looks like a fallen tree.'

As we get closer I see it. It's a tree, or more like a log, lying across the whole width of the road.

'I don't like the look of it,' says Luc, as he brings the AV to a halt, squinting ahead into the fading light.

'Don't worry,' I say. 'I'm sure we can shift it. We've got some rope in the back. We could tie it to the AV and drag it to the side of the road.' I make to open the door.

'Stop, Riley!' Luc cries, grabbing my arm and making me jump.

'What?'

'Look.' He points into the hills.

'What is it?' I follow his line of sight to see twinkling lights. 'What are they?'

'It could be a raiding party.'

'What!'

'I didn't want to mention it before. I hoped we wouldn't run into any.'

'What do we do?'

'It might be a trap,' he says. 'That log didn't fly into the middle of the road on its own. Someone wants us to get out and try to move it.'

'But those lights are miles away.'

'Yeah, but whoever put the log there is probably really close by and watching us.' As he's speaking, he flicks on the blackout mode to shield us from view.

I look out of my window and see that our ambushers could be hidden anywhere. Darkness is seconds away and there are any number of dense trees and bushes to hide behind. I shiver.

'We could drive over it,' Luc ventures, 'but we might damage the underneath.'

'I don't want to break down here.'

'Me neither. I don't think we should risk it.' Luc switches the headlights onto full beam. 'Oh God, look closer, Riley.'

'Look where?'

'At the log. It's got nails or something sticking out all over it.'

I stare and sure enough in the gloom I can make out hundreds of evil little spikes along its length, confirming Luc's theory that this is indeed an ambush. We're in a tough, virtually impenetrable armoured vehicle but it doesn't stop an unwelcome fear from inching through my body.

'Maybe ... Could we shoot at it?' I ask, feeling the tremor in my voice. I don't really take my suggestion seriously and wait for Luc to tactfully dismiss the idea.

'Hmm. That's not a bad idea. If we gun a weak spot near the middle, we might be able to split it in two. It might shift out of the way as we drive into it. What a waste of bullets though - shooting at a tree.'

'We can't worry about that,' I say.

'And the run-on-flats will get us out of here if we get punctured from the spikes.'

'Can we do it quickly?' I ask. 'Cos sitting here is really freaking me out.'

'Yep,' Luc agrees. 'Thank God we brought shed loads of ammo.' He reaches behind and unclips the gun case, passing me the PK and taking the heavier M60 for himself.

'Should we both fire at it?' I say, beginning to panic. 'Or ... I don't want to get out though. Maybe we should open the roof and stand up.'

Luc turns to me. 'Look,' he says softly, realising I'm about to go to pieces. 'I'm going to shoot at the tree and you're going to cover me. If you see anything moving, shoot at it. If you hear any shots apart from mine, shoot in that direction.'

I nod, feeling numb.

'I doubt they've got any automatic weapons, but when they see ours they're gonna start drooling. They'll want what we've got. Here are the binoculars, keep scanning around for trouble.' He smiles. 'We'll do this, okay? It'll be fine.'

I nod again, mute, and sling the bins around my neck as Luc opens the roof hatch.

At least I've had good training, as have all of us Perimeter kids. Pa taught Skye and me from the age of eight. We had advanced driving lessons, comprehensive weapons training and survival skills. At the time it had all been great fun, but I see now that Pa was equipping us for every eventuality.

It all feels like it's happening in slow motion. There's no time to feel scared anymore. One minute Luc and I are discussing what we should do. The next minute we're firing off rounds into the dark, silent countryside.

They come at us from the far distance, to the left, where the sun has recently set. From what I can see, most of them are on horseback, but there are a lot on foot, swarming down from the hills. I can't see how Luc is doing so I just spray bullets, even though my targets are way out of range. But if the raiders keep on coming, it won't be long until I hit something ... or someone.

The riders are wearing what appear to be old fashioned riot-police helmets and bullet proof vests over their clothes. They look like futuristic cowboys. Surreal and menacing. They've got weapons, but I can't feel bullets anywhere close.

After what must be less than thirty seconds or so, the raiders turn tail and disappear back up the hillside. Luc stops firing and so do I. I check the fallen log. It's been decimated, reduced to a million splinters. Luc grins at me.

'That was quick,' I gasp, the adrenalin still racing around my body.

'You okay?' he whispers in the sudden silence.

Just then, something cold presses at the side of my head. Luc swings his weapon towards me, but he's too late.

'I'll shoot.' It's a man's voice, steady and confident. His breath smells rank, his body odour sickening. I don't dare turn my head to look at him. His arm slithers around my shoulders and his gun presses harder into my temple.

Luc lowers his weapon as the man relieves me of my machine gun with his left hand. I'm rigid with fear, hardly able to breathe. He must've crawled up the other side of the AV while we were distracted by the raiders coming down the hill. Why on earth hadn't we anticipated something like this? We should have activated the shockplates before carrying out our hasty plan. Luc must have the same thought as me, because I see his hand snaking down inside the AV towards the shock button.

But before Luc has a chance to do anything, another man appears over the top of the AV and cracks Luc on the side of the head with his gun. Luc crumples down into his seat like a rag doll and I see thick globs of blood on the roof-opening.

'No,' I moan. My vision blurs and I feel like I'm about to pass out.

'Don't worry,' says the man next to me. 'He'll just have a bit of a headache when he wakes up and I feel so much better now he's asleep.' He's well-spoken and, when I glance at him, he smiles, smug and in control of the situation. I reckon he's in his twenties; he's clean shaven and good looking. Pity about his personal hygiene.

He slings my Kalashnikov over his body and reaches past me into the AV to pull Luc up by his hair so he's now slumped upright in the driver's seat. But he hasn't done this out of any concern for Luc; he's trying to reach Luc's weapon which fell onto the floor when he was knocked out.

I weigh up my options and find them very limited. The revolver is still jammed against my head, my gun hangs from the man's malodorous body and my lovely Luc is unconscious, with another raider trying to reach the M60 down in the footwell. Then things get suddenly worse.

'Nice work, Solly.' Another man's face materialises over the top of the AV and my heart plummets even further. Then, from behind the rustling trees and bushes the hidden raiding party appears. There are about twenty to thirty men and women of varying ages and attire, all modestly armed and some carrying lanterns. They look almost civilised – grubby, but not too unkempt, not like the people I saw outside the Charminster Compound. I hear distant shouting and see the mounted raiders waving and cheering from the hillsides.

We're done for. We hadn't scared them off before, as I'd mistakenly thought. They were just waiting for Solly to do his worst. I'm paralysed with fear, surrounded by hostile strangers capable of who knows what.

CHAPTER FIFTEEN

RILEY

Now the raiders are crawling over the AV like dirty ants. They climb up on to the roof to congratulate Solly, their hero. They're surprisingly well-spoken and intelligent sounding. From their aggressive behaviour, I wrongly assumed they were all stupid and half-wild.

Solly removes the metal gun barrel from the side of my head and grabs me by the waist. I gasp as he lifts me out of the vehicle, about to pass me down into the waiting arms of his friend. There's no time to think, I have to act quickly and so, with all the strength I can muster, I kick out as hard as I possibly can with my heel. Unfortunately I'm only wearing my flip flops, but I manage to hit the sweet spot I'm aiming for and he drops me back into the passenger seat. I could almost smile to see him doubling up in agony, half sliding off the roof.

'You little bitch,' he wheezes.

Meanwhile, his companion is leaning down into the drivers' side, grappling past Luc's body to reach for the elusive gun. I've got another surprise in store for them and, from my safe position inside the AV, I quickly flick the switch that activates the shock plates. There's a split-second of teasing silence, followed by a highly-charged hum - a ramping up of power.

Solly and his companion peer down at me in horror as it dawns on them what the low, menacing sound means. I'm too wired to savour my victory.

The raiders who've crawled onto the vehicle are quite literally about to receive the shock of their lives. Their hair begins to lift in slow-motion and then, suddenly and violently their bodies are thrown from the AV at the same time, like startled flies.

The darkness is almost absolute outside, apart from the headlights and weak lanterns. Static from the electric plates showers sparks of light which accompany the raiders on their unexpected flights. Arms and legs splayed, hair standing on end and mouths open in silent screams and yells. They fly through the air at frightening speed, upwards and outwards; a cascade of human bodies.

Has the electric current killed them? Or are they just badly stunned? I realise I'm shaking and I try to get my brain to unfreeze. I still have to get us out of here. The metal plates buzz and crackle and I thank God for old technology.

Those who were thrown are now strewn on the ground about twenty feet from the vehicle, either in the middle of the road or on the grass verges. Some collided with those standing around the vehicle and are now lying unconscious on top of them. Others are just standing slack-jawed in amazement.

But shock soon turns to anger and one idiot boy charges towards me and tries to open the passenger door. He immediately finds himself lying incapacitated with his friends, face down in the dirt.

A woman picks up my Kalashnikov from Solly's prone body and fiddles around with it for a while, before firing it at close range on the AV. I give a short scream as bullets bounce off the windows. The vehicle shudders horribly under the impact.

Then she has a brainwave and lowers her aim to the tyres. I'm seriously freaking out now. I need to stop shaking and squealing and *do* something. I'm lucky - the woman's ammunition runs out before she's able to hamper my chances of a good getaway. She throws the gun down in disgust, the smirk, wiped from her face. There's nothing any of them can do and they're furious.

All my thoughts now are of getting out of here, but Luc's still slumped unconscious in the driver's seat.

'Luc! Luc, wake up. Please, Luc!' I shake him, but he doesn't respond and there's no way I can shift him out of the way quickly enough. I close the roof and do the only thing I can in the circumstances - I improvise.

Although I'm still in the passenger seat, I release the handbrake and stretch my right leg over Luc's, onto the accelerator. I dip the clutch with my left leg and reach past Luc to grab the steering wheel. His face rests on my back as I lean in front of him.

The keycard clicks and I feel the engine hum. I stare at the road ahead illuminated by the yellow headlights still on full beam. The log now resembles nothing more than a jumble of broken wood, but there are also several stunned bodies sprawled in amongst it. Hearing the engine, some of the raiders run into the road to lift the injured out of the way.

I slide the gears into first, overdoing the accelerator so the engine roars as the AV leaps forward. I'm aware of several sickening judders beneath the wheels and I don't know if I'm driving over bits of machine-gunned log and nails or if it's the raiders' bodies I'm mangling. I crunch into second gear and then third.

Leaning across the still-unconscious Luc, I drive awkwardly for about ten or fifteen minutes until I can no longer see the glow of lights in the hillsides. My heart is racing and my body is trembling in fear and shock and from the unnatural position my body is forced into. When I can stand it no more, I swerve over to the side of the road and pull on the handbrake.

I leave the engine running and make sure the plates are still activated. I have to move Luc across to the passenger side, I can't drive like this and I'm worried about the unnatural position Luc's sitting in.

'Luc!' I whisper loudly, still really scared in case there's anyone around. 'Luc! Can you hear me? Are you okay?'

Nothing. *Please God let him be okay.*

The small crescent moon gives off a weak glow as a cloud moves to reveal it. On Luc's head is a huge egg-shaped lump and a livid bruise where he was hit with the revolver. Blood is congealing down the side of his face, but miraculously the wound seems to have stopped bleeding. I'm freaking out about him. It's obvious he's in a bad way and needs proper help.

If I was braver I'd turn back right now, but the thought of another encounter with the raiders is too much for me. I wish I'd been thinking straight back there - I would have done a three point turn and headed straight back home to the Perimeter. But I was too scared to think about which direction to drive in; I'd just wanted to get out of there.

I stretch, rolling my neck up and down and from side to side and then I lean across to examine Luc. His breaths come slow and even. I scent the warmth from his skin.

I want to lay him across the back seat, but he might roll off with all the jolting around and, besides, it'll be too difficult for me to get him there. My only other option is to put him in the front passenger seat and hope the upright position will be okay for him.

I climb into the back and hook my arms underneath his armpits. He's so heavy and I'm worried I might be making things worse for his poor unconscious body. But even more worrying would be the imminent appearance of other raiding parties or worse and anyway, it's impractical and dangerous to carry on driving the way I have been. A dog or maybe a wolf howls in the distance and I try not to think about the horrors of the night as I concentrate on trying to slide and heave Luc into the passenger seat.

Sweating and breathless, I finally manage to get him where I want him to be. Then I swing his legs across one at a time, climb into the driver's seat and fasten both our seatbelts.

I rest my head on the steering wheel and try to get my

breathing back under control. A few tears drip onto my cheeks and when I look across at Luc I feel immediately guilty. This is my fault, this trip which originally seemed so glamorous and heroic. And now I might have gotten Luc seriously and permanently injured. Killed even. Please let him be okay. But right now we have to get out of here, so I drive in a semi-stupor, relieved to be away from the beautiful floodplain.

The road soon narrows, becoming hillier. Summer-coated trees line the road, bowing over to greet each other in the middle. I drive through this long, rustling tunnel, eerie and muffled in the dark, headlights shining strangely in the green murk. The way twists and turns, it rises and then drops away sharply.

I grip the wheel, periodically stretching my fingers out where they ache from being locked into such a tense position. I drive in a terror of so many things: Luc's unconscious state, the appearance of more raiders, or driving off the edge of the road - it seems so precarious in the unpredictable darkness. But I know so far we've been lucky to escape with our lives.

Every time I look at Luc, my heart lurches. It seems as though he's sleeping peacefully, his breaths are regular and his face is so serene. But in the dim light, I can clearly see the huge lump and vicious cut on the side of his head. Panic tries to jumble my thoughts, so I take some breaths to calm down. I need to put all the negative thoughts out of my head, to tell myself he's just asleep and will wake up soon. If I let myself think anything else, I'll throw up, pass out or have a full blown panic attack.

Suddenly, a yellow eye and a white ribbed wing fill my vision for a split second, as a huge brown owl nearly smacks into the windscreen. I slam my foot on the brake and the AV skids on the gravelly road with a sound like white noise.

Luc and I pitch forward against our seatbelts, to be yanked backwards into our seats again. Luckily, the force isn't great enough to set off the airbags. Luc's head lolls to one side. The owl hoots and swoops off into the night, unharmed.

I pull on the handbrake with shaking hands and my breath comes in noisy and uneven gasps. What else could possibly happen tonight? The AV is skewed across the road. I look up and notice the beam from the headlights is shining directly onto a narrow and overgrown dirt track leading off the main road.

I realise I'm too shaken up to drive out here tonight, so I re-start the engine and steer the AV onto the track. Once I'm out of sight of the road, I park up in the tangled undergrowth.

With trembling fingers, I switch off the engine, kill the lights, open the door and climb out. It takes what little courage I have to creep back onto the main road. I shiver and my teeth chatter, though the night air is warm. My nerves are shot to bits but I have to force myself into the middle of the deserted road to make sure no passer-by will be able to see our vehicle. A cool breeze plucks at my hair and the leaves rustle and sigh. I can't wait to get back to the security of the AV.

Once satisfied we're truly hidden from view, I come back to check on Luc. He's still unconscious. I would rather he was lying flat, but I don't dare attempt to lift him again, so I recline his seat as far as it will go and then crawl into the back seat to fall into a restless sleep.

The following morning, I awake to the strange and unfamiliar sound of a cow mooing. I stretch, peer up out of the rear window and see a herd of black and white cattle leaning their thick necks over a five-barred gate about two hundred yards away. Between me and the wooden gate, towers an even higher wire fence topped with rolls of barbed wire. I'm lucky I didn't drive or stumble into it last night.

Someone's whistling. I follow the noise and see a woman with short fair hair wheeling a red push bike across the field towards the cows. The AV is in plain view through the gate - she must have seen us. A million things race through my brain at once, from the events of last night, to whether Luc has recovered this morning.

I sit up quickly to check the passenger seat and my stomach lurches to find it empty. Perhaps Luc has slipped down into the passenger footwell. I lean forward to look, but no. Luc has disappeared.

Fumbling, I unlock the AV and, in my haste, I fall onto the wet grass. I scrabble to get upright and then scan the area for Luc. The woman is now riding her bike as she herds the cows back across the field. How could she not have spotted me or the huge AV? She hasn't even glanced in my direction. What am I supposed to do now?

CHAPTER SIXTEEN

Eleanor

My brother David ran into the house at five pm on Thursday August 10th.

'Turn on the news!' he shouted. I heard the crackle of the TV being switched on in the lounge. 'Come and look at this, Ellie!'

Everyone else had been at work that day as I lounged around the house in summer holiday mode and daydreamed about Connor. He was also at work, helping Dad at the factory.

'Do you want a cup of tea?' I yelled from the kitchen.

'No, just come and look at this will you! It's hit the fan!'

I poured a few drops of milk into my tea and dismissed my brother's over-dramatic tone. I sauntered into the lounge, where David knelt in front of the television. He looked up at me and shuffled backwards to give me a better view of the screen.

An anchorwoman stood in front of what looked like a shopping centre. Behind her, people were running and screaming. A stream of text scrolled across the bottom of the screen: *so far there have been explosions in London, Manchester, Leeds, Birmingham, Bristol* ... The list went on. The anchorwoman spoke,

'It's the same story throughout Europe. Also, the U.S., Australia, South Africa, India ... A global attack, the like of which has never been seen before ... thousands feared dead ... as I am speaking I am getting reports of still more explosions in Scotland, in Cardiff ...'

Sirens screamed behind her and she wore a crazed look, like she couldn't believe the enormity of the story she was relating.

'Oh my God.' I felt sick. 'David, what's happening?'

He turned to look at me and we both exhaled slowly through our mouths, at the same time. There had been a couple of terrorist attacks earlier in the summer, but nothing compared to the stories we now witnessed on the screen. I sensed this was something that wouldn't be forgotten anytime soon.

The next couple of weeks were odd. No one we knew of in our village had been hurt. But we all obsessively focused on the news. Four days after the first attacks, there were more bombings. Again, they were worldwide. Not as extensive as the first round of attacks, but still horrific, and enough to refuel a mass panic of the population. Nobody felt safe. There was none of the distance that normally accompanies big news stories. It all felt real and close. Most of us knew people who had been directly affected.

Because the police had now diverted most of their efforts to stopping the attacks, there were too few of them to deal with the rapidly escalating crime wave that overtook the country. To try to prevent total chaos, the armed forces came onto the streets. Soldiers on the beat meant the police force could concentrate more fully on investigating the terror attacks. But, even though they had intercepted a couple of plots, the enormity of the task they faced was plain for all to see.

So far, there had been twenty-eight bombings in the first wave of attacks and nine in the second. And this was just in the UK. The devastation had been wrought by a combination of suicide bombers, sophisticated car bombs, plane hijacks and vicious nail bombs left in public areas. The attacks occurred in airports, sea ports, shopping centres, transport systems, office blocks and bars.

The damage and suffering grew beyond anything anyone could have imagined and the world could only watch in horror as the death toll mounted each day.

CHAPTER SEVENTEEN

RILEY

I climb back into the AV and sit here, trying to decide what to do. Suddenly, there's a sharp rapping on the windscreen. I jump and look up. It's Luc with a smile on his face. Standing next to him is a small wiry man in a worn tweed jacket and matching cloth cap. I open the door, ecstatic to see Luc. I get out, wanting to wrap my arms around him, but I don't. The air smells of wet grass and manure.

'You're alright!' I say. 'I thought you were never going to wake up and then when I woke up and saw you weren't in the AV I didn't know what to think. Are you okay?'

'Hey, Riley, I'm okay. Just feel a bit sick and I've got a banging headache. I woke up and needed a pee. I didn't know where I was. When I saw you lying on the back seat I didn't know if you were alive or dead. I had to check you were breathing.'

'What?'

'Well I still don't know what happened. When I realised you were safe, just asleep, I didn't want to wake you. What happened? How did you get us out of there? Sorry, I haven't introduced you. This is Fred. It's his land we're parked on.'

'Morning.' He tips his cap and gives a tight-lipped smile, but his eyes are warm and humorous. 'I found your man watering my field and was wondering if you'd care to take some breakfast with us. Jessie's just gotta take the cows across for milking.'

'Umm, great, yeah. If you're sure that's okay,' I stammer, taken aback by the man's apparent friendliness after the hostilities of last night.

Luc looks at me and shrugs as if to say 'why not'.

'How are you?' he asks me again. 'Tell me everything. Are you alright? How's the AV? Does it still drive okay?'

'I'm fine, the AV's fine. It drove okay last night, but it took a bit of a battering. Maybe we better look underneath and we should check the tyres.'

We give the AV a brief once-over and the only damage we can see, is a bent wheel arch and scraped front bumper. The engine still starts fine and miraculously the tyres are unpunctured.

Fred waits while we're doing this, then he explains we'll have to take the long way round as his fields are electrified and wired-off and there's a five-foot-deep ditch around them as well. It crosses my mind I could have easily fallen into this ditch last night. He gestures to us to follow and then strides on ahead, leaving Luc and me to stumble after him.

We make our way across the dew-soaked field. I'm still wearing my flip flops – the most impractical footwear on the planet - and have to skirt around prickly thistles and large steaming cow pats. As we walk, I fill Luc in on what happened last night after he'd been knocked out.

'God, Riley, you saved our lives! You're amazing and I was completely useless.'

'Well, there's not a lot you can do when you're unconscious.' My cheeks flush under his gaze.

'True.' He grins.

'Changing the subject though, do you think it's safe to follow these people?'

'Well, I spoke to both of them for about half an hour before you woke up and they seem normal and decent. And they're offering us breakfast. I'm starving, aren't you?'

I realise I am.

We're nearly at the barn. The cows are still mooing and I spot a cockerel on the fence, crowing for all he's worth. A couple of collies sit to attention in the yard and then circle the woman as she exits the field with the cattle. They make me think of Woolly. It feels like ages since I've seen him, even though it was only yesterday. I almost wish we'd brought him with us.

She wheels a large scaffold tower out of the barn and across the smooth surface of the yard, over to where we're waiting outside the fence by the ditch. Fred pulls out a long wide plank from under a nearby bush. It has a thick groove in the top and he swings it up so it slots into a bar on the top platform of the tower. The bottom of the plank rests on the ground by our feet.

Jessie climbs up the tower and throws us down a rope which is tied to the top of the tower. Fred uses the rope to haul himself, hand-over-hand, up the plank and onto the scaffold platform.

'Up you come!' he shouts. Luc and I look at each other and follow him up the plank. I've got slight doubts about following strangers into a place that obviously has no immediate route for escape. But I follow his instructions anyway and so does Luc. When we reach the top, Fred pulls up the plank and passes it down to Jessie. Then we all climb down the tower and Jessie wheels it away, back into the shed.

'Cor, I'm getting too old for that climbing malarkey,' Fred chuckles. 'Haven't done *that* in a while. We've got another way in and out, but I don't know you well enough to show you it just yet, no offence.'

'None taken,' Luc says.

Jessie beckons us and we follow her past the barn and round the back, to a sweet Georgian-style farmhouse built from mellow grey stone and half-covered in Virginia Creeper.

'Fred's going to do the milking. He'll be along later,' she says in a gravelly voice.

We enter the house through a side door, which takes us into a freezing scullery. The dogs trot after us and lie down on a doggy-smelling rug where they stay, somewhat dejected. Jessie slips off her Wellingtons and slides a pair of espadrilles on. We wipe our feet on the mat and follow her into the main, warmer part of the kitchen. She gestures to a chipped Formica table with six mismatched wooden chairs and we sit down gratefully and glance around.

It's a large, but cosy room with a slate floor and awful green textured wallpaper - functional, rather than aesthetic, but with a nice homey feel. On the shabby Welsh dresser sit framed photographs of children - a boy and a girl in various stages of childhood. I feel strangely comforted by the dresser's warm honey and treacle tones. Its gleaming brass handles rest on backplates shaped like birds with their wings outstretched and I think back to the second scare I had last night when the owl nearly collided with the AV. If it hadn't been for that startling encounter, I wouldn't have stopped here, scared and exhausted. I get the superstitious thought that maybe the owl was Skye guiding us to kindness and shelter.

Jessie reaches into a kitchen cupboard and takes out an ancient-looking bottle. 'Hydrogen peroxide,' she says. 'I'm going to dilute it to clean that wound on your head,' she says to Luc.

I see him wince. 'Okay, thanks,' he says.

She dabs some on the cut and the liquid starts foaming. Luc doesn't make a sound, but I notice he's gripping the sides of the chair.

'There,' she says. 'I'll brew up some comfrey root tea to help the bruising. It'll take about an hour or so. Remind me after breakfast.'

'Thanks,' says Luc.

'Now, on to more pleasant things. Tea? I'm afraid we've only got mint, but it's quite delicious.'

'Yes please.'

'I've got some homemade bread and jam, if you'd like, or would you prefer bacon and eggs?'

I'm absolutely starving. I hadn't realised how much, until she started talking about food and now I can feel the build-up of saliva in my mouth and the giant-sized hole in my stomach.

'Tell you what,' continues Jessie. 'We'll have the lot.'

She starts to prepare the food on a cream wood burning stove. It radiates a gentle heat, taking the edge off what would have been a very chilly room, if the freezing scullery is anything to go by.

As she cooks, we sip our tea and I tell her about the previous night's unwelcome encounter. She listens without speaking; just nodding or shaking her head at the appropriate times.

'And then I woke up and saw you with your cows in the field,' I say, my story complete.

'Unfortunately, your tale doesn't surprise me,' she replies, as she serves up our delicious-smelling English breakfast and joins us at the table. 'When we go into the village, we always hear some awful tale about run-ins with the raiders. It's getting worse and there's no one to keep them in check. I don't feel as safe here as I used to.'

'Are they your children?' I point to the photographs on the dresser.

'Yes, that's Freddie Junior and that's Melissa.'

'How old are they?'

'Freddie's nineteen now and Lissy's sixteen.'

'Same age as me,' I say. 'I'm sixteen.'

'When's your birthday?' asks Jessie.

'Beginning of May.'

'Same as Liss.' There's an awkward silence.

'This is absolutely delicious, Jessie,' says Luc.

'Mmm,' I agree. 'It's so kind of you to go to all this trouble.'

'Not at all, it's my pleasure.' She smiles. I like her face. It's kind and sweet. But she looks sad. I suppose it's a hard, lonely life. I wonder where her children are.

We're on to our third cup of tea and all but licking our plates clean, when Fred comes in through the scullery door.

'Finished?' Jessie asks him with a smile.

'As if!' Fred replies.

'I'll give you a hand after breakfast. Wash your hands and sit down. Yours is in the pan. I'll serve it up.'

'Lovely.' He turns to us. 'I see you're enjoying the produce - all home-grown you know.'

'It's fantastic,' I say.

'Really good,' Luc agrees. 'Thanks so much for inviting us.'

'You stay as long as you like,' Fred offers. 'We don't get many visitors.'

'You forgot to remind me about the comfrey root!' scolds Jessie. She takes a cloth and soaks it in the brewed tea. Then she places it on Luc's head.

'That feels great,' he says. 'Really good. Thanks.'

After breakfast, Luc goes back to the AV to check it's still safely hidden from view and to do a more thorough check for damage, while Jessie gives me a tour. Fred says he has farm business to attend to, but will see us later this evening.

The farm is a decent size and they've got cattle, pigs, a tiny flock of sheep, ducks, chickens and rabbits. They also have an enormous kitchen garden which is charming, as well as practical.

Luc returns at about 10.30am. We offer to help out with the chores, but Jessie won't hear of it and tells us to go into the lounge, take a sofa each and have a sleep. She brings us in a couple of quilts, covers us over and draws the curtains.

'Help yourselves to food and drink. I'll be out in the yard if you need me.' And she closes the door behind us. We're alone again and I want to talk to Luc, but I'm so tired I can barely keep my eyes open.

'She's nice,' says Luc.

'I know,' I yawn. 'They don't even know us. They're really kind people.' I snuggle down onto the soft floral sofa, pull the quilt up to my nose and sleep.

CHAPTER EIGHTEEN

RILEY

I wake to the sound of the grandfather clock striking four. I'm completely disorientated. The events of the past twenty four hours unfurl slowly. Daylight spills in from behind one side of the heavy velvet curtains so it must be four in the afternoon.

Luc's still asleep on the sofa opposite me. Fred and Jessie haven't even asked who we are or why we're on the road alone. They seem such nice people and I feel we owe them an explanation, but I get the feeling they wouldn't approve of what we're doing. Luc stirs and interrupts my musings.

'Hello,' I say.

'Hi,' he replies. And we both fall about laughing at the bizarreness of the situation.

Later, we sit at the kitchen table and help Jessie prepare the vegetables for dinner. She clucks around us like a mother hen, asking us to sample various delicious foodstuffs. The room has warmed up and is thick with steam and cooking smells.

'We'll be stuffed before we even start dinner,' says Luc

'I know,' says Jessie. 'But you have to try a couple of slices of this cucumber, it's really good.'

We still haven't seen any sign of their children and I don't like to ask. Maybe they're visiting family or friends. It's odd they haven't said where they are. But then I suppose we haven't told them what we're doing. So I decide to mind my own business and just be thankful we've met this hospitable couple.

Soon dinner is ready and Jessie calls to Fred, who's upstairs getting changed out of his work clothes.

I feel relaxed and well-rested. I'm not so worried about Luc's health anymore. He seems to be recovering really well, although the bruise still looks nasty.

Jessie's telling us about the surrounding area. 'There's a compound just north of here, but we always preferred to be independent. We do some good trade with them and nowadays they're friendly enough, not like it used to be at the beginning. In any case, we have to stay here just in case ...'

Fred walks in and touches her arm. 'We're in a bit of a situation,' he says to us. 'Something happened a while ago.'

'You don't have to explain anything to us,' Luc says.

'No, it's okay. We'd like to tell you. You might've thought it strange our kids aren't around.'

I'm intrigued, but neither of us speaks.

'It happened nine years ago,' continues Fred. 'We'd got used to the way things were, with all the troubles and everything. This place was secure; locked tight against raiders and looters. We'd already abandoned a lot of land over the years and most of our livestock had been stolen. We're lucky to have what we got really. But at the time we were considering leaving the farm and moving into the compound so the kids could go to school and we wouldn't be so cut-off.

'Freddie was ten and Liss was seven. One day …' He broke off and paused for a moment. 'One day, Jess and I were tending to the animals as usual. We asked the children to sweep out the yard and feed the chickens. Jessie came back down to the house to cook breakfast, but the children weren't in the yard and it was still unswept. She got cross and went into the house to see what they were playing at, but they weren't there neither. She assumed they must have been with me, helping with the cows. They weren't, and we never saw 'em again.'

I realise what he's telling us – that their children have gone missing. There's a heavy silence. Luc breaks it.

'So they disappeared?'

Jessie sighs. 'We didn't have the same security measures on the farm then that we have now. We were stupid, naive. It's the not-knowing that eats you up inside. I mean they could be anywhere. I refuse to believe they've gone for good. This morning. We thought, well for a second when Fred saw Luc …'

'Oh God!' I say, comprehending. 'You thought we could have been them coming home! I'm so sorry.'

'That's right,' Fred replies. 'We wouldn't normally invite strangers into our home, but we saw you two and thought of our children and Jessie's a big softie and begged me to invite you both in for breakfast. So you see, we can't move to a safer location in case they manage to find their way back to us.

'The local compound is secure now, with home grown provisions and new amenities and we wouldn't have to live on our nerves like this. They've already offered us a cottage that's just come available, but we can't leave because we have to be here when Freddie and Liss come home, else how would they find us again? We're stuck here, in limbo. Waiting.'

I feel awful and don't know what else to say. The rest of our dinner stays cold on the plates. I get up to put my arms round Jessie, who gives me a kiss and pats the back of my hand.

How will they ever be able to move on with their lives when they don't know what's happened to their children? I think about my sheltered upbringing and compare it to the most people who live in fear and uncertainty, like this poor couple. I've seen nothing on our journey that comes close to the life I've led and I feel an overwhelming rush of gratitude to my parents.

Then I get a stab of guilt. Aren't they too, worrying themselves stupid about our safety? They don't know if we're alive or dead. The note we left will do nothing to calm their fears; it will only make them worry more. I decide to contact them as soon as we can. But the next opportunity probably won't be until we reach Century Barracks in Warminster.

Then something occurs to me. Something so obvious, I wonder why I didn't think of it the second Fred and Jessie mentioned their children's disappearance. It must have occurred to Luc too, because we look at each other and mouth the same word, 'Grey.'

I'm itching to tell them what we know, but I wonder if it's the right thing to do. It's too late to keep it from them though, as they've missed nothing of our unsubtle exchange.

'Do you think it might've been James Grey's lot?' I ask Luc, not sure if I should have spoken.

'Who?' Fred and Jessie answer in unison.

'Umm.' I start to feel nervous about what I'm going to tell them, but I continue anyway. 'James Grey. From Salisbury.'

'Never heard of him,' says Jessie. 'Fred?'

'No. Doesn't ring any bells,' he answers. They turn to look at me, as Luc still hasn't spoken.

'Please, tell us what you can,' says Jessie.

I hesitate. Not sure where to start.

'Tell us.' Her voice is barely a whisper now. She's shaking and tears roll down her cheeks. 'I don't even want to let myself hope there's a chance you might know what happened after all this time.' She pushes back her chair and stands up unsteadily. Fred rises and put his arms around her. He turns to face me and Luc and there is anger in his eyes.

'If you know something, please tell us. I like you two kids, but you better not be upsetting my Jess for nothing.'

'I'm sorry,' says Luc. 'We shouldn't have said anything. It's just, what happened to your children happens quite a lot around here and my father has a theory about who's behind the abductions.'

'Spit it out, lad.' Fred speaks more gently this time and guides Jessie back to her chair. He sits next to her and holds her hands in his.

I feel uncomfortable that I blurted out Grey's name without thinking. But it's too late and anyway Luc seems to be gearing up to tell them about James Grey, Salisbury and the rumours.

CHAPTER NINETEEN

Eleanor

With thousands of people either dead or missing, we gave thanks, hourly that our loved ones were still beside us. My emotions fluctuated between a blissful euphoria that Connor and I were so consumed with each other, and the growing worry that world events were about to catch us up.

The centre to everybody's lives had shifted. Priorities changed. The tainted summer air held a mixture of urgency and recklessness. Samuel decided to join up. The military had issued a public announcement for more people to defend our besieged country and the TV advert gave a list of recruitment offices where you could just turn up to enlist.

Samuel was sold on it, and Abi was all at once, proud and distraught. She'd taken to calling him, *My Samuel.* They accepted him on the spot, pending his security checks and, all being well, he would go through fast-track basic training and then start serving.

He took to his new career like a cockerel to a five-barred gate, crowing loudly to Abi and me about his new responsibilities. I suppose at the time, I thought he was basically a loyal, good-hearted bloke - just not a very bright one. And he was easily seduced by power and beauty. He wanted to be at the heart of the action, the first to know everything and he craved the status and power newly up for grabs. It became harder for me to like him though, as he openly hated Connor.

One afternoon, Connor and I were walking back from the corner shop to my parents' house. It was quite chilly and we were looking forward to getting in out of the gusting wind. He had his arm around me and I leant into his body, revelling in our closeness.

'Still in your civvies, Connor. Not gonna help out your country then?'

We both turned around and saw Samuel with a couple of his army buddies. Connor ignored him and we carried on walking. A thousand and one retorts hovered on my tongue, but I couldn't spit any of them out.

'Talking to *you*, mate,' Samuel called out. I heard him say something to his buddies and they all laughed.

I prayed Samuel would leave it alone. We carried on walking, but I felt Connor's stride slow down. We could hear them close behind. The road was quiet and I had a stomach-lurching feeling this wouldn't end well.

'Connor! Mate! Is it because you're a coward? Is that it?'

Connor looked at me and gave me a reassuring smile. He didn't appear at all worried. He seemed calm and unbothered.

'I said. Is it because you're a coward?' This time, Samuel's voice was right behind us.

'Ellie,' Connor spoke to me quietly. 'You go on home. I'll be there in a bit.'

'No way,' I replied and turned around to face the three soldiers. The wind whipped my hair around my face and I pushed it behind my ears. 'Samuel Bletchley, you're being a twat. Why don't you just shut your ignorant mouth.'

This provoked laughter and jeers from him and his mates.

'Hey, Connor! Guess that proves it then. You really are a coward. Gotta get your woman to fight your battles.'

'Is that what this is then?' Connor asked. 'A battle?' He dropped his arm from around my shoulders, stood in the middle of the pavement facing the three of them and took a long swig from his can of lemonade.

Samuel and his mates didn't reply, they just smiled and nudged each other like the immature idiots they were.

'So. You think I'm a coward, yeah? That's what this is about?'

'Pretty much,' Samuel replied.

'That's an easy issue to sort out, Sam.'

'Only my mates call me Sam.'

'And what are your two mates called?' Connor asked.

Samuel looked confused for a second. 'Them?' He gestured to his mates.

Connor nodded.

'Mark and Rich. What's that gotta do with anything?'

'Mark, Rich,' Connor looked at the beefy soldiers. 'Why don't you two do one so I can prove to Samuel I'm not the coward he thinks I am. But if all three of you stay, I think that would prove *you* are the cowards. We can settle this one on one or you can all three start laying into me and we'll know for a fact I'm right.' Connor stared hard at Samuel, not breaking eye contact for a second.

Samuel looked away first. He smiled and shook his head.

'You wanna fight me, Connor? Nah, you don't wanna do that mate. You might get hurt.'

He patted Connor on the shoulder and then all three of them barged past us and carried on down the road.

I looked at Connor and saw a brief flicker of cold hate in his eyes, but then he instantly softened and winked at me. He draped his arm back around my shoulders.

I was still really unnerved though. I knew Samuel still thought Johnny had been wronged and Connor was to blame. He wouldn't accept it had been my decision to end the relationship, and Johnny was too dignified to pursue the matter. As a loyal friend to Johnny, Sam still wanted his revenge and, as we were soon to find out, his new career put him in the perfect position to exact it. Samuel just couldn't help himself.

CHAPTER TWENTY

RILEY

Luc and I heard the history of James Grey's rise to power from Luc's Uncle Rufus, who's one of the few people outside Salisbury to have met the man. Salisbury Cathedral is the focal point for devout Christians across the country. The reason it's so important, is that it's now the very last cathedral left in Britain. Because of this, after the main terror attacks, Salisbury attracted pilgrims who travelled through unpredictable countryside to reach its walls and help preserve it against looters and vandals.

We all knew the rumours surrounding one of these pilgrims - Mr James Grey. Luc's uncle once had the misfortune to dine with him a few years ago, as a guest in his grand house in the Cathedral Close.

Luc's Uncle Rufus is based at our Perimeter, but only ever comes home about once a year, as he's heavily involved in the family business. He spends his time managing perimeter security around the country, but also in his more secretive occupation of weapons production.

Rufus was hand-delivered a request to dinner, by one of James Grey's personal messengers. Rufus assumed he wanted to discuss perimeter business and so he accepted his invitation.

He arrived on time at the heavily guarded Cathedral Close, where they passed an interesting evening. Grey told Rufus his story or, as he liked to call it, his 'epiphany.'

'I was called to save the people,' he said.

But Rufus told us there was something manic about Grey. He got the feeling he was more than slightly unhinged, that it was obvious to see the fearful respect everybody paid him.

It turned out it wasn't security Grey was after from Luc's Uncle, but information on weapons production. Rufus was shocked that Grey knew anything about it, as it wasn't supposed to be common knowledge.

Grey suggested it would be mutually beneficial if Rufus were to set up a munitions factory within Salisbury's walls. Grey said he knew it wasn't a very Christian business but it was a necessary evil needed for protection. Rufus lied, politely denying all knowledge of the weapons industry and beat a hasty retreat. But he left behind a very angry man.

Rufus now has strong opinions on Grey:

'He's a man who is wholly sure of himself, an evil dictator disguised as the saviour of mankind. He's the worst kind of charlatan, but unfortunately he's got that place sewn up tight with his priestly warriors, disciples and slaves running around doing his bidding. It's a closed society and it's fuelled by fear.'

Under no circumstances will Luc's Uncle arm this madman with weapons and we're all praying that no one else will help him, for who knows how powerful he might become?

Thankfully, four years after his meeting with Rufus, Grey

isn't yet crusading against the rest of Britain in a holy war. So we can only hope his weapons production never gets going.

According to Rufus, James Grey, a one-time hospital worker, came down to Salisbury from his hometown, Durham, where the Cathedral and many churches had been taken over and, in Grey's words, 'desecrated by the masses.' They were being used either as places of shelter, as fortresses, or they had been targeted by terrorists, demolished or dismantled.

'... But nowhere, nowhere I tell you, were they being respected as Houses of God. Blasphemy everywhere I turned!' Luc's Uncle had pounded the table with his fist to add weight to his impression of Grey.

Grey was furious with this blatant disrespect to his God, but he received word from his sister, who lived outside Salisbury, that their ancient Cathedral was still intact. She could still see its four hundred and four foot spire from her little house. Rumour spread that it was being protected against terrorists and other ignorant heathens, by people such as himself, who were flocking to its aid to 'preserve Christianity in these barbaric times.'

After he received this message from his sister, Grey felt something he had never felt in all his thirty nine years - hope, in the form of a spiritual calling. He packed up his sparse belongings and trailed his frightened wife and four children more than halfway across the country until they reached the little village on the outskirts of the city where his sister lived.

His sister's house had been demolished and there was no

sign of her, so they assumed the worst. They hiked the five extra miles to the Cathedral Close to find it bolted shut from the inside against the outside world. No amount of begging, cajoling or shouting gained him entrance from the guards. He and his family had to make camp outside the walls, along with the hundreds of other homeless families and pilgrims, many of whom were injured, mortally ill or just plain crazy.

He made sure he and his family camped well away from the others, wary of attracting the wrong sort of attention or catching some vile disease. Occasionally, one of the gates would open to allow somebody out, or back in, but he could never catch a glimpse of the person, as they would always be surrounded by a heavily armed security force. Grey traded some of their precious food for a map of The Close.

He prayed night and day for God to admit him to His place of worship and one day, seven months later, his prayers were answered. The inhabitants of the eighty acre Cathedral Close were struck down by an unknown illness.

One morning, the gates opened wide and a robed man staggered out calling for a doctor. Weak, crying and sweating profusely, he had hideous, swollen lumps on his neck and black bruises on his face. He suddenly broke down into a coughing fit, clutching his chest in agony. As soon as Grey saw the distraught man he knew what he was witnessing - the plague.

He went straight to find his wife, children and meagre possessions and they left the area. They slept rough for several weeks and avoided all contact with other people. One day they stumbled across a deserted, mouldering two-bedroom mobile home hidden by trees in the corner of a field. They cleaned it up and moved in. Grey waited patiently, planning his next move.

Three months later, he was confident Salisbury Cathedral would be his to restore to the good Christian people of Britain. He told his family to remain in the mobile home for their own protection. He said he would return for them within a year. If he did not come back within the allotted time, they were to 'make a life for themselves.' (He never saw them again. When he finally did send someone to find them, the messenger returned saying the mobile home was empty with no sign of recent habitation. Grey assumed they must all be dead, kidnapped or fled).

When he returned to the Cathedral Close, the area outside the walls was as he had expected it to be - deserted. The stench of rotting bodies overpowered him, and Grey repeatedly threw up every time he tried to approach the St Anne Gate. However, he persevered and, when he reached it, he found it unlocked.

And so, after months of waiting, he had finally made it into The Close. At the entrance, a shallow pit was overflowing with partially burnt, decaying bodies. He jogged past with his face averted, but he knew he would soon have to deal with it.

He saw deserted buildings - Bishop Wordsworth's School, The Sub-Deanery, Sarum College; he knew the buildings and the layout by heart, from the worn and crumpled map he kept in his pocket. He went straight into the cavernous cathedral and dropped to his knees to give thanks to God for entrusting him with this holy task to undertake.

Over the next few days, he began the unforgiving and near impossible task of burning the corpses. He slept each night in the North Canonry and scavenged food from the empty buildings. One day, he hit the jackpot and found huge rooms in The Bishop's Palace piled high to the ceiling with bottled water, tins of fruit and vegetables and all manner of supplies that would have taken an army several months to get through.

But then, during that first week, he contracted strong flu-like symptoms. He knew this was inevitable and had expected it to happen. A couple of years previously, after the initial terror attacks, he'd had the foresight to steal an array of medicines from his place of work. He prayed for forgiveness every night, but saw the theft as a minor transgression, needed in case he or his family should need treatment in the future.

So, sweating and in fear, he prepared a syringe and gave himself his first shot of antibiotic, straight into his thigh. He had enough for two shots over a ten day course and prayed this would be enough to protect him from the disease.

He sweated it out, not having anticipated feeling so awful. He thought he would die, but the plague didn't manage to take hold. He was ill for two weeks, with dizzy spells and a strange deafness and light-headedness that disorientated him. But he attributed this to the pitiful amount of food he had consumed. The food was abundant, he just hadn't the energy to eat it.

At the end of his second week, he had a visitor - a middle-aged man who turned out to be one of the Cathedral Close gardeners by the name of Dickinson. He had survived the plague without the help of antibiotics. But, unlike the other survivors who had fled, he remained, not sure what else to do. When he found Grey on the brink of death, he took on the task of nursing him back to health.

Soon, Grey's mind cleared enough to focus upon the huge task ahead of him. Although he was impatient to start, he knew that he would have to get fit and healthy before the real work could begin. Dickinson offered to help him. It took months.

First they daubed the exterior walls will the words 'PLAGUE, KEEP AWAY'. Next, they dug pits and burnt the dead. It was exhausting, stomach-churning work, but they kept at it until every last corpse was just a charred remain. Thankfully, there can't have been that many people within the walls in the first place, but even so, it was almost six months before Grey decided to remove the warning graffiti and open the gates.

During that time he had amassed a small group of some twenty five or so followers. They had each ignored the warnings and entered the Close by cunning or brute force; either because they had already survived the plague, or because they felt it worth the risk. Either way, they were greeted warily by Grey, who interrogated each of them at gunpoint while deciding whether or not to let them remain. They all ended up more than willing to do Grey's bidding. How or why? Who knows? Were they brainwashed, bribed or threatened?

These first inhabitants became his core disciples and Grey considered them to have been chosen by God for him, as they had made it into the Close without fear of the plague.

He had some weaponry left over from the deceased security forces and so they all took up arms and prepared to receive their first influx of residents. Each visitor was grilled thoroughly on arrival and, if they were worthy, they were housed within the walls and given a role to fill, be it gardener, farmer, cook, child carer or tradesman.

The one common factor required was the willingness to embrace Grey's new religion. Few people refused to stay, as his way of life promised an easier existence than the one they faced outside the walls. He planned to disregard all previous incarnations of Christianity and devise a new, all-encompassing faith, to unite every denomination. And in true Grey style, he named it 'Grey's Church of the Epiphany'.

His Church grew quickly and soon the eighty acre Close became overcrowded. So Grey expanded his new empire. Before five years had elapsed, his walls enclosed almost the whole of Salisbury and beyond. He's as strict about letting people out as he is about letting them in. The army allows him to get on with it, as long as he doesn't cut off their transport routes and he pays them to turn a blind eye.

This is the gospel according to Rufus. But he still knows very little about what actually goes on behind The Close walls. Maybe it's all peace and harmony. But Luc's uncle is a good judge of character and he thinks we haven't heard the last of James Grey, not by a long way. He's a man out for glory and he'll get it by any means necessary.

CHAPTER TWENTY ONE

RILEY

Luc has just finished telling Fred and Jessie about Salisbury's recent history. He left out the bit about his Uncle Rufus' weapons production, just giving them the bare facts about James Grey and Salisbury. I see him pause as he thinks about how to tell them the next bit.

'So what has all this got to do with our Liss and Freddie Junior?' asks Jessie. 'Unless you think they may be with this Grey character.'

'We only know about him though rumours,' I say. 'My Pa always put the fear of God into us about Grey. He said if we ever set foot outside the Perimeter we could be snatched. He's like the bogeyman, or something.'

Luc continues. 'My uncle saw someone when he was in there. It was a girl, who'd gone missing from a local compound. She just disappeared, like your children. And then, a month later, my uncle recognised her in Grey's courtyard. He managed to smuggle her out and I'm not sure of all the details, but she had definitely been abducted. She said there were hundreds of other children who'd been taken or lured in, now trapped or brainwashed. And anyway, over the past few years there have been a lot of unexplained disappearances of children.

'I don't know what to think,' Jessie says. 'It's a possibility, but then again, it could just as likely be raiders that took them, or ...' She starts to cry again.

'Jess, darlin', don't cry.' Fred wipes her tears.

'I know we don't know for sure, but it makes sense that it could've been Grey,' I say. 'Raiders want food, weapons or valuables, not more mouths to feed. Grey isn't trusting anymore; he turns people away from his gates. But he's got hundreds of followers and they're mostly children or young adults. Children are easier to brainwash and train up to be loyal to him and his religion.'

'Anyway,' Luc says, 'we've told you what we know about Grey and I don't know if we've made you feel better or worse, but maybe there might be some hope for you that ...'

'That what?' Fred interrupts. 'That we can march up to Grey's house and say, 'excuse me, Sir, but have you got our kids? We think you might have took 'em without asking and we'd like 'em back'.'

'I don't know,' Luc says. 'I'm sorry.'

'Oh Go-o-od!' says Jessie, exhaling loudly. 'This is just too much. I can't deal with this now. I can't *think* anymore. Thank you Luc, Riley, for what you've told us, but I can't listen to any more.' She trembles as she stands and makes a move to clear the table.

'Just leave them dinner things, Jess.' Fred gives us a glare. 'No offence, kids, but would you mind going upstairs and leaving me and Jess to talk. We'll see yer in the morning.'

We stand up awkwardly and say goodnight, not really knowing if we should add anything more to ease the situation. But Fred wants us gone. As we walk up the stairs, Luc gives me a look I can't decipher, but I don’t think he’s too happy.

‘We shouldn't have mentioned Grey,’ he whispers. ‘I think we've just given them false hope. Even if Grey has got their kids, there's nothing they can do about it.’

‘I know,’ I reply. ‘But we had to tell them. It’s their kids. Surely they have a right to know all the possibilities.’

His jaw clenches tight. ‘Yeah, I guess. But I feel bad for them.’

‘I know. Me too.’

To make matters worse, the rooms we’re going to sleep in tonight are Liss and Freddie's bedrooms. When Jessie showed us to our rooms earlier, we hadn't known their children were missing. We just assumed they had moved out or were with friends. Now I know the truth, I’m a little creeped out that we’re sleeping in their bedrooms.

‘Hope you sleep okay, Riley,’ he says, squeezing my hand. ‘Sorry if I seemed a bit off.’

‘Don’t worry about it. It’s a weird situation. You sleep well too.’

My room is immaculate, but looks exactly as it must have been nine years ago. It’s a seven-year-old girl’s bedroom, with cuddly toys, dolls and pretty things. A shrine. A pink and mauve delight that makes me sad. I gaze out of the window into the black night, the darkness relieved by starry pinpricks and a sliver of moon. I close the fairy curtains and lie on top of the covers, thinking of Luc in the next room, of Fred and Jessie's lost daughter and of my Skye.

We spend the following morning helping Fred and Jessie with their chores around the house and farm. I get stuck in, pleased for the distraction the physical work provides.

'There's always too much to do,' says Jessie. 'It's amazing how much more we can get done with you here. Thank you.'

They haven't mentioned last night's conversation and I don't feel it's my place to bring it up. An awkward feeling hovers in the air between us and our hosts. Luc and I agree we should probably head off soon. In the cold light of morning, I feel as if I've made a huge error in judgement by telling this sweet couple what we know. Luc was right, we shouldn't have said anything.

Jessie looks pale and tired and Fred is cordial, but tight lipped. I know I've opened old wounds. Did I genuinely think I was doing something good? Or was I just excited at the thought of giving them the news that could lead to a dramatic reunion with their children?

They ask us to join them for a sandwich in the kitchen and we politely follow them in. The easy good humour from yesterday has completely gone. We all sit down around the Formica table, not knowing what to say. After a long minute of silent chewing, Fred clears his throat.

'Jess and I didn't get much sleep last night, as you can imagine.'

'We're sorry,' Luc says. 'It was insensitive of us to ...'

Fred raises his hand. 'Let me finish, lad.'

Luc and I cast our eyes downward while Fred continues.

'We're grateful you told us about Grey. It's a lot for us to take in. We really never expected to hear anything about our children again. We'd sorta said goodbye to them a few years ago, you know, in our heads. Your revelation has changed everything. We had no leads before, nothing to go on, no help; they could have been anywhere. But now . . . We can't go on like before, not if there's the smallest chance they could be alive; if there's a chance they're there. We have to try. We have to.'

Jessie is staring at me and Luc. 'We need your help,' she says. 'We could try by ourselves, but we'd have more of a chance if you would tell us how we could get in there. We wouldn't expect you to put yourselves in any danger, but if you could just help us to formulate a plan. Advise us how to go about it. You know about the place.'

'We'll do anything we can to help,' I say. 'Of course we will.'

'Hold on, Riley,' Luc says. 'Of course we'd love to help, but I don't see how we can.'

'Luc,' I start to reason with him. 'Surely we can ...'

'No, Riley,' he snaps. 'This isn't fixable. None of this is fixable. Not finding abducted children or bringing in escaped murderers and not bringing Skye back to life.'

I raise my eyes to Fred and Jessie, who return my look of shock. I've never seen Luc like this. I've seen him irritated and annoyed, and after Skye, I saw him sad beyond measure, but this anger is an entirely different Luc. He's biting his lip and shaking with emotion. I can see he hadn't meant to blurt out our business like that.

'I don't even wanna ask,' Fred says.

'This is such a mess,' sighs Luc, his rage dissipating as quickly as it flared up. 'The whole thing is just completely screwed up. Riley, we must be mad to be doing any of this.'

'I'm sorry, Luc,' I say.

'Not your fault.'

We've got no choice but to tell them what Luc and I are doing. It would feel wrong not to say anything. We tell them a watered-down version of our story, starting with Skye's murder, but leaving out the part about not having our parents' permission. Jessie now looks even more stricken than before, if that's possible.

'What kind of world are we living in? Riley, I'm sorry about your sister, you poor girl. And there's us, trying to rope you into our affairs, when you've already got so much on your plate.'

'Sorry,' Fred echoes. 'Looks like we're not the only ones suffering.'

We all sit quietly, lost in our own thoughts for what feels like a long time.

'Okay,' Luc breaks the silence. 'I'm definitely going to regret this, but Riley's right.' He turns to me with a smile that doesn't quite reach his eyes and then returns his gaze to the couple. 'We should help you. You've been really kind to us and we're here now, on the road. There's no going back for Riley and me.'

'Luc,' I smile at him. He looks at me but doesn't return the smile this time.

'Riley,' he says. 'We'll do this, but everyone will have to do exactly what I say. No questions, no hesitation or doubts. If we do this, it's serious and we'll do it my way.'

'Luc, lad,' says Fred. 'Just give us some information and we'll do the rest. We can't ask you to put yourselves in danger for us. It's not right, you're kids yourselves.'

'Fred, no offence, but you've got no chance of doing this without us. The very fact we're *kids* is what's going to make this plan work.'

'I hope you're not suggesting what I think you are.' Fred is worried and so am I. I'm just starting to realise what Luc's plan is going to involve.

It's all very well, telling them about Grey and our theories on all the missing children, but now we have to actually do something about it and that's the scary part. We've never been to Salisbury before. We've only heard of Grey through Luc's uncle. Of course we have to help them, but what are we going to do about Chambers and our own search for answers?

Our parents will now be frantic with worry and every day we delay our search, means more stress for our families. But it's too late for us to think about that now. At least the road to Salisbury is the route we were going to take anyway. We've made our choice and have to follow it through. I want to help these people and, besides, I like them and want more than anything for them to find their children.

CHAPTER TWENTY TWO

RILEY

Luc and I stand outside the walls of Salisbury Cathedral. We're on foot and we've dressed to make ourselves appear as young and vulnerable as possible, in scruffy, stained t shirts and shorts. I'm not wearing a scrap of makeup and my hair is pulled back in a ponytail. This morning, Luc shaved his fine stubble with Fred's cut throat razor until his skin was peachy soft. We're unarmed and carry no bags or possessions.

We knocked and shouted several times with no response from the main gates and so we followed the high wall along for about three hundred yards. Now we've arrived at a small wooden door with thick metal studs. I'm hesitating, but Luc bangs on it twice with his fist. Almost instantly, a woman opens it.

She's small and pretty with shoulder-length dark blonde hair. She doesn't look anything like the dark-robed religious zealots I had imagined. In fact, the only religious-looking thing about her is the small gold cross hanging neatly around her neck, nestling below her collar bone just above her pastel blue shirt. I'm guessing she's in her thirties and she has an open friendly face.

Luc and I had psyched ourselves up so much for this

moment that I'm quite taken aback to be greeted with such courtesy and lack of security.

'Come in,' she says. 'The road's not a good place to be these days. Would you like a drink?'

We step through the small wooden door in the wall and glance around. There's no security that I can see and we're in a small beautiful courtyard, fragrant with flowers and herbs. She motions us towards a wrought iron patio set and we sit down.

'Be back in a minute.' She smiles. 'Lemonade okay?'

We nod and watch as she passes through a half-glazed door in the side of a house, its red bricks faded and crumbling.

'This is odd,' I whisper to Luc.

'Not really,' he replies. 'Think about it. If you want to recruit children or young adults, heavy security isn't going to make them want to stay. Grey's a smart man. He'll try the carrot approach first. This first impression will look like paradise to most kids used to living rough on the outside. You can guarantee if we were anything other than two defenceless kids at the gate, we'd have got a very different welcome.'

The door creaks open and the woman returns carrying a tray with a jug of lemonade, three glasses and a plate of biscuits. A large ginger tom cat runs out of the door with her and scampers across to where we're sitting. He purrs loudly, winding himself around our legs, his nose in the air, asking to be petted.

'Don't mind Tigger,' says the woman. 'Shoo him away if he bothers you. He just loves company.' She sits and pours out the cloudy lemonade.

'No,' I reply. 'He's lovely, really friendly.' I reach down to stroke the cat.

'Help yourselves to biscuits.' She gestures to the plate and Luc and I take one each. They're obviously really delicious, but nerves stifle the taste and my dry mouth makes it feel like crumbly cement on my tongue. I reach for my glass and swallow a mouthful of the acidic drink.

'It's all homemade,' says the woman. 'I'm Rebecca.'

'Luc.'

'Riley.' I cough. We decided earlier that we didn't need to change our first names, as nobody would know who we are anyway.

'We're sorry to bother you,' says Luc. 'But we've got nowhere to go and we saw your gate and we're so hungry and thirsty. It's really kind of you.'

'It's no bother,' Rebecca smiles. 'Relax. Enjoy your drinks. You don't have to rush off on account of me. I have work to do anyway. I'll be in here if you need me.' She points back to the door she's just come through. 'Please stay as long as you like.' She swigs down the last of her lemonade and goes back into the house.

We wait a few minutes. All I can hear is Tigger's insistent purring, the breeze ruffling the leaves of the trees and a distant hammering sound of metal on metal. It's a warm afternoon, still early and the sun's high in the sky.

Things still feel a strained between me and Luc after what happened at Fred and Jessie's. I don't know if he's a little mad at me for telling them about Grey, but now's not the time to have *that* discussion.

He stands and has a look around the small courtyard. It feels like we're in a private residence. If you didn't know any better, you would never guess this place belonged to The Cathedral Close. A jumble of pots and troughs contain flowers and herbs. Ivy clings to the walls of the house and creeps around the dark blank windows. A couple of wasps buzz sleepily around us and a line of ants stream across the cracked terracotta flagstones.

Now we're inside the walls, there's no going back. Luc stares up at the house, as if attempting to unravel its secrets and I try hard not to think about what we're doing. Luc told me my only task is to locate Liss and try to keep her close to me. He's going to do the rest.

CHAPTER TWENTY THREE

Eleanor

Suddenly, the speed at which worldwide events unfolded was like someone had pressed a fast-forward button, spooling us crazily towards a too-scary ending. The attacks hadn't stopped and no one knew if they were carried out by the same networks, or if new terror groups around the world were taking advantage of the confusion.

Three weeks later at four in the morning, an army convoy of trucks rolled through our sleepy village on their way to assist with all the border closures being put into effect. But not all the vehicles kept on rolling.

One camouflage truck stopped at the end of our lane and a small unit of soldiers silently jogged up the pavement towards our house. Samuel was among them.

Crisis point had been reached and so all traditional military protocol had been abandoned. NCOs and Privates had been automatically upgraded to make way for the newly enlisted. Nothing familiar could be relied upon and personal freedom was now a thing of the past.

The military unit came into our house. They told my parents they wanted Connor. My parents told the officer in charge that Connor wasn't in the house, but they didn't believe us and searched each room.

We remonstrated with the soldiers. Sleep was misting up my brain but outrage woke me up. I followed one of the soldiers into my room, asking him what he thought he was doing. I wanted to run to Connor's camper van and warn him, but I knew that to do so would be to reveal his whereabouts. It was too late anyway. Connor had heard the commotion and had opened the shiny red door to his van.

I stared out of my bedroom window as he stood there in his boxer shorts, confused and sleepy. He pulled an old grey t shirt over his head. One of the soldiers outside shouted to the others. They poured out of the house. Connor looked small and alone, squinting downwards and he shielded his eyes with his arm, as they shone a torch over him. They took him away immediately, with no regard for his dignity or comfort.

'What are you doing?' I screamed from my bedroom window and ran, almost falling downstairs. My brothers shouted at them and my parents tried to calm us all down. 'What's going on? Why have they got you, Connor?' I ran across the front lawn towards him in my bare feet. Two fresh-faced soldiers barred my way, unmoved by my tears.

I saw Samuel and my hopes soared. 'Sam!' I shouted. 'Why have they got Connor? Tell them! Tell them they've got the wrong person!'

But he refused to catch my eye and didn't say a word. It hit me then with a bitter punch. I couldn't believe it, but I knew the truth.

'You bastard!' I wanted to bite and scratch and kick and hit him until there was nothing left. 'You did this! Connor has done nothing! Nothing. Why would you do such an evil thing?'

It was clear to me then, that this was all Samuel's doing. He had gotten Connor arrested under some false pretence. I could only pray and hope they would find no evidence to back it up. That Samuel was only trying to scare him and would release him soon.

My father spoke to two of the soldiers, but they wouldn't give him any reason for the arrest. They took Connor's camper van and drove it away. My brothers picked me up off the dew-sodden lawn and carried me back into the house.

CHAPTER TWENTY FOUR

RILEY

About twenty minutes later, Rebecca returns. 'You two alright?' she asks.

I nod.

'You're brother and sister are you?'

'Yeah. Our mum and dad were killed a few months back, by raiders.' Luc feeds her the cover story we worked out earlier.

'Oh, you poor things.' She sits down and gives us a sympathetic smile. 'Where are you staying?'

'Well, we're looking for a place. We've been on the road for a while.'

'How old are you?'

'Sixteen,' Luc lies.

She turns to me.

'Fourteen,' I say, colouring. Obviously I'm not as good an actor as Luc.

We're banking on the fact that as we're roughly the same ages as Freddie and Lissy, we'll be housed with or near them. We're also assuming that accommodation will be according to gender and so we're prepared to be split up. That's the part I'm dreading - being alone without Luc to back me up.

I'm quickly becoming more and more in awe of him. He's

rational and practical, while I'm hot-headed and impulsive. He seems so focused and certain while I'm a mass of nerves. My head is swimming with fear at what could happen to us.

'You know,' she says. 'You're very welcome to stay here for the night. We've plenty of room.'

'Really?'

'It's no problem.'

'Is this some kind of compound then?' Luc asks.

'Yes, in a way it is. We've rescued hundreds of people who have no place left to turn. We think of ourselves as an oasis in the wilderness, offering food, shelter and protection.'

'Sounds amazing,' I say.

'Well, come on, you must be tired. Shall I show you to your quarters?' She stands and gestures to the building behind her.

We follow her into the house, which is actually some kind of work room. Several women, maybe ten or twelve of them, all similar in appearance to Rebecca, sit at desks and tables. Some are writing and some are reading; the majority are sewing clothing. None of them talk, they're all quietly engaged in their tasks, but most of them glance up and smile as we thread our way through to the door on the far side of the room.

As we walk through the door, a young man in his late teens greets us. His appearance is unremarkable and he's dressed in unflattering beige trousers and a short-sleeved white cotton shirt. He asks Luc to follow him. I make to go after them, but Rebecca touches my arm.

'I'm afraid the men and women's quarters are in separate

buildings. Don't worry, you'll see your brother later.'

Luc gives me a reassuring smile and a penetrating stare that gives me some comfort. Suddenly, I have an inappropriate image of us together, his lips on mine. I don't know where it came from but I shake the thought away.

'Don't worry, Riley,' he says. 'I'm sure Rebecca will look after you. I'll see you later.'

I take a breath and study my surroundings as Luc told me to do. We're in a gravel courtyard, much bigger than the one at the entrance. It's rectangular, with a building on each side, mostly in shade, with just a few small squares of sunlight on the ground. A cloud blots the sun for an instant and I shiver and hug my goose-bumped arms. I'm only dressed in a t shirt and shorts, and wish I'd thought to bring a jumper or cardigan.

Luc is taken off to the right, to a long low red brick house. His trainers crunch loudly over the gravel, until he disappears through a dark green painted wooden door. Rebecca watches them go and then she asks me to follow her. We walk directly across the courtyard into an imposing building, four storeys high, with wide steps leading up to a set of grand double doors.

We enter a dim wood-panelled hallway with a wide staircase. It smells musty and slightly of sweaty feet. The kitchen must be somewhere at the end of the hallway, as I can hear clanking pots and pans and distant busy voices. Rebecca leads me up two flights of stairs to a shabby landing with a worn patterned carpet and about eight closed doors. It's gloomy and quiet.

She knocks on the door immediately at the top of the stairs.

A plump girl opens it. She's wearing a dark grey A line skirt with a grey shirt tucked in. Around her neck hangs an iron cross, the same colour as her shirt. Her hair is pulled back into a lank ponytail and she's got angry-looking acne on her cheeks and chin.

'Martha,' says Rebecca. 'This is Riley, she's staying tonight.'

'Riley, is it?' Martha glares at me, her mouth pulled downwards. 'Is that short for anything?'

'No, it's just Riley.'

'Right.' She hmmphs. 'Follow me then. We'll get you settled.'

'I'll see you, Riley,' says Rebecca, turning to go. 'Martha will look after you now.'

'But I'll see you later won't I?' I ask Rebecca, unwilling to have a seemingly kind woman replaced by this unfriendly girl.

'I'm afraid not,' Rebecca replies, already halfway down the stairs. 'You don't need me anymore.' She gazes up regretfully and then hurries down and out of view, her footsteps receding.

I brace myself. This is, after all, what I was expecting from the outset anyway. But our welcome softened me up a bit. I must remember why I'm really here and what I'm supposed to do. Martha points towards a room in the middle of the corridor.

'There's the bathroom. Take a shower. There are some clean clothes on the back of the door. If you leave your clothes in the basket, I'll have them washed for you. Come and knock on my door when you've finished.'

I do as she asks and soon I'm clean, smelling of the harsh soap, and dressed identically to Martha, minus the cross and still wearing my flip flops. The clothes fit me okay, but there's no mirror so I can't really tell how awful I look. I take a deep breath and knock on Martha's door. She regards me and hmmphs her approval. Then she steps out onto the landing and locks her door.

'Follow me,' she orders.

I follow her to the other end of the corridor where she opens another door. I expect to see another room, but instead there's a small dark, wooden, winding staircase leading down.

It's been two days and I've heard no mention and seen no trace of Luc, Liss or Freddie. Everybody I've met so far has biblical names and it's entirely likely that Freddie and Liss's names have been changed, which will make it an almost impossible task to locate them. I hope Luc's having more luck than me; the alternative doesn't bear thinking about. What if I never get out of this strange half-asleep place?

I've been assigned to the Nursery, which is actually an okay job, if exhausting. All The Close's children are taken from their parents at the age of two and housed together in the Nursery. They're separated into age groups until they're nine, when they are split by gender. I'm taking care of the three to five-year olds. There are twenty four of them, looked after by four of us: myself, an older woman and two women in their twenties.

Nothing has been explained to me, other than the actual duties I've been assigned. Any questions I ask are met with a vague smile and an unenlightening change of subject.

Everyone's on autopilot and there's no small talk, chatter or gossip - they simply get on with their duties in a kind, but firm manner. The children all behave immaculately.

I sleep in one of the dormitories on Martha's floor. There are four bunks in my room, sleeping eight girls who are around the age of fourteen. I've hardly spoken to any of them, as they come in after I go to bed and are still asleep when I get up for work at the Nursery. They obviously work a different shift to me.

I tried talking to a couple of them last night, but they were just as vague and dreamy as my co-workers. I'm getting panicky now, worrying I might be stuck here forever, turning into a version of these half-alive women and girls. It's not so scary here, but it doesn't feel right either. It's too quiet and emotionless. Like the life has been sucked out of everyone.

It's my third morning and I've just reached the bottom of the dark staircase that takes me from my dormitory to the maze of buildings where the Nursery is located, when I see a figure in the corner. My heart skips a beat as I realise it's Luc looking a little nerdy in borrowed clothes. I was beginning to think I'd never see him again.

'Looking good, Riley,' Luc grins at me.

'Back atcha, Lucas.'

He turns serious. 'You okay? Sorry I couldn't get here sooner and I can't stay long, I'm supposed to be getting paint cans.'

'What's happening?'

'It's not good news, Riley. I'm pretty sure we've been tricked.'

CHAPTER TWENTY FIVE

RILEY

'Tricked? I say. 'Tricked how?

Luc shakes his head slowly, a scowl on his face.

'Luc, tell me what's happened.'

He steps closer and starts talking in a fast whisper. 'Our first night here, I climbed up on the roof to get an idea of the layout of the place. I didn't see anybody. No security guards or anything. There's another courtyard round the back and there was a vehicle in there. It was parked under some trees.'

'A vehicle?' I say with a growing feeling of dread. I think I know where this is heading.

'Riley, it was our AV.'

'Are you sure?'

'Hundred percent.'

Fred and Jessie were supposed to be waiting a mile away in their jeep with our AV parked close by. They were going wait there for us and if we didn't show up after ten days they would drive to our Perimeter in Bournemouth and alert our parents who would send in help.

But if our AV was now in Grey's Close, something had gone very wrong.

'There wasn't a lot I could do from up on the roof,' Luc

continued. 'I had to get back and try to find out what it meant.'

'So they must've caught Fred and Jessie,' I say. 'What shall we do? We'll have to find them. Get them out as well as their kids.'

'Hang on, Riley. I haven't told you the rest.'

As I wait for him to continue, I hear footsteps coming down the stairs.

'Quick,' I hiss, yanking open the broom cupboard and dragging him inside with me. I pull the door closed behind us, hoping whoever's coming doesn't open the door and discover us.

The footsteps get louder and then they stop. We're in total darkness and there's a strong smell of wood and disinfectant. Luc's body is pressed up close to mine. He takes my hand. My heart is crashing against my ribs.

Any minute now, I expect the door to open. We'll be hauled out and turned over to James Grey. I hold my breath and squeeze Luc's hand. And then the footsteps continue on, moving further away until I no longer hear them.

Luc inches open the door and peers out. 'All clear.'

We step out of the cupboard and give each other a look which says it all.

'God, we need to get out of this place,' I say.

'Yeah, might be harder than we thought,' Luc replies. 'I found out some other stuff which you're not going to like.'

I wait for him to go on.

'The next day, after I'd spotted our AV, I planned to try and get some sense out of somebody. There was this boy a bit younger than me - Michael. I told him about Fred and Jessie's kids being kidnapped. Hoped he might know who they were.'

'Was that such a good idea?'

'I was running out of options. I couldn't wait around for answers to fall into my lap. Anyway, get this - Michael doesn't know Fred and Jessie's kids, but he does know Fred and Jessie.'

'He knows Fred and Jessie?'

'Yes.'

'That can't be right,' I say.

'Yeah, it was a shock for me too, but there's no mistake. Michael described the farm and said what a nice couple they were. He said they were the ones who sent him here, and that was months ago.'

'No!'

'Yes.'

'But that means ...'

'It means Fred and Jessie must have known about Grey all along.'

As Luc whispers his discovery to me in the dark doorway, I experience a sweep of hopelessness.

'But they seemed genuinely upset,' I say, raising my voice. 'Jessie was in tears.'

'Shh, Riley,' Luc says, glancing around. 'I know. It's sick. They tricked us.'

'So there probably *is* no Freddie Junior and Liss. They must've made them up. How could they do that?' I wonder, did they do it willingly? Or have they been coerced? Brainwashed too maybe? Well, it makes no difference now. They fooled us completely and now I feel stupid and angry. I thought I was a good judge of character, but I was completely taken in by them.

'Riley! Riley, are you okay?' Luc shakes my arm to get my attention back.

'What should we do?' I say. 'We're trapped here.'

'We'll get out. I'll find a way. Security seems laid back. It's just the outside wall we need to worry about. But we'll have to do something fast before they move the AV. If we lose our transport we've got no chance. Day five is the start of *Integration Week* for newbies and I don't want to stick around for that or we'll end up like zombies.'

'I should've been at the Nursery ages ago,' I say. 'They'll be wondering where I am.'

'Yeah, I better get back too.'

'So what now?' I ask.

'Okay,' Luc says. 'How about, each night between two and four in the morning, you wait in the bathroom. Hang a rag or a piece of clothing from the window to let me know you're there. Once I've got a plan, I'll come and get you.'

I nod and we briefly hug before he leaves. I wait a moment and then hurry to the Nursery, my mind spinning out with everything he told me.

This is the fourth night I've waited for Luc to come and meet me. But he hasn't shown up yet and each morning I've staggered back to bed, weary and disappointed.

Tonight, as usual, I've hung a small hand towel outside the bathroom window. It's chilly and all I'm wearing is a cotton nightshirt. I wish there was a large towel or something I could wrap around me. I couldn't risk getting dressed in case someone saw me.

I get up and stamp my right leg which is full of pins and needles. I'm still angry with myself. Luc's gut instinct was to leave well alone and not even mention James Grey to Fred and Jessie, but I opened my big mouth and now we're both in danger of a lifetime of incarceration.

But it's too late to regret stuff. We just have to hope we can get out of here. And then what will we do? Continue on our way to find Chambers? Suppose Luc doesn't want to carry on. I wouldn't blame him if he's had enough and wants to go home. Do I want to keep going?

I give it some thought and decide I'm not ready to give up on our mission despite the danger. This realisation surprises me and gives me a surge of fresh courage. The alternative is to go back home and live with regret. Skye is dead, she had no choices, but I'm alive and I really want to do this for her. I have to get out of here, if not for me, then for her and anyone else who might fall foul of Chambers.

Now, in the quiet murk of the bathroom, I'm willing Luc to come for me, but an hour passes and there's still no sign of him. Each night, I worry that I've arrived too late or returned to my room too early.

I'm almost dozing off on the chilly linoleum floor, when I hear a soft tap on the window. I give a start. I'm cold and stiff, but my heart beats fast and I jump up and go to the window.

Luc's face is such a welcome sight. He climbs into the bathroom, slides the window shut and passes me a pair of worn navy jogging bottoms. I pull them on gratefully. They're too long, so I roll them up a bit. We hug awkwardly and I return the towel to the hook.

'Okay, we haven't got much time,' he whispers. 'Come on, I hope you've got a good head for heights.' I follow him out of the window and try not to look down. 'Wait till I've reached the ledge before you start coming down,' Luc says. 'I don't think the drainpipe will take both of us at once.'

I don't share his confidence in my climbing ability and my right leg shakes uncontrollably. But I grit my teeth and attempt to emulate his cat-like agility. We finally make it down to the ground. This side of the building adjoins a different courtyard. I glance around and spy our AV parked under some trees. It seems too good to be true – there's no one in sight.

'Why aren't there any guards?' I whisper. 'A place like this, you think there'd be loads of security.'

'Yeah, you're right.' He thinks for a minute. 'Maybe there's something we're not seeing, or maybe they don't think they need security on the inside. I mean, with everyone here wandering around in a daze, they probably don't need to worry about people escaping. It is a bit weird though. You think there'd be *someone*.'

'Any ideas about how we're going to get out?' I ask. 'We seem pretty well locked in.'

'There's a delivery van arriving later. Well, it's come in the last two mornings. It's not a great plan, but it's all I've got. I thought we could just make a break for it when the gates open and hope they don't catch us. We have to hope we can get into the AV and that it's got enough fuel to get us away.'

'It sounds like a plan to me,' I reply. The fresh air and the climb down from the bathroom has woken me up and, with a heavy shot of adrenalin thrown in, I feel on heightened alert. 'Luc, you're amazing. I wouldn't have thought we had a hope of escaping.'

'Thanks, but we've got a way to go yet. Okay, when I say go, we need to run to the AV. You flatten yourself up behind one of those trees, while I see if the keycard's still there. Once I'm in, you get in the passenger side as quickly and quietly as you can.'

I nod.

Luckily for us, there's no artificial lighting in the courtyard and none of the lights in the surrounding buildings are on either, but we know it won't be too long before everyone is awake and the bells start ringing for morning service. Luc and I haven't attended service yet as we're not allowed to go until we've completed our 'Integration' course, whatever that entails. Hopefully we'll never have to find out. The sun is rising fast and a milky light begins to flood the expanse we're about to cross.

We go for it, crouching low and running fast. I feel vulnerable and exposed, expecting to hear a shout or running footsteps at any moment. But we reach the AV without incident and I scoot behind a large horse chestnut tree. Its green spiky pods remind me of more innocent autumns, of hard-baked, vinegar-coated conkers smashing into each other.

Luc tries the door of the AV. It's locked. He scrabbles beneath the vehicle, searching around for the spare keycard which is normally magnetically fixed to the underside. We didn't check if it was still in place after the run-in with the raiders on the floodplain and I'm praying it didn't get dislodged during my bumpy getaway. Luc's mother always keeps a spare under there, much to the disapproval of his father, Eddie, who thinks it's a dangerously obvious thing to do.

Luc is taking a long time and I peer out from behind the trunk. He beckons me over. 'Riley,' he hisses. 'I can't find it. It's not in the usual place. Come and give me a hand, quick.'

I creep over and slide under the vehicle on my back. 'I wish we had a torch,' I say. 'It's too dark under here. It's impossible to see.'

'I don't think it's here.' Luc slides out from underneath and I join him. His fists are balled up tight and he has smears of oil on his eyebrows and cheek.

Then I see a movement out of the corner of my eye and a streak of fear flashes up my spine. I tap Luc on the arm and point.

He turns around to see what has me frozen in terror - a procession of black robed figures streaming out of a small door in the outside wall and heading towards us.

CHAPTER TWENTY SIX

Eleanor

The following day I took the bus up to Abi's house, sure she would have some information from Samuel about what had happened to Connor. The story she gave me was so ludicrous, I could hardly believe she said it with a straight face.

'Ellie, you won't believe it - Connor's a terrorist!' She looked at me, waiting for my reaction, but I couldn't speak. I didn't understand why she would say such a thing. 'Ellie, you're in love with a murderer.' She was clearly joking. 'God, he could have killed us all.'

'Are you joking?'

'Do I sound like I'm joking? I'm really sorry, Ellie, but they're going to interrogate him and then they'll probably shoot him.' She spoke with no regard for my feelings. No words of comfort. She treated it like a piece of juicy gossip. Something to be savoured.

'You spiteful, evil cow!' I slapped her on her smug face as hard as I could. Her hands flew up to her cheek. I looked at her and shook my head. 'Why would you say those things? Why are you being so horrible to me?' Tears escaped with the shock of what was happening.

Still holding her cheek. Abigail raised her head and looked at me. 'I'm telling the truth and you'll regret doing that, Eleanor.'

When I got home, I sat down with my family and we tried to piece together what had just happened. After several hours of tears and speculation, we all reached the same awful conclusion - Samuel and Abi had probably cooked up the accusation out of sheer spite.

'In which case,' said Oliver, 'the army will realise they have no evidence against him and let him go.'

'But what if Bletchley (I couldn't now call him by his first name, Samuel, because it was too friendly and familiar. And I accompanied his surname with a retching sound, for good measure) has planted some evidence?'

'He doesn't have the brains. He wouldn't have thought that far ahead,' reassured David.

'No, but Robbins does.' (Ditto the retching sound for Abigail).

'They wouldn't go that far, darling,' Dad said. 'Look, give it a week and I bet we'll hear Connor's van puttering up the Lane and he'll be telling us all about his adventures. He's a sensible lad. He'll realise what's happened and he'll plead his case well.'

My family did a good job of trying to calm me down. They had known Connor and I were fond of each other, but it wasn't until the previous night that they'd seen the true extent of my feelings towards him. I think my cries and tears had shocked them almost as much as his arrest had. I was so relieved they hadn't believed Abigail Robbins' ridiculous accusation and my brother Tom was almost as upset as I was. Connor was one of his best friends.

But Connor's van didn't come puttering up the lane any time during that week, and I could get no news of his whereabouts. My father called Samuel's dad for me, but he said they'd had no news from their son and didn't expect to hear from him until Christmas.

I knew I would have to swallow my pride and my hatred and go and visit Abigail once more. But the thought made me feel sick and I was afraid I would physically attack her if she so much as looked at me with that smug expression ... But then I thought of Connor and knew I would do whatever it took to get him back and if that meant sucking up to Abigail, then so be it.

CHAPTER TWENTY SEVEN

RILEY

The black robed figures are flocking towards us. We realise, too late, that some parts of the wall are hollow in the middle. Now the sun has risen higher, casting a stronger light, I can see odd bricks missing here and there. Eyeholes for the guards inside to peer out and see what's going on while remaining undetected. They can probably see through to the outside in the same way.

'Holy crap,' says Luc.

'Holy, is right,' I reply.

As they glide closer, I see their guns. There's no point in running. There must be at least twenty of them, all with heavy metal crucifixes swinging over the top of their homespun cloaks. They surround us and the AV. Deep overhanging hoods conceal their features, giving the impression of being looked upon by a black sea of faceless creatures.

It is the most chilling sight I have ever seen and to add to the terror, they are chanting in some unknown language. They don't raise their weapons, but their chanting is growing louder, more insistent, almost deafening. Suddenly they stop and the ensuing silence sounds worse than the eerie voices.

Two of them step forward and put us, unresisting, into arm and leg shackles which clink and rattle. They lead us away and we stumble across the courtyard. We are taken along pathways and across gardens, through corridors and into a huge echoing hall. I'm too shocked and afraid to think about exactly where we are headed.

They shepherd us through a bare antechamber into a large, austere room. The walls and floor are of grey stone and the ceiling is high with a central circular metal pendant light. Small high windows stud the walls. It feels like a large cell. Morning has barely dawned, but Grey looks very much awake, sitting alone at the head of a large wooden refectory table set for breakfast. I know it's him. Who else would it be?

'Well.' The man smiles at us down his patrician nose. He would be aristocratically handsome if it weren't for his cold, dead blue eyes. 'My new children,' he smirks. 'What? You don't like my hospitality? Were your quarters not satisfactory?' He laughs.

Luc stares down at his feet, his fists still clenched and his ears red with anger and humiliation. But I can't take my eyes off this *man*. This bogeyman we have heard tales of for most of our sheltered lives. James Grey. How have we ended up here? Shackled and alone.

'Were you looking for this?' He picks up the AV keycard from the table and waves it in front of us. 'You can't have thought we'd have left this in its hiding place. That would have been remiss of us, wouldn't it? And that's quite a cache of weapons you have in there. I wonder what two such young ones are doing with such a fine vehicle and so much valuable cargo.

Stolen I imagine.

'I very much look forward to hearing your stories. They did very well, sending two such lost souls to me.' He pauses. 'I am sorry about our little deception, but you really *will* thank us in the end. I promise it. And I did enjoy your early morning shenanigans. Climbing out of bathroom windows, shinning up and down drainpipes. Very enterprising. Must have been cold in that bathroom, Riley.'

My skin crawls with the knowledge that he's been watching us, that he knew all our plans in detail. That he is, in fact, laughing at us. I feel humiliated and stupid, which I suppose is his intention. Luc must be livid. I can feel the anger radiating off him. The whole episode of our escape has been documented by Grey and here he is gloating. Revelling in our helplessness.

In front of him sits a large plate of food - toast, eggs, bacon, sausages, beans and tomatoes. Somewhat different to the thin, grey, salty porridge that *we* call breakfast in this place. He loads up his fork and eats noisily. A thin line of runny egg yolk travels down from the corner of his mouth to his chin. I've got a direct view of the gross mashed up contents of his mouth as he continues to speak.

'Come closer, children, I wish to talk to you.'

His affected way of speaking would be laughable if we weren't in so much danger. The two guards at our shoulders push us forward and force us to shuffle up until we're close enough to smell his scent. A repugnant odour of soap and something else, something sour and rank which rises up above the smell of fried food. I lean back a little.

'Leave us please.' He waves the guards back and I hear them softly swoosh away. 'I see you inspecting my breakfast. Are you hungry? We can remedy that in a moment, but first I need you to understand something.' He pauses and stares hard at each of us. 'My disciples *want* to be here. I am their saviour. You run from me now, but soon you will run *towards* me. You think I am taking you against your will, but you are young and you have no idea what you want from life.

'It's an evil world out there and I can save you from it. In a few weeks you won't want to be anywhere else, I guarantee it. Just one month, that's all I ask. Embrace my way willingly for thirty days and if you still want to leave after that time, you will be free to go.'

'A month so you can brainwash us, I don't think so,' Luc spits out the words. I silently cheer his defiance, but it also scares me. I don't want to see this man turn angry.

Grey holds up another forkful to his mouth, unfazed by Luc's outburst. He closes his eyes, anticipating the flavours. He's enjoying our discomfort and revelling in his power. I can tell there is something really wrong with him. Not just the obvious power trip, but something more. It's like he's a totally different species to us, as if his brain is wired in another way. It is paralysing and terrifying to be in his presence. The one word replaying in my mind is *evil*. This man is evil.

The room remains silent, apart from Grey's hypnotic voice and the occasional clink of our shackles. Grey is unhurried in his sermon. He takes long pauses to savour his breakfast, his fork held to his lips, his eyes closed again.

Luc glances at me and I have the nervous feeling he's about to do something.

I'm right.

As Grey holds his fork aloft, Luc lunges forwards with his shackled hands stretched out in front of him. He shoves as hard as he can and sends his whole body weight forward, towards the fork poised in front of Grey's open mouth. Luc rams the loaded fork down Grey's throat with gruesome consequences. Grey gurgles and chokes, grasping at the fork and at his neck.

I cry out. I can't help myself. But that wasn't the smartest thing to do in the circumstances, as it instantly alerts the two guards who come running in.

Before they can grab us or check on Grey, Luc seizes one of the heavy pewter candlesticks from the table. He has to hold it in both hands because of the shackles. He spins around, swings it upwards and catches one of the guards under the chin with it. The man instantly goes down.

At the same time, the other guard grasps me around the neck and tries to pull his gun out from his robe. I elbow him backwards in the stomach as Luc shoves the end of the candlestick into his face. The man releases me and doubles up. Luc then brings his metal cuffs down onto his head with a dull thud.

The guards are both out cold in under thirty seconds. I can't believe it. I know that, as a trained guard, Luc knows some stuff, but I'm shocked to witness it first-hand. Luc doesn't stop. He reaches down to the first guard's waist, trying to get the keys off his belt.

Shaking myself out of my shocked stupor, I shuffle over towards him. I hold my shackled hands out next to the guard's belt as Luc goes through the keys. At the sixth attempt we hear a beautiful click and my hands are free. We soon unchain our hands and feet.

Luc swiftly disrobes both guards and tosses me one of the cloaks. I put it on and try to block out the sickening sounds coming from Grey, who is writhing on his back on the floor, his hands still clutching at the fork. Luc throws me the guard's pistol and picks up the machine gun. We hide the weapons under our cloaks.

'Mustn't forget this,' says Luc, picking up the AV keycard from the table. 'Let's go.'

We race back through the empty antechamber and across the echoing hall, through the maze of buildings we hope will lead us back to the AV. Luc seems to know exactly where he's going and only pauses briefly, before resuming his confident navigation. Then I hear the inevitable – hurried footsteps and loud, gruff voices behind us.

CHAPTER TWENTY EIGHT

RILEY

'Run!' Luc shouts.

I hitch up my robe with one hand and clutch my weapon in the other. We run along a narrow hallway and Luc shoves open the door at the end. It leads out into the courtyard where our AV gleams in the sunlight. The footsteps behind us are growing louder now, crunching across the gravel. A shot rings out. I don't dare turn around. I hear shouted instructions and a burst of machine gun fire, but we don't stop. Luc pushes me ahead of him and at the same time he presses the keycard into my hand. He turns and sprays bullets in an arc around him.

'I'll drive,' Luc shouts to me. I wave the card at the vehicle and see the lights flash. I leap into the passenger seat and slam the door shut. Never have I been so glad to smell the warm leathery interior of that vehicle. It feels like home.

I push the card in all the way and the engine purrs to life. I inch down my window and fire a few shots in the guards' direction. I know I'll never hit them from this distance with such a small revolver, but I hope it'll delay them until Luc's safely in.

Luc dives into the driver's side and pulls his door shut. I bang on the blackout mode switch and Luc activates the shockplates. The guards re-enact their original manoeuvre, starting up their spooky chanting and glide forward to surround the AV. The main difference is that this time we're inside the vehicle, shielded by heavy armour and high voltage shockplates.

'Hold on!' Luc yells and slams the vehicle in reverse, knocking down several of the dark-robed figures. Sparks fly, where the shockplates have buzzed into action. The guards' frenzied chanting soon degenerates into shouts of alarm and warning.

My stolen gun has no more bullets, so I scrabble down into the footwell, under the mat and find the catch that opens the hidden cavity where our emergency provisions are stashed. My shaking fingers eventually close around cold smooth metal and I lift out the small loaded revolver and click off the safety. Luc screeches to a halt and accelerates hard to the left. He guns it across the courtyard.

With immaculate timing, the gates are already open and a dark green delivery van has its nose through the opening. A couple of robed figures run across the courtyard to try to close the gates. Our engine roars and I poke the barrel of the gun out through a crack in my window. I fire a couple more shots, immediately triggering a volley of machine fire in response.

'You don't need to shoot anymore, Riley, they can't get us in here,' Luc says. I close my window as shots ricochet off the electrically charged AV.

The green van slowly enters the courtyard and I see the driver staring around in confusion. He stops midway through the gates, unsure how to proceed. He glances from our vehicle, to the robed guards. Luc puts his hand on the horn and holds it down, flashing his lights and driving directly towards the van. It works, and the driver reverses out of the courtyard. Our AV is almost on top of him and we power our way through the gates, smashing into the front corner of the van as we go. The van spins around and careens into a shallow ditch outside the gates.

Luc turns right onto the bumpy road, away from the bright morning sun in the east and towards Warminster and Gloucestershire to the west. In the jumbled chaos of my mind, I hope this is a conscious decision to carry on with our quest and not head back home.

Glancing behind, I see a few robed figures flapping and gesturing like demented crows. Shots still follow us and I wait for vehicles to zoom out in pursuit, but miraculously the road behind stays clear. For now, we are safe.

After a manic fifteen minute drive over the potholed road, there's still no sign we're being followed. We hope that with Grey seriously injured, perhaps even dead, they'll have more important things to deal with than a couple of escaped kids. Although our reacquisition of the AV will be a serious loss to them.

I peer into the back of the AV and see nothing. They've taken all our possessions. I hadn't expected anything less, but it's still a huge blow to know we're miles from familiar territory with only limited emergency provisions.

'It's all gone,' I say.

Luc looks at me with a resigned shrug.

'All of it,' I repeat.

'We've got our lives, Riley, and that's more than I thought we'd have a couple of hours ago.'

'You're right.' I sigh. 'I don't know how you were so calm back there. You didn't freak out at all. I don't know how you thought of that thing with the fork. I feel ill just thinking about it.'

'It was a spur of the moment thing. An opportunity. And well, you saved me from psycho raiders, so I thought it was only fair to save you from religious nutters.'

'Cool.'

We drive on in silence for a while, each adrift in our thoughts. After a while, I speak.

'I know it's probably too late to ask this question, but do you think it's too risky to carry on? I mean if I knew what it was really going to be like ...'

'Put it this way, if we head back home we'll have to go past James Grey's place again and then we'll have to try and get past the raiders, who'll want a bit of revenge for the shockplate thing. And didn't you say you drove over a couple of them?'

'I'm so sorry Luc.'

'Why are you apologising? It's not your fault.'

'I mean for suggesting we come on this trip in the first place. It's been a nightmare and we haven't even got anywhere near finding out about Chambers.'

'Riley, don't be stupid, I wouldn't have come if I didn't want to. I think we *had* to make this trip ... Hey!'

I have rather annoyingly started to cry. Luc pulls over to the side of the road and switches off the engine.

'I'm sorry,' I sob. 'And now I feel really pathetic for crying. I feel so guilty.'

'Guilty about what?' Luc's eyes widen with worry.

I feel like such an idiot and a drama queen, but I can't put into words the panic that's clutching at me and the guilt that's hovering above me, ever present, always poking and prodding at me. Guilt for putting him in danger. Guilt for making my parents sick with worry. Guilt for being alive when Skye is dead. Everything.

I choke back another sob. And now I feel like a fraud for getting his sympathy with my distress.

'Hey, Riley, don't cry.' He clumsily tries to wipe away some of my tears. 'We're so close to Warminster. It would be a waste if we gave up now. Maybe we can get some information when we get there and then we can, I dunno, either follow it up and try to get Chambers, or ... we can accept the trail's gone cold and head straight to your grandparents' place. Okay?'

I don't reply.

'*Okay*?' he repeats. He's staring at me, holding both my hands in his, but I can't look him in the eye.

'Okay,' I agree. 'Sorry.'

'And stop saying sorry, you've got nothing to be sorry for.'

He kisses my cheek and smoothes a stray curl away from my face. I look up at him and he smiles, his fingers still on my face.

Then he leans forward and kisses my lips. Gently. Softly.

I sink into his kiss. It makes my body feel light as though I might float away. Everything else disappears. It's just me and Luc and this kiss. And I want more. But then I realise what's happening and immediately pull away. I'm out of breath. Shocked. It felt so right, but I can't do this. Luc isn't mine to have.

'I'm sorry,' Luc says. 'But you must know how I feel about you? How I've always felt about you.'

'About *me*? No. I don't know anything about that. I can't. We can't.'

'Why not?'

'You know why not,' I say.

'But, Riley. You kissed me back. It felt amazing.'

He's trying to make eye contact but I can't look at him. If I look at him my resolve will crumble.

'Tell me why we can't,' he says again.

I take a breath.

'Riley ...'

I finally look up at him and utter one word. 'Skye.'

There's nothing he can say to that. After a moment he starts up the engine and we get back on the road.

On the way to Warminster we see little sign of life. Dense, overgrown greenery borders the road, concealing the surrounding countryside. The route sometimes leads past a walled compound or perimeter of some kind. I can only wonder and guess what lies behind their blank exteriors. Are they like our own Talbot Woods Perimeter where the inhabitants live in peace and safety? Or do they hide something more sinister? After recent events, I'm convinced it's the latter.

It's strange to think of all these hidden communities dotted around the country. What problems do they face? What are their means of survival? These are all thoughts and questions that have never troubled me before.

It suddenly dawns on me, the dangers Luc's father faces in his job. I've never questioned what he does for a living. It's just something he's always done - organising security for wealthy compounds and setting up new perimeters. But it now occurs to me that each time he scouts for new business he's travelling into the unknown and risking his life. He has no notion of what he'll find inside each one. This danger is going to be Luc's career too and I worry for his long-term safety.

I'm also realising that, for most people, living inside a secure perimeter doesn't come easy or cheap. The majority have risked something big in order to afford to keep their families safely inside.

But all these thoughts are just a distraction to keep me from thinking about the one thing that's pounding my brain like a jackhammer - Luc.

That kiss was the last thing I expected to happen. Part of me acknowledges that these feelings have always been here within me, but Luc was Skye's crush. I never allowed myself to think of him like that.

My lips burn where he kissed me and I scrape my teeth over them, trying to erase the memory. It cannot happen. No matter how much I want it, I can't give into these feelings.

By the time we approach the Century Barracks at Warminster, it's late afternoon and I'm exhausted. My eyes are heavy with sleep and my body feels like it's got no bones. I'm taking a turn at the wheel and it's more tiring than I thought it would be. Luc's taking a nap on the back seat. We haven't really spoken since we kissed.

When we reach the turning to take us up to the entrance, I brake and pull over. I turn and look at him asleep on the back seat, his face smooth and untroubled.

'We're here,' I say. 'Luc.'

He opens his eyes and stretches out across the back seat. 'Okay.' He yawns. 'Let me just wake up and get my head straight?' Pillow creases line his cheek and his hair sticks up on one side.

'Yeah, no problem,' I reply, glad to take a moment before we have to meet more strangers. I'm still freaked out from the last few days and from this morning's events in particular. I turn away and stare out of the windscreen at nothing.

'Don't worry,' Luc says, catching my expression. 'I've been here before with dad. They know me. The Major seemed like a decent bloke from what I remember.'

'Good,' I say. 'It'll be nice not to have any drama for a change.'

We've already discussed what we'll say when we arrive,

deciding that Luc would do most of the talking.

I shuffle across to the passenger seat and Luc climbs into the driver's side. We both check our appearances and Luc smoothes his hair down. We've removed our guards' robes but Luc is still dressed in his grey outfit from Salisbury and I look ridiculous in navy jogging bottoms, and a white cotton nightshirt.

I'm nervous but hoping that we might finally get some positive information on Chambers. This could be the first step towards justice for Skye - the reason we embarked on this journey in the first place. I try to put all the chaos of the past few days out of my head and focus on the evening ahead and on how the army is going to help us.

CHAPTER TWENTY NINE

RILEY

After the repeated terror attacks all those years ago, most of the British Army was recalled from overseas to take care of the increasing threats to public safety. But soon afterwards, our government more or less collapsed into nothing. The cabinet ministers fled from a decimated and dangerous London.

A new emergency Security Council established itself in the capital, made up of minor politicians and business tycoons whose empires had been destroyed. But the predominant members of the Council were, of course, the military men.

Over the years, the armed forces have been reduced to several ragged units scattered throughout the country, only as good or bad as the generals who lead them. The local Dorset Barracks liaises amicably enough with our Perimeter guards, so I'm assuming the army is welcomed by most of the population.

A few secure compounds refuse to acknowledge the army's authority and deny them access but in these situations the army's policy is to back-off. Anything could be going on behind those walls, but the soldiers don't interfere. They're now the only remnant of legitimate power left in the country and they do a passable job of preventing the total disintegration of society. But chaos and terror are always simmering away beneath the scarred surface, ready to erupt given the tiniest exit to explode out of.

We drive alongside a double layered barbed wire fence until we reach a set of closed metal gates. The armed soldier at the checkpoint moves his finger up and down to tell Luc to open his window. Two other soldiers have their machine guns lightly trained in Luc's direction. My nerves kick in. The soldier bends his head slightly, to hear what Luc has to say.

'Hi, I'm Lucas Donovan and this is Riley Culpepper. My father's Eddie Donovan. We've come up from the Talbot Woods Perimeter on the South Coast. Can we speak to Major Driscoll?'

'Turn off your engine please and wait here,' the soldier says, ignoring Luc's question. He enters a small hut and speaks on the radio. I can't hear the content of the conversation. While we wait in the AV, three soldiers approach us.

'Can you vacate the vehicle,' one of them says.

I look at Luc who nods. We get out and stand by the hut as they thoroughly check over the AV.

'It's routine,' Luc says. 'They would do it whoever we were.'

'Okay,' I reply, only slightly reassured.

They complete their task quickly and efficiently, even using small mirrors on sticks to check the underside of the vehicle. They finish their search and take the machine gun which we hadn't been able to fit in the hidden compartment.

'You'll get this back on exit, Sir,' one of the soldiers says to Luc, completely ignoring me.

Next, they pat us down, making us stand with our arms out.

It's humiliating and I flush with discomfort. When they're done, my heart rate speeds up. What if they don't believe our reason for being here and they contact Eddie? We can't be turned away now that we're so close to getting somewhere. But I needn't have worried. The soldier in the hut soon returns.

'You'll be escorted through in a moment. Please return to your vehicle.'

After about five minutes, two soldiers in a jeep drive up. They turn their vehicle around before they reach us and the soldier at the checkpoint, motions for us to follow them.

We drive through what appears to be a small well-tended, but bleak, town, made up predominantly of black and green prefabricated buildings. It's good to be gliding along a smooth road for a change and my body welcomes the transition from the relentless bone-jolting it's become accustomed to.

We pull up behind the jeep in front of a long, low, single-storey brick building. The two soldiers exit the jeep and come to greet us. We both get out of the AV and stand awkwardly waiting to make our introductions.

'Hello, Lucas, Miss Culpepper, I'm Major Robert Cornell and this is Captain Michael Lewis.'

The Major is a tall, thick-set man in his fifties, with a florid face and broken veins that suggest he likes a drink or two. The Captain is of a similar build, but with a healthier tanned complexion and small, piercing blue eyes, which he trains on Luc and me with suspicion.

'This is an unexpected pleasure,' the Major continues. 'Good to meet you. What brings you all the way up here?'

'I'm meeting my father, Eddie Donovan here. He should arrive tomorrow. Could we wait for him?'

'Your father? That is a surprise.' He smiles at his colleague as he shakes Luc's hand and nods in my direction.

I take an instant dislike to both of them. It's as though they're in on some private joke at our expense and I feel out of my depth and ill-at-ease.

'I met Major Mark Driscoll when I was last here with my father,' Luc says, his voice strong and confident.

'Yes,' replies Cornell. 'He is no longer with us.' He doesn't elaborate. Does that mean he's dead or merely stationed elsewhere? 'You must be tired after your journey.'

Another soldier appears at our side and Major Cornell gives him orders to show us to our accommodation.

'A bit basic I'm afraid, but with such short notice ...' He tails off. 'Anyway, freshen up and Rogers here will bring you to dinner at twenty hundred hours. Until then.'

Rogers shows us to a small dilapidated terrapin. It consists of a bedroom with two single beds and a grotty bathroom that smells damp despite the hot summer. But it's spotlessly clean, even if it is in dire need of redecorating.

We each take a hot shower and then sit on our beds to rest for an hour or so. Neither of us mentions what happened between us. In fact, Luc hardly says a word. He closes his eyes and lies back on the bed until we're summoned to dinner in the Officers' Mess. But over the past few minutes a banging headache has been building over my right eye and then my left. I suddenly feel light headed and I can hardly see.

'Luc, I don't feel well.'

'What's wrong?'

'It's my head … it's pounding and I feel like I'm going to throw up.'

'Can I get you anything? Water?'

I nod. 'Please.'

I close my eyes again and after a moment, Luc returns with a bottle of water. He sits on the bed next to me and rubs my shoulder while I sip the lukewarm liquid.

'You better stay here,' he says. 'I'll go to dinner. Don't worry, Riley. Take it easy. I'll try and get the information we need. Just … just try and get some sleep.'

'You can't go on your own. That's not fair. I'll be okay.' I swing my legs around and try to stand, but my legs buckle and the room sways. Luc catches me before I hit the deck.

'You're not going anywhere,' he says, helping me back onto the bed. 'Sleep. I'll be back soon.' He takes my hand and kisses my cheek. Then he leaves to join the soldier who will escort him to dinner.

I lie back on the bed on top of the scratchy brown blanket. My head feels like it's being tightened in a vice and I try to relax. But there's so much stuff swilling about in my brain that I'm sure it's about to explode. Ma says she thinks of the sea when she wants to unwind. I've never seen the ocean in real life. Only in DVDs and maybe in my dreams.

I close my eyes and try to picture myself there: Honey-coloured sand, wet and smooth and cold. Next I think of blue green water lapping at the shore. Soothing. Restful. Calm. It works and soon I am asleep.

I can't breathe and I'm struggling to remember where I am in my semi-conscious state. I feel like I'm suffocating and now, with rising panic, I realise someone's hand is covering my mouth. I open my eyes.

'Mmmphf!' I try to scream, but the huge hand is clamped too firmly. Bewildered and terrified, I stare into the dark eyes of a black, uniformed soldier. To him, I must look like a frightened pony - eyes wide in fear and hyperventilating through my nose in noisy puffs.

'Quiet!' he whispers loudly. 'You're in ...'

'Mmmmph!' I try to yell for somebody to help me. His hand is still over my mouth and I do my best to open it so that I can bite down along the side of his forefinger. But he gets wise to this straightaway and squeezes my mouth closed with his fingers, bruising my cheeks painfully.

'For Christ sake, just listen a minute or you're gonna get hurt,' he hisses with a strong country accent I can't place. He pulls my face up close to his and I try to twist away. He looks African or Jamaican. I've never even seen a black man before.

Sleep still clings to me and I feel disorientated, wondering where the hell I am and why I'm being attacked. Then it all comes flooding back: I'm at Century Barracks, Luc is at dinner with the big brass and I fell asleep. Now, here I am, being jerked awake by this huge soldier who's in my room with his hand crushing my face. I stop struggling for a moment, so I can breathe through my nose and also because I need him to relax the grip he's got on my cheeks.

'God, that's better,' he relaxes too. 'I don't want to hurt you, but I can't let you scream or they'll have us both.' He glances anxiously towards the door. 'You're in the crapper if you stay here. I can help you and your boyfriend get out, but we haven't got much time. They'll be here in a minute and you won't like what they got planned for you.'

His words start to register and a new kind of fear replaces the one I felt just a second ago.

He seems genuine. Scared and anxious, but with a kind-ish face. But, what do I know? He could just as easily be a mad man out to kill me. After the last few days, my mind is all over the place. Miraculously, I realise my headache has gone.

'Right,' he says, 'I'm gonna let you go and then I'll back away from you. Please God don't scream or we're finished, okay?'

I nod and show what I hope to be assent in my eyes.

'And letting go, and backing away,' he says slowly with a sardonic half smile.

We stare at each other warily, for about five seconds.

'Right. Hello, Riley, I'm Denzil. Here's the short version.' He speaks quickly and quietly. 'As of about three months ago, Luc's dad became Century Barracks' number one enemy. I don't know the details, but he must've done something to seriously piss off the Major because, for weeks now, they've been planning some kind of retaliation.

'Your bloke obviously has no idea of this or he wouldn't have brought you within twenty miles of this place. They can't believe their luck up at the mess hall and they're humouring him till they decide what to do. They knew he was lying about meeting his dad, and now they're dreaming up how they can use him to ruin Eddie and get some revenge.'

'We've got to get him out of there,' I whisper back. 'But do they know who *I* am? My father's on really good terms with the army. He's one of their main suppliers.' Even as I say the words, I know I'm kidding myself.

'Who knows you're here?' asks Denzil.

I don't reply.

'Exactly,' he says. 'They know you're AWOL. Your parents would never in a million years let you out of your Perimeter alone. Right now, you're a fine-looking female in a barracks full of frustrated men, whose boyfriend's family business is seriously irritating them. I don't fancy your chances.'

'Okay.' I swing my legs off the bed. 'How do we get out?' I hear the shake in my voice. 'What's the time? Is Luc still eating with them?' I bend down and slip my flip flops onto my feet. 'Why are you doing this anyway? Helping us, I mean.'

'Selfish reasons,' he replies. 'I'll explain later, when we get out of here.'

'You mean you want to come with us?'

'You won't escape without me.'

CHAPTER THIRTY

Eleanor

Calling Abigail from my mobile, I swallowed my anger and tried to adopt a friendly, apologetic tone. I asked if she'd meet me at the recreation ground that afternoon. She agreed.

I waited for her in the deserted playground and sat on a cold, wet swing. She was twenty five minutes late, but I smiled at her when she arrived, hands in her pockets, the hood from her parka covering her platinum hair. She glanced at the swing next to me, but it was covered in raindrops so she stood where she was.

'Grotty day,' she said.

'Hi Abi,' I said, trying to be breezy.

'Hi. You alright?'

I brought my swing to a stop and stood up, forcing myself to say the next few words. 'I'm sorry I slapped you before.' I gave her what I hoped was an apologetic smile. 'I must have been in shock or something.'

'Don't worry about it. I knew you weren't yourself.'

I tried to restrain myself from slapping her again.

'You know,' she continued. 'I get you were upset about Connor. He tricked us all and you must've felt pretty used and stupid when you found out.'

Good God, it took all my strength not to punch the smug smile off her face. I took a deep breath and hummed a tune in my head trying to ignore the self-satisfied crap pouring from her spiteful mouth.

'Finding out he was a terrorist must have been a hideous shock,' she said.

I stifled the many retorts that came to my lips and just nodded.

'I feel like I haven't seen you for ages,' she breathed. 'Let's forget about boys and do something fun.'

'Yeah, good idea,' I replied. 'But, Abi ... Do you know what actually happened to Connor? Is he still under arrest or have they let him go?'

'Oh for God's sake,' she said. 'Connor, Connor, Connor! You've only known him for a few weeks and it's all you go on about. It's so bo-ring.'

'I know.' I smiled and tried to stay upbeat and act like I didn't care. I knew if she sensed my desperation, I wouldn't get anything out of her. God, why had I had her as my friend for so long? I must have been blind. She was a monster. 'I just want to know so I can put him out of my head. It's bugging me, you know?'

'Yeah, fair enough. But you won't like it, Ellie.'

I heard the blood pound in my ears. What was she going to tell me? I swallowed down bile in the back of my throat.

'Look, Abi,' I pretended to be bored. 'I don't really care, but I need to know for Tom. Connor's a good friend of his and he wants to know what's going on.'

She eyed me sharply.

'Anyway,' I tried a lighter tone. 'I'd like to know if I've been going out with a convicted terrorist or not.' I pulled a lopsided face.

'Yeah, not cool,' she relaxed her gaze and actually laughed. 'Look, he's dead okay? There, I've said it.'

Her words hung between us.

'I'm sorry. I know you liked him and everything.'

'*Liked* him,' I repeated. '*Liked* him? He's the love of my life. I love him and he's not dead. You're lying.'

'I thought you said you didn't care ...'

'Liked him?' I looked at her with what must have been pure loathing, because she backed away. 'You are a jealous, vindictive cow. This is you and Bletchley pretending to be soldiers. What I want to know is why I ever had you as a friend in the first place?'

'Now hang on,' she interrupted. 'If it wasn't for me ...'

'If it wasn't for you, I would never have gone out with Johnny in the first place. You only hooked me up with him so we could be a foursome with you and Bletchley. If you hadn't been such a bossy cow, I would've been free to see Connor ...'

'Don't call me a cow, you psycho bitch ...'

'... and Soldier Boy Sam wouldn't have had some pathetic idea about avenging Johnny's hurt pride.'

'Yeah, well blame me if it makes you feel better, Ellie.'

That stung. I knew in my heart it was my own stupid fault

for being so easily led by her. I felt disgusted with myself, defeated, tired, bereft. There was nothing left for me, nothing that mattered anymore. I was too numb to even cry.

'How do you know what's happened to him anyway?' I suddenly asked. She looked angry and uncomfortable, shocked by the strength of my feelings.

'Ellie, I'm sorry. Sam called me. Connor tried to escape at Portsmouth and a soldier shot him. I don't know the details.'

'It's all gone mad,' I muttered. 'Connor isn't a terrorist. It's all bloody stupid.'

Abi looked like she was going to leave, but then she changed her mind and put her arms around me. But my body was stiff and unyielding, and I wouldn't sink into her clumsy, cold embrace.

CHAPTER THIRTY ONE

RILEY

I study Denzil, taking in the intense expression on his face, and through my fuzzy panicked senses comes a cold knife-cut of realisation. I have no choice. No one else can do this. It's up to me and I can't afford to muck it up. I put my fear into a box and clear my mind of everything except what I know I have to do.

Our lives are at stake, but this time I'm not afraid. I feel like I've been plucked me out of reality and given a shot of calm.

Minutes later, I walk into the dining hall and up to Luc, who sits at the far end of the room next to some scarily important looking men in uniform. They blur into a sea of khaki and I've no idea who they are or what rank they hold. My heart thumps, but I do my best to plaster on a smile for everyone seated at Luc's table.

'Sorry to disturb you.' I smile apologetically. 'Luc, could I borrow you for a second. There's some stuff in the AV I need.'

'Are you okay?' he asks. 'Feeling better?'

I nod. All I can think about is getting us the hell away from Warminster.

One of Luc's dining companions speaks. 'Go on, son, help the young lady out. We'll keep it warm for you.' They all laugh at this, though what's so funny, I can't tell. They remind me of a pack of hyenas I once saw on a wildlife DVD, laughing hysterically before tearing into another animal's kill.

As we walk out of the room, Luc hisses, 'I think they were just about to give me some useful info on Chambers. Are you sure you're okay? You've got a weird expression on your face.'

'Sshh,' I answer. 'We're in trouble.' I quickly fill him in on the details.

Like me, he doesn't know whether to believe Denzil's story or not, but if it's true then we'll be in greater danger if we stay. We make up our minds quickly and decide to leave.

Luc and I walk the five hundred yards to the AV. It seems like five miles in the humid electrified air. We slide into the vehicle and Luc drives out, back the way we came in, less than three hours ago. As we approach the checkpoint, Denzil emerges from the hut. Through the door, I see the body of a soldier sprawled on the floor. Denzil sees us eying the body.

'Don't worry, he'll live. I just clocked him on the back of the head.' He jumps into the back seat, throwing us each a machine gun, one of which is our confiscated weapon.

'Keep those handy,' he says. 'I'm deserting my post and I reckon we got about fifteen minutes before they realise you're not having any pudding. I should put my foot down hard on that pedal if I were you,' he says to Luc. 'I'm Denzil, pleased to meet you.'

'What the hell's going on?' asks Luc, clearly shaken by this turn of events. 'Why do we have to leave? You said my father's not welcome here anymore. It all sounds like a load of crap to me.'

'Can we drive and talk?' Denzil says.

Luc shakes his head but he does as Denzil asks and turns back onto the road.

'I just need you to trust it's also best for *me* if I get you out of here alive,' Denzil says. 'I know you got no real reason to trust me yet, but you must have known something wasn't right back there or why would you be escaping with me now?'

'I trust Riley. She said we needed go, so here we are.'

'I gave you back all your weapons didn't I?' Denzil says. 'I wouldn't have done that if I was gonna hurt you.'

'Well, it doesn't look like we've got much choice now,' says Luc. 'Not now we're fleeing from our hosts and you did something nasty to that soldier back there. And Riley seems to trust you.' Luc glances across at me and I shrug non-committally, which isn't any help at all. He presses his lips together and his jaw tightens.

'We'll go along with you for now,' he says, braking suddenly as we reach a junction. He turns to look at Denzil, who almost fills the whole of the back seat. 'We're heading west. That okay?' Luc asks. 'Tell you the truth, I'm a bit drunk. They loaded me up with spirits back there.'

'It doesn't matter which way we go. They'll send units in both directions. May as well head towards Westbury, and go as fast as you can. I've topped up your tank.'

Luc and I both peer at the fuel gauge, which is showing 'Full'.

'Nice one,' Luc says grudgingly, looking at him in the rear view mirror.

'Are you alright to drive?' I ask. 'Do you want me to take over?'

'I'm sobering up quickly, but thanks for the offer.'

Night is falling around us and the AV's beams are on full. We're climbing in altitude and the road winds above the surrounding countryside, which spreads out all around us in dark splodges of field and woodland. The road quality is better than we'd been used to and we manage to hit thirty miles per hour, but I still feel every jolt and accidentally bite my tongue. It hurts like hell, but I don't say anything.

'We'll have to get off the road in a minute,' Denzil says. 'Once they've discovered we've gone, they'll send out the Lynx.'

'What's a Lynx?' I ask. 'It doesn't sound good, whatever it is.'

'It's not. Not for us anyway. It's a helicopter and it'll pick us up straight away if we stay on the road. Lucky for us, they've got no more anti-armour missiles, but we still got the door guns to watch out for.'

'So why are we still on the road? Let's find somewhere to hide.' I'm panicking now.

'We still got time,' Denzil reassures. They might not even bother to come after us.'

'Really?' Luc asks.

'Nah, man. They'll come after us, no question.' He laughs a deep belly laugh.

'Great,' says Luc, massaging his temple with his right hand.

We pass tiny terraced brick cottages perched on the side of the road, obviously abandoned and completely dilapidated. They look sinister in the black night, like huddled old crones plotting our downfall. We drive towards a bridge with faded graffiti daubed across its length: *TURN BACK OR DIE.*

'That's a bit dramatic.' Luc brakes suddenly, unsure whether or not to continue.

'Don't worry. That graffiti's years old,' says Denzil. 'This is Westbury. It used to be a compound, but everyone got wiped out in the plague.'

'Everyone?' I ask.

'It was bad. About twelve years ago they all got sick and nearly everyone died. Anyone who didn't get it fled the place and no one ever came back. Westbury's deserted now, apart from the odd traveller. It's a ghost town, literally. Loads of the lads swear they've seen weird stuff going on down here.'

'Thanks for that, Denzil. You've made me feel so much better.' Goosebumps prickle all over my back and arms.

He laughs his loud surprising laugh, unexpected for such a softly-spoken person. It would be infectious if I wasn't so scared for my life.

'I'm glad you think it's all so hilarious,' says Luc. 'Are we going into the joyous ghost town of plagues and death then?'

'We'll hide ourselves there till morning.' Denzil confirms my fears.

'Why did I know you were going to say that.' I'm not happy with the thought of spending a night in this creepy, deserted town. But then I suppose it is marginally better than being shot at from a military helicopter.

The AV crawls under the bridge and along the silent narrow street. I can't see any signs of habitation. Thick foliage lines the road. I don't even want to think about what I would do if I was alone here. We turn off the main track into an overgrown wilderness of rubble and tangled greenery, bumping over goodness- knows-what and straining our eyes to spot somewhere to hide.

'This is no good,' Denzil says after a couple of minutes of trying to penetrate our way through the debris in the AV. 'Got a torch?'

I scrabble about in the footwell and release the catch on the hidden compartment. My hand finds the torch straightaway and I pass it back to him.

'Stop the vehicle and kill the lights. I'm gonna go find us somewhere proper to hide.'

'On foot?' I ask, horrified he could be so brave.

'Yeah. You two wait here. I won't be long.'

'I'll come with you,' Luc says.

'No need. You stay with Riley. It'll be quicker if it's just me.' And he's gone, eaten up by the shadows.

'Do you think he'll come back?' Luc asks.

CHAPTER THIRTY TWO

RILEY

Leaves and branches swish and clatter against the windows of the AV.

'A storm's coming,' says Luc.

'Fantastic. We're in a ghost town at night, with thunder and lightning on the way.' My sarcasm is covering up an impending meltdown. *Please God, let me manage to keep it together.* 'I hope he comes back soon.'

It's a strange thing, but after only a few minutes in Denzil's company, we've already been won over by his confidence and unpretentiousness. Luc and I have both adapted our attitudes to mimic his good humour, despite our nightmare situation.

A loud rapping on Luc's window makes me squeal.

'It's okay, Riley. It's Denzil.'

Now I feel like an idiot. Luc puts his hand on my arm for a second and then opens his window.

'Mind if I drive a minute?' Denzil asks.

'Be my guest.' Luc slides effortlessly into the back seat, while Denzil eases into the driver's side.

'I found the perfect place, man,' Denzil says, reversing loudly onto the main track again.

We drive up to a large vine-covered concrete warehouse of

some sort. It's mainly intact, but hidden from plain view by the encroaching forest. The huge rusted garage door is open and Denzil drives inside. Luc jumps out of the AV and pulls the metal door closed behind us. Denzil kills the lights and turns off the engine. It's dark, but a few holes in the roof cast a faint glow of moonlight into the AV.

'Right,' says Denzil. 'We just have to be quiet and hope they don't discover our hidey hole. Got any grub? I'm starving.'

Although we're under the cover of the old warehouse, we stay inside the AV and Denzil and I share a very light unappetising supper of dry crackers, water and freeze-dried strips of meat, some of the few supplies still left in the footwell. Luc says he's too stuffed to eat any more. He already ate a massive dinner at the Barracks. We push the boat out for pudding and share a slab of chocolate.

'The main course was pretty ropey,' Denzil says. 'But I haven't had chocolate for, well ... must be ten years. I'm getting a good sugar rush. Thanks, guys.'

Once we've eaten, Luc asks the question we both want to know:

'So, Denzil, how come you helped us to escape? And why do you want to leave the Barracks?'

Denzil Porter is thirty four years old. He grew up in the St Paul's area of Bristol, in a steep unlovely terrace, with his large extended family. He spent his early teens trying to dodge the front-line drug-dealing activities all around him and, at the age of seventeen-and-a-half, he finally managed to escape inevitability, and took his eight GCSEs into the army with him.

He trained as a soldier in The Royal Military Police, doing his Basic Training at Winchester and his Trade Training at Chichester. Once trained, he was promoted to Lance Corporal, moving quickly to Corporal and he hoped to make Sergeant within the next six years. He loved army life, working hard and playing hard. I could tell from his cheeky humour as we fled the barracks, that he's a good man to have around in times of stress. His family was proud of him and he was happy in his career.

He undertook a six month operational Tour in Afghanistan, but only stayed for four, as he was pulled back to England during the prolonged terror attacks to put his Royal Military Police Training into effect.

'The Middle East was bad, but England was worse,' he tells us. 'Afghanistan was this unknown foreign country and we were briefed on what to expect over there, but England ...' He exhales heavily. 'To come home and face that level of chaos in your own country, well it was unreal. I managed to get most of my family out of Bristol and into a compound in Thornbury, just north of the city, but I lost a lot of my cousins and friends. I haven't been able to visit my family for six years now - no fuel allowance, no leave. The last message I got from them was eight months ago, begging me to find somewhere else for them to stay. My dad's really ill. I don't even know if he's still alive.'

'Surely the army would help you to move them somewhere

else?' Luc asks.

'You're joking aren't you?' Denzil shakes his head. 'I don't know how they even have the nerve to call themselves the army anymore. They're nothing more than legal terrorists. They're corrupt and racist, and the decent one's have either left, been driven out or are trying to get the hell out as soon as they can.

'My life these last few years has been a nightmare. I don't know how I've stood it this long, living with that bunch of ignorant... See, I don't lick arse enough and I've got no money and no connections, which is how you get on in this game nowadays. I'm a bit of a joker though. I reckon that's what's seen me through. The lads think I'm good for a laugh and it's saved me from a few beatings.'

I'm shocked by what he's telling us. If the army can't be relied on, that means nobody's looking out for our country. Nobody other than people like Pa and Eddie.

'Maybe it's just the bunch of losers at Century Barracks,' Denzil adds, reading my thoughts. 'I don't really know what the other bases round the country are like. Maybe there's some good guys left. All I know is I've had enough and I want out.'

'So what do you need us for?' Luc asks. 'Surely you could've escaped years ago if things are that bad.'

'It's not that simple. Like I said, I've got no connections. First, I needed a way to escape. But mainly I was waiting for a decent opportunity to take me somewhere good. I mean, if I just escaped, where would I go? What would I do? I'd be absent without leave, on the run with no way of helping my family and if they caught me trying to leg it, they'd either shoot me for desertion or worse. I've got to be able to go where they can't touch me. This way, with your help, I've got a decent vehicle to escape in and ...' He pauses and scrutinises our faces.

'What?' we ask simultaneously.

'I need your help.'

'We are helping you,' I say.

'No, I mean I *really* need your help. I want to become a guard. I want to work in a perimeter town, far away from this shithole - 'scuse my language - where I can keep my family safe. Your dad owns a security company.' He turns to Luc. 'I know he needs trained men like me, but I haven't had the opportunity to meet him. Maybe ... if you could get me a job with accommodation for my family? I'm a professional. I'm hard-working ... loyal.'

He tails off and stares at us expectantly. I realise just how powerful our families are. We've got the means to make and break lives. This man's hope rests in Luc's hands.

Guards are usually made up of ex-police, military and security, but they're prized jobs which pay well and mean your family will be well-housed and provided for - a rarity nowadays. Positions aren't given away easily as you have to be able to trust the guard you're employing with your life. In our perimeter, any potential guard has to first have two sponsors, who are guards themselves, to vouch for him or her. These sponsors are hard to come by as they risk dismissal or even imprisonment if the new guard lets them down. In this way, we're almost guaranteed to get trustworthy men and women looking after us.

Denzil obviously doesn't know anyone willing to sponsor him and he has no other means of proving himself. The opportunity to help us was too valuable for him to ignore.

'If we manage to escape from your lovely ex-work colleagues, then I'm sure I can sort something out,' Luc says.

With his flippant reply, Luc has managed to lighten the atmosphere and give Denzil the hope he needs.

'Man, you will never regret it.' He settles back, a sudden sigh of relief smoothing out the lines on his satin forehead.

We sit in silence for a while, listening to each other breathing. Thunder grumbles in the distance and then, through the part-opened roof, lightning illuminates our surroundings, shocking our gloom-adjusted senses. Rows and rows of rails, covered in clear plastic, are briefly thrown into sharp relief.

'A clothing warehouse,' I say. 'Ma would love to go rummaging around in here.'

Thunder again, nearer and louder. Again the lightning flashes, daylight bright. Then the rain comes. Widely-spaced-out heavy drops gathering speed and finally drumming down onto the roof of the warehouse and onto our AV, as we're parked directly under one of the roof's enormous holes.

'This should help keep them off our trail,' Denzil says, loud enough for us to hear him over the rattling rain. It turns out to be a short storm though and within ten minutes or so the rain has eased to a gentle patter.

'Have you heard of a man named Ron Chambers?' I ask.

'The killer who escaped?' Denzil replies. 'Yeah, I heard of him.'

'My heart lifts at his words. This could be the breakthrough we've been searching for.

'Two of the lads nearly picked him up. Stupid tossers - they let him go off on his merry way. He probably bribed them. They were lying if they said they never knew who he was. Hold on.' He raises his hand for quiet. 'Here we go.'

'What?' I ask.

'Sshh.' He puts his fingers to his lips and I feel a snaking, creeping sense of dread. 'Listen.'

Sure enough, I hear the unwelcome sound of helicopter blades whirring overhead.

'They're here. We'll just have to sit tight and hope they pass us by.'

I want Denzil to carry on with his story about Chambers. I'm sure he can tell us something to lead us to his whereabouts, but it isn't the right time. I'll just have to be patient and hope we got out of this predicament so I can question him further.

It's chilly and damp now and I'd give anything for a warm jumper. I shiver. Denzil sees, takes off his jacket and passes it to me. I shake my head, but he shushes me and presses it into my hand.

I think about our situation here and realise it depresses me. This is the army, our supposed protectors and law-and-order keepers. If they're corrupt then what chance does our country have? We really are living in a world gone to hell. Forced to trust another stranger to help us out. But will he also let us down like Fred and Jessie?

Over the intermittent drips of rain, we hear a convoy of vehicles drive past, close to our hiding place. Then voices. A shout. I shiver again.

'Building-to-building search!' We all make out the words and I feel sick.

'Milligan.' I don't like the way Denzil says the name.

'Building-to-building search?' asks Luc. 'Do you think we'll be safe here?'

'Not any more. Milligan won't leave this village until every structure is searched thoroughly. He'll have sent the Lynx ahead to check the roads.'

'What should we do?' I really don't fancy our chances if we get caught, and I'm terrified for Luc's life after what Denzil said about his father.

'There's no way we'll all be able to escape together,' says Denzil. His next words make my heart sink. 'I'll have to leave you here.'

CHAPTER THIRTY THREE

Eleanor

Connor's face and smell was still so familiar to me. I had previously borrowed a checked shirt of his and, when I took to my bed, I inhaled his scent as I wept. I pictured his perfect face, terrified in case I forgot what he looked like. My own face was pasty and blotched, my eyes dull and swollen from continuous crying. I couldn't stir myself to even wash and I felt hideous and grotty. I just kept thinking, what's the point?

Over the next few days, my family was tender and consoling. Mum brought me up comfort food, like warm chicken noodle soup or creamy mashed potato, throwing my windows open, 'for fresh air' amidst my half-hearted protests. My brothers tried to tempt me with chocolates and glossy magazines, and Dad just held me while I cried oceans. All I wanted was to hibernate under my duvet.

My family tried to discover exactly what had happened to Connor, but although they contacted the army and the police, nobody knew anything. Or if they did, they kept it quiet. The Press weren't interested. Well, they were interested, but only in the angle that we had been harbouring a suspected terrorist. And they soon lost interest when there was nothing more to learn.

The media kept giving us more bad news. Thousands of people had either fled the country to return to their native homes, or had returned to Britain, to get home before the border closures came into effect, which they now had. Plenty of people were still stranded though, unable to get a flight or passage on a ship. And no one knew when the borders would re-open.

Like most countries, Britain was officially closed off to the outside world. For now, public transport had stopped running and petrol was severely rationed. A state of emergency had been declared. The summer was ending and the leaves were changing along with everything else.

CHAPTER THIRTY FOUR

RILEY

'What are you talking about?' Luc says.

'Sshh. For God's sake, man, keep your voice down,' Denzil hisses.

'Sorry,' Luc whispers. 'But where are you going? You can't just leave us here. What are we supposed to do?'

'I've got an idea,' says Denzil. 'I don't like it. I'm gutted about it, but it's our only chance.'

'What?' asks Luc. 'What's your idea?'

'I could make out that you took me against my will and now I'm escaping back to the barracks.'

'But won't they want to know why we escaped in the first place?' I ask. 'Why would we have thought we were in danger if it wasn't for you telling us?'

'Good point.'

'How about you tell them that Riley heard soldiers walking past her window talking about how they were going to do us some serious harm?' Luc says. 'She panicked and came to fetch me.'

'That would work,' says Denzil. 'Then you knocked out one of the soldiers and took me at gunpoint from my post at the checkpoint. I'll tell them you tied me up in the back of your AV, but I untied my ankles and threw myself out the back of the moving vehicle. Sound believable to you?'

We half nod, half shake our heads, wearing doubtful expressions.

'Well, it'll have to do,' Denzil says.

'Maybe you could throw them off our scent,' says Luc. 'Tell them you saw us stop and pull off the road. That we're driving cross-country in the other direction, heading back down south.'

'Yeah, I can do that,' Denzil replies. 'Meantime, you stay put till dawn. By then I should've been able to draw them south, away from here. I'll tell 'em you're probably heading back to Bournemouth, frightened out of your stupid minds.'

'Hey!' I say with mock indignance. 'Are you sure there's no other way? I don't like to think of you going back there when you hate it so much.'

Denzil smiles and shakes his head. 'We're running out of time. It's the only plan I can think of that's got a chance of working. I need this guard job, so I need you to get out of here alive.' He points at the jacket I'm wearing. 'I'm gonna need that back.'

I shrug it off and hand it to him.

'We have to make it look authentic,' says Luc.

'No holds barred then. My life depends on it.'

We bind his hands together with rope and give his ankles rope burns, so it looks as though they've been bound.

Denzil turns to Luc, 'I'm relying on you to give me what you got.'

Luc takes a breath and punches Denzil hard on the mouth. I flinch. He's bleeding from the lip, but he doesn't make a sound.

Luc finds a jagged piece of metal from the warehouse floor and uses it to rip down one side of Denzil's uniform. Luc rips the bottom of his shirt and makes a gag for Denzil's mouth. Lastly, Denzil rolls in the dirt.

We stand awkwardly silent for a moment.

'Thank you, Denzil,' says Luc. 'But you know you really don't have to do this. We could all just make a run for it.'

'Man, you didn't just mess up my uniform and give me a fat lip for nothing. I've been with these sorry-ass soldiers for years now, a few weeks longer won't hurt and then I can get to Bournemouth no problem. Anyway, didn't you hear me before? I need you to escape so you can give me the job of highly paid guard with chunky Christmas bonus.'

'The job's definitely yours,' Luc says. 'Thanks, mate. Good luck. We'll see you soon.' They shake hands and Luc presses some gold pieces into his hand. 'To help you find your way back to us.'

I give Denzil a hug and kiss his cheek. He passes me the gag and I tie it around his mouth, mindful of the purple bruise and split lip.

He smiles, lifts up the garage door a fraction and rolls out into the dangerous night. All we can do now is sit and wait.

It's quiet. Not once do we hear soldiers nearby. Hopefully Denzil has thrown them off our trail.

‘I'll sleep in the front, you take the back seat,’ offers Luc.

‘No way. You’re definitely taking the back seat, you're still recovering from your bang on the head.’ Luc doesn't think I notice each time he winces at the pain the raiders inflicted. ‘Anyway, you need a decent night’s sleep more than I do. I already had some kip back at the barracks.’

‘Riley, if you don't take the back seat, I'll sleep on the floor outside.’

‘Urrgh, you're such a gentleman,’ I huff, feeling guilty. But I know he will actually sleep on the floor if I don't do as I’m told, so I climb into the back seat and make myself comfortable.

‘Night, Luc.’

‘Night, Riley. Sleep well ... if you can.

‘Thanks.’

‘You did really well tonight, coming to get me in the mess hall. That was a horrible call to make, knowing whether or not to trust Denzil. I don't know what would've happened if we'd stayed.’

‘I'm sorry I was such a wimp before. Leaving you to go and eat with those hideous soldiers.’

‘It wasn’t your fault. You were ill.’

‘I’m still sorry.’

‘Well, it's a good thing you didn’t come otherwise we would’ve been stuck there. And it turned out fine, so don’t worry about it. I just hope Denzil’s alright.’

‘He saved us,’ I say. ‘And he didn’t even know us.’

The rest of the night is long and strangely lonely. Denzil has left a big gap. Luc and I had quickly gotten used to his company. I pray he's going to be alright, that he'll manage his escape to Bournemouth soon. We owe him our lives.

Luc and I chat about nothing until finally we manage to doze off for an hour or two.

Now early morning has crept up on us and I feel cold and stiff. I'm worrying about Denzil and wonder if he's succeeded in fooling his colleagues.

It's strange spending the night alone with Luc. I hope things will go back to normal between us. I hope our feelings for each other will subside and we can be friends again with no awkwardness. But that kiss keeps trying to replay itself over and over in my mind. It's just the stress of the journey, I tell myself. That's all it is. Nothing more.

I regret not asking Denzil sooner about Chambers. I should have got more answers. Now it's beginning to look like a lost cause on all fronts. Last night was probably the end of the trail.

We've got no plans of action left. We've got no new leads to follow. Our prime goal was Century Barracks, relying on the soldiers to point us in the right direction. Now we've reached a dead end. We'll have to keep going onwards to my grandparents' house.

Maybe we can stop at settlements along the way and show Chambers' picture to everyone we meet. After all, he's rumoured to be somewhere in the West Country and we are heading west, so it's possible someone might recognise him. But I don't really believe this is going to get us anywhere. It's all so hopeless.

I'm deflated. My bones are damp and I feel grubby and irritable. Watery sunlight filters through the trees and into the hole in the warehouse roof, but it isn't enough to warm the chilly space. As well as everything else, I'm really conscious our parents will now be sick with worry. I've got to face it, this trip has been a hideous mistake causing nothing but grief and distress. I shiver for the millionth time and try to think of something to make me feel less miserable. But I'm on a real downer.

Luc has been rummaging around for ages in the front, trying to find something.

'What are you looking for?'

He lifts his head and passes me a large bar of whole nut milk chocolate. 'Breakfast? Half each?' he grins.

'Damn good idea,' I say, a reluctant smile escaping at the thought of such decadence.

At seven o'clock we risk opening the garage door. The sunshine streams into the gloomy warehouse. The brightness, combined with a sugar rush from breakfast, does a lot to lighten my mood.

'Wait here,' says Luc. 'I'm just going to have a little scout around and make sure there's no one about.'

'Can I come with you?'

'Yeah, course.'

We crawl under the garage door and stand up, blinking and squinting in the light. The sun on my skin feels good and I stretch my body, catlike in the warmth. Then I turn around three hundred and sixty degrees to take in our surroundings. We're standing in a sun-drenched clearing encircled by trees and bushes. The vine-covered warehouse has almost merged into the surrounding forest.

Last night's storm has washed away our tyre tracks, so we head towards a gap in the foliage. We walk for only a few seconds before finding ourselves back on the narrow main road.

Gentle birdsong permeates the air and a startled squirrel spirals up a tree next to me. It's like we're in a completely different place to the eerie ghost town we reluctantly entered last night. This morning we've awoken to the heat-hazed jungle of a lost civilisation. A dappled light plays through the trees and I half-expect to see fairies and goblins or perhaps a unicorn come trotting through the forest. Steam from last night's rainstorm rises in soft billowing puffs from the drying land and the morning air smells fresh and loamy.

We stand for a minute, staring down along the track at the shimmering, half-ruined buildings that have sunk back into the soft earth.

'I don't think there's anyone here, do you?' says Luc.

'Doesn't look like it. But what if we start up the engine and someone hears?'

'Mm.' Luc pauses in thought. 'The thing is, I don't think it's a good idea to hang around here for much longer. We're too close to Warminster. They might come back when they don't find us to the south.'

'You're right,' I say. 'Let's just go. Come on.'

Luc gazes at me for a moment and then catches my infectious urgency. We run back to the AV, laughing hysterically and almost tripping ourselves up in the process. I've got that silly-scared feeling, like when Skye and I were young and Pa would pretend to be a bear, chasing us up the stairs and we'd scream and squeal in terror. Only this time, the terror is partially real. Well on my part, anyway.

We push up the warehouse door, jump into the AV, breathless with recklessness, and Luc starts up the engine. Bouncing back onto the track, we drive lightning fast out of Westbury, hearts pounding, hoping to God no one's following us.

CHAPTER THIRTY FIVE

RILEY

One hour on the road and we start to relax and to believe we might have eluded the soldiers. Denzil has saved our lives and we're indebted to him.

We drive through beautiful open countryside swathed in rolling hills of pale green, cinnamon and gold, textured like billowing raw silk. After our exhausting confrontations and escapes, I suddenly feel exhilarated and untouchable. The road widens out, smoother and less-potholed, so we fly over the tarmac at nearly forty miles-per-hour in some places, laughing at the freedom.

At this point, I think we both realise our mission is doomed to failure due to a complete lack of information. Also, if I'm totally honest, we've got no real plan for what we would do if we did happen to stumble across our fugitive, other than pull out a gun and shoot him, which now seems like another unrealistic piece of fantasizing.

After a majorly depressed start to the day, I quickly reconcile myself to the fact that there are too many elements beyond my control and the best I can do is to soak up this adventure to the full. Skye would understand that events have conspired to work against us. Perhaps it's her, protecting us from crossing paths with this evil man. I know we won't find him. Maybe I knew this all along, but refused to accept it.

In my new realistic frame of mind, I try to kid myself that what I feel for Luc is circumstantial lust – he's the only person I'm with, so of course I'm attracted to him. There's no one else to compare him with. But one glance across at him and I'm in freefall. I turn away and think instead of Skye, seeing her face in my mind.

We change places so Luc can have a break. I begin to enjoy the drive, gazing out of the window at the endless scenery. Bottle-green woodland pins down the edges of the landscape with not even a hint of autumn in the leaves yet.

Up ahead, I spot a small bright shape on the horizon and try to work out what it is. It doesn't look like a helicopter and it's too large and slow to be a bird. Soon it's out of sight behind a distant hill. I dismiss it and don't think it important enough to wake Luc who's fallen asleep. Ten minutes later I see it again, only this time it's much closer and I think I now know what it is.

'Luc, look!'

He opens his eyes, on instant alert.

'A hot air balloon!' I say.

'What? Where?'

'There, over to your left. I saw it a while back, but I couldn't work out what it was. It's amazing.'

'Mm,' says Luc, stretching. 'I hope it doesn't get any closer.'

'What do you mean? Why?'

'Nothing, I'm just being paranoid. It's just a balloon.'

But his paranoia is catching as half an hour later the balloon has drifted nearer and is travelling parallel to our route. It's close enough for us to see its white and orange diamond pattern and we can also make out several figures standing in the basket.

'Okay, I don't like the look of that at all,' says Luc. He reaches down into the footwell and takes out the binoculars. I pull over to the side of the road as he stares through the lenses, adjusting the focus.

'There are two, three, four people in there, as far as I can make out. And they've got binoculars trained on us too.'

'What?' My heart speeds up and I hear the blood whooshing in my ears.

'We need to hide,' he says.

I look around. It's a clear bright day and we're travelling on probably the only road for miles in a metallic grey vehicle that glints like a beacon in the sunshine. We may as well have plastered a big sign across our roof that reads 'come and get us'.

'Do you think it's the army?' I ask.

'It would be a bit weird for the army to travel around in an orange balloon, but we can't take any chances. I don't want to hang around and find out.'

'Me neither.'

'Let's find somewhere to hide and let's do it quickly.'

'We could drive back the way we came,' I suggest. 'They must have to go with the wind and they won't be able to turn as quickly as we can. I saw a track about five minutes back there.

Maybe there are some trees we could shelter under.'

'Do it,' he says.

I perform a clumsy seven point turn, sweating and apologising. Luc puts his hand on my arm and leaves it there.

'You're doing great. They're probably nothing to do with us anyway. We're just doing this to be on the safe side.'

'Thanks, I'm okay. It's just, after those raiders and Grey and the army and everything.'

'I know.' He leans over and kisses my cheek. Even in my terrified state, my heart beats double time for a whole new reason.

'I'll put the shockplates on this time, just in case.' I turn to look at him and he holds my gaze. I look away first, a jumble of emotions coursing through me.

'There!' He points. I scan the middle distance and see the roof of an old barn.

'Brilliant.' Revving the engine, I nose the AV up a steep bank and through the trees. There, we find just what we're searching for - a dilapidated grey stone barn surrounded by trees. It's really just one wall and a roof with a couple of rusted supports at the front.

I park the AV under its concealing roof and turn off the engine. We sit in silence, listening to the faint ticking and clicking of the tired engine as it cools down.

Hunger distracts us from danger, so we spread the rug out on the grassy barn floor and feast on crackers with marmite and apples from a nearby tree. We pick some juicy blackberries from a hedgerow next to the barn and gorge ourselves silly on them, until our hands and tongues are stained purple.

Luc takes the binoculars and creeps onto the road to search the sky for our floating friends. A minute later he returns.

'I can't see them.'

'Do you think they've gone?'

'I don't know, but we should wait here for a bit, until we're sure. They won't be able to spot us from up there anyway.'

'God, that was scary,' I reply. 'I was convinced they were after us.'

'A hot air balloon can't really compete with the AV. Let's just chill here for a bit.'

We lie side by side on the rug in the cool shade of the open barn, listening to the wind sweep through the long grass.

We don't speak and my heart thumps in my chest. I can't feel the ground beneath my body and yet, at the same time, it feels like I'm connected to the earth itself.

Luc's hand is so close to mine that I feel the heat from his skin. And then he moves it the thousand miles required to hold my hand. I don't know how long we lie here like this, just holding hands. It could be seconds or minutes or hours.

I want him to make a move, but at the same time I don't.

'Riley ...'

'Yeah?' My voice comes out as a whisper.

'What you said, before, about Skye. About us. Did you really mean it?'

'Yes,' I say. I let go of his hand and sit up, hugging my knees to my chest.

He sits up too and faces me, cross-legged. He reaches forward and tilts my chin up so I'm forced to look at him. His eyes are blue, his face is beautiful and I want nothing more than to lean forward and kiss him. But I can't.

'I love you, Riley.'

My heart fills up with a feeling I've never known before. I can't believe he's spoken those words.

'Luc ...'

'It's okay if you don't feel the same. I just had to tell you.'

'It's not that. It's just ... I would feel like a bad person if we took this further. Skye was my sister and she had feelings for you.'

'Me and Skye would never have happened. I loved her like a sister. Nothing more.'

'I know that. I do, but ...'

Luc stands up and takes a breath. 'I don't want you to feel any pressure, Riley. Not after everything you've been through. That's the last thing I want. I just need you to know that I could make you happy. We both loved Skye and she loved us. I don't think it would be wrong.'

His words are seductive and I want so much to believe them.

'I can't,' I say. Even though in my head I'm saying the words, 'yes, yes, I love you too'.

He bows his head and walks away.

Luc is gone for a while, but I don't go after him. I figure he needs to be alone. And although I think I've done the right thing, I also feel like a bitch for rejecting him. I admit to myself that I do love Luc and I know that we could be really happy together.

Skye wasn't a jealous person. She was good and sweet and generous. She would be happy for us. I know she would. But something is still stopping me. As much as I want to be with him, I know my decision is the right one. I can't betray Skye's memory.

But I don't know how much longer I can keep doing this.

Luc returns before it gets dark. He gives me a sad smile. 'We should stay here tonight,' he says.

'Okay.'

Those are the only words we speak that night.

We wake early, but the awkwardness from last night still hangs heavy like morning mist. Our meagre breakfast of dry crackers tastes like dust in my mouth and it feels as though there's a stone sitting where my heart should be. It's jagged and heavy and it hurts.

We pack up in silence and get back on the road. Thankfully, we see no sign of any army vehicles or of yesterday's balloon. The road is wide and empty. I'm trying to think of something neutral to say to break the silence, all the while wondering if Luc hates me now.

'Can we get back to how we were?' I say.

'What do you mean?'

'This feels horrible,' I say. 'I want us to be friends again.'

'Yeah. Course,' he says. But it's the fakest sentence I've ever heard him speak and we sink back into silence.

At Melksham, we pass a large grey-walled compound and decide to stop and show Chambers' picture to the guards. We pull up outside some thick wooden doors and wait nervously in the AV for someone to come out. A letterbox-sized opening appears at head-height and a face appears behind the grille.

'State your business,' comes a bored voice.

Luc opens his window and holds out the picture, explaining why we're here. The man beckons Luc forward. He gets out of the AV and passes the picture to the guard, along with a couple of silver bits.

'I'll go and ask,' the guard says.

The grille disappears as the opening slides shut. Half-an-hour later, a shout and a hand beckon Luc back to the door. The guard thrusts the picture back out through the bars.

'Sorry, no sightings,' he says mechanically and the grille closes again.

Luc and I look at each other and shrug, in growing acceptance of the lack of information. The same story greets us at three further settlements. Some guards are friendly and others are as curt as those at Melksham, but they all have the same response: 'Sorry, no.' At least doing this gives us something to focus on other than our feelings toward each other. Makes us feel a little easier in each other's company.

We're heading towards the Chippenham Compound and Luc says we're over halfway to my grandparents' house. I'm happy at the thought of seeing my family, despite the trouble I'm in.

On the approach to Chippenham, we have to really start paying attention to the route, as we've reached a complicated series of junctions and roundabouts and a lot of the roads are completely overgrown. There are no signposts anywhere and Luc has to concentrate hard to remember which route to take.

'This is it, I remember now,' he says, relief in his voice. 'There are sometimes raiders up on the bypass.'

'What?'

'Don't worry. If we head closer to the town's compound, we should avoid them. We have to pass under an old railway bridge ... Should be down here if I'm remembering right ... Yep, there it is. I thought we were lost for a minute.'

We inch under the bridge and around a blind corner only wide enough for one vehicle at a time. The road is clear as always and we press on towards the compound.

As we round a bend, we're faced with an impossibly high wall made from steel, or metal of some kind, with huge rivets all over it. It looks like a massive water tower, but Luc says this is the main Chippenham Compound.

High, square towers, like castle turrets, protrude periodically from the top of the walls and, against the bright sunshine, I make out the small silhouettes of armed figures on guard. Several gun barrels track our progress as we turn and wind our way past the metal fortress, but no one opens fire.

Then, up ahead, we see a sight that makes Luc skid to a halt – armed men blocking our path.

CHAPTER THIRTY SIX

Eleanor

At the end of September, Tom came home one night with some horrendous news. 'Johnny's parents were both killed last week in one of the Southampton bombings.'

'Oh no.' I sat down, shocked. 'No! I can't believe it. What? Both of them?' I asked, feeling so bad for Johnny.

'Yeah.'

We all just looked at each other. Nobody knew what to say anymore. It just seemed like bad news on top of bad news.

'He's gonna be driving back home tomorrow,' Tom added.

'D'you think I should ring him?' I asked. 'I mean, would he even want to hear from me after everything?'

'I think that would be a nice thing to do, darling.' My mother came over and stroked my hair.

'You dumped him,' David said bluntly. 'He might not need reminding of *that* after what's just happened to his family.'

'That's a bit harsh, Dave,' said Tom. 'I don't think he'll be thinking about that. He'll just be glad she cared enough to call.'

'I say call him,' Oliver shouted from the other room.

'Oh my God, now you've all confused me,' I said. They began arguing among themselves, so I left them to it, trudging upstairs to think about what Johnny must be going through.

It turned out I was spared making a decision as he called round half an hour later to say goodbye. David shouted up the stairs while I stared out the window at a double-glazed sunset. It made me squint and turn away; its beauty an irritation. I felt and looked awful, but was past caring about my appearance. David shouted again, impatient. Yelling that Johnny was here.

I slouched downstairs in my tatty old tracksuit and toxic slippers, my hair scraped off my face in a ponytail. I felt shaky.

Johnny stood in the hallway with rounded shoulders, his hands clasped in front of him. When he looked up at me, I could tell he was surprised by my appearance. I was shocked by his. His face was haggard, he had dark circles under his eyes and his hair had grown out into an unfashionable fuzz. He gave me a warm hug and we went and sat in the lounge, which everyone tactfully vacated, after passing on their condolences.

'I'm so sorry about your parents,' I said. 'If there's anything I can do …'

'Thanks. I'm going home tomorrow, finally. I had to wait for my petrol ration. My brother and his wife are meeting me at mum and dad's.' He swallowed and took a breath to steady the wobble in his voice. 'So, I should be okay for a while.'

'That's good. That you'll have family there to look after you, I mean.' I felt like I'd said the wrong thing.

'Yeah.' There was an awkward pause and then Johnny surprised me. 'I heard what happened to Connor. I'm sorry. I mean, I know you really liked him. I tried to find out what happened to him for you, but I haven't got Sam's number, and his parents don't know when he'll get leave.'

'You didn't have to do that.' I couldn't believe he'd tried to do such a nice thing for me. I certainly didn't deserve his help. 'I want you to know, I'm really sorry, Johnny. About everything, how it all turned out ... you and me. You must think I'm a horrible person, and now your parents ...' It was no good. I tried to stop them, but the tears streamed down my face. Johnny's parents were dead. Connor was dead. The world was going to hell, and now he'd think I was a weak, self-centred bitch for crying all over him.

'Don't cry.' He picked up his jacket and used the lining to dab my tears away.

'Your lovely jacket ...'

'It's not lovely. I don't even like it. Sam made me buy it. Said it made me look cool. I think it makes me look like a twat.'

I giggled through my tears. 'No, you don't.'

'No? Okay, but I made you laugh though.'

I nodded.

'Look, Ellie, I've got to go back and face some pretty unpleasant stuff, and I don't know if, or when I'll see you. My uni course has been suspended, so ...' He shrugged. 'I just wanted to come and say goodbye, and no hard feelings. I hope everything goes well for you.' He got up to go.

'Thank you. Same to you. Okay, well take care of yourself.'

'You too.' We hugged and kissed on the cheek and then he left.

But that wasn't the last I would see of Johnny Culpepper.

CHAPTER THIRTY SEVEN

RILEY

There are four of them that I can see. Big looking guys dressed in khaki with black boots and berets. They're standing around next to a rusty old caravan and a barrier with a sign. It looks like quite a hastily-put-together operation. Luc and I both peer through the windscreen to try to make out the word on the square sheet of warped plywood.

'Toll,' we say in unison.

'I suppose that means we have to pay to get through,' I say, dreading the thought of approaching the barrier.

'Yeah. I've been this way before and it wasn't here then. They look like privateers.'

Privateers are men who set themselves up as freelance guards. You pay them to escort you through dangerous areas. Some of them are the real thing, but usually it's just a scam to extort money from scared travellers.

'I don't want to risk it,' says Luc. 'We'll try our luck at the compound and maybe they'll let us cut through. I'd rather pay the compound guards than a protection racket.'

He does a u-turn and we head back to find the compound entrance. An ominous droning sound follows us and I turn to see two privateers on motorcycles coming up behind the AV and flanking us. They smile and motion for us to slow down.

'Shockplates,' I hiss through my teeth.

'Done it,' Luc replies, slowing our vehicle to a halt, but leaving the engine running. He opens the window a crack and one of the privateers draws up beside us and peers in. Although he's built like a wrestler, he doesn't look much older than us.

'Nice day,' he says.

'Mm,' agrees Luc.

'Where you headed? We'd be happy to escort you through to the other side of town. Lots of nasty folk about these days. Wouldn't want you to run into any raiders, or the like.'

'Thanks, but we've got business in the compound.'

'Don't worry, you can get access to the Compound from our strip. Follow me, I'll show you how to get in.'

'It's okay,' Luc replies calmly. 'I've remembered where the main entrance is. Thanks anyway, for your help.'

The privateer draws his weapon, but Luc is faster and manages to close the window before he can get a shot.

I realise we've just had a very narrow escape. That boy could have shot Luc in the head if he'd been quicker.

Luc revs the engine and accelerates, leaving the privateers behind. But the two boys start off in pursuit, firing rounds at our vehicle, their cohorts following on behind. Shots ricochet off the AV, accompanied by showers of sparks and the electric crackle of the shock plates.

As Luc drives, I scan the unbroken metal walls for any type of opening to escape into, but I can see no entrance. Then, above the din, I hear faint shouts and see the bikers gesticulating to each other. The compound watchmen are shooting at the privateers from their towers, using powerful, mounted semi-automatic guns.

'Hallelujah,' says Luc, as two of the bikers drop their speed. Soon, all four finally cease their pursuit and turn back towards the shabby toll gate.

Without warning, a concealed door in the wall slides open and we nearly drive straight past without noticing. Luc slams on the brakes and reverses, so we're now directly outside the yawning opening. I peer out of my window to get a better look inside. An elderly man in a royal blue frock coat and matching top hat stands inside and motions wildly for us to enter.

'What shall we do?' I ask Luc. 'Is it safe in there? That man looks crazy.'

'It should be safe. It's a compound. Safer than out here at the moment anyway.' Luc backs up, swings around and accelerates through the narrowing entrance, as the door slides shut.

We find ourselves in a vast deserted field bordered on three sides by high green hedges. I glance back at the wall and can't even see where the opening was. Luc brings to AV to a stop as I stare through the windscreen at the frowning, whiskered man who has ushered us into the compound. He's tapping his foot and glancing down at his watch.

Luc reaches for his revolver and opens his door.

'Come along, come along. Quickly now,' the man orders, like an impatient headmaster. 'You've interrupted me from my judging and they shall all be wondering what's keeping me.'

His walkie talkie suddenly demands his attention. 'Sir, do you require close range assistance? Over.'

'No, no, Luis, I told you I'm perfectly capable of welcoming our guests myself. Tell Marcia I shall be along momentarily. Oh, over. Yes. Over.'

The man stares upwards, and we follow his line of vision to one of the wall's turrets, where I make out the small figure of a guard holding a walkie talkie. The other guards have their gun sights trained on our AV which makes me remember one of Pa's fond sayings about frying pans and fires. But for some reason, I don't feel at all scared. Maybe I've used up my quota of fear.

'You'll have to leave that in your vehicle,' the man says, pointing to Luc's gun. 'Luis gets twitchy if he sees weapons.'

Luc hesitates before replacing the revolver.

As we climb out of the AV, our strange host clips the receiver onto his coat and it dangles there, awkwardly. 'Jolly useful device.' He pats the walkie talkie. 'I always like to personally greet any visitors we get to our little town. I've got a nose for riff raff and I can tell you're not.'

We walk around the vehicle to join the odd Dickensian man who's standing next to a small motorised golf cart. He climbs into the driver's seat and motions to us to do the same. I stretch my arms and roll my neck which feels as though it's got a thousand kinks in it. I hear a couple of clicks.

'Hello, I'm Lucas Donovan and this is Riley Culpepper. We're grateful to you for helping us out back there.'

'Not at all,' the man replies.

'We need to find a route to avoid the toll outside. If you could point us in the right direction ...'

'Yes, very good, very good,' the man replies absently. 'The name's Aubrey Rowbotham, Mayor of Chippenham. Welcome. But can we get a move on. I'm holding up proceedings. Jump in and we can talk on the way.'

We don't seem to have much of a choice and so I sit next to the Mayor, while Luc balances precariously on the back of the little golf cart.

'Will our vehicle be okay here?' Luc asks.

'Have you locked it?'

'Yes.'

'Perfectly safe then.'

We trundle across the vast field and, as we approach the hedge at the far end, I make out the murmur and hum of a large crowd of people.

'Where is everybody?' I ask. 'I can hear voices, but I can't see anyone.'

'It's a big day today,' answers the Mayor. 'You timed it just right for your visit. It's our Autumn Harvest Fair. Everybody's making their way to Lowstone Castle Field. Been there since eight o'clock myself, being Mayor and all. I'm judging the livestock. Some damn fine beasts, let me tell you. Are you familiar with pigs?'

We both answer in the negative. I'm trying desperately not to giggle. Luc shoots me a warning glance and I bite my lip and look down.

'Shame. Learn a lot from pigs, you know. Learn from most animals, but I do have a soft spot for our curly tailed friends.'

'Who are those lads outside your walls?' Luc asks. 'Are they privateers? Are they charging a genuine toll, or were they planning on robbing us?'

'So many questions! Blasted nuisance those ruffians. I've known them since they were potty trained and they're still behaving like two year olds. Bloody awful disgrace. Don't get me started.'

'You know them personally?' I ask. 'Are they from here?'

'They are. Unfortunately one of the stupid nitwits is my great nephew. We tried locking them up for their misdemeanours, but it didn't do any good I'm afraid. They kept right on with their wicked ways, egging each other on, you know. I don't think our gentle way of life suits them very much.

'Some of our less charitable citizens wanted to turn them over to the army, but we erred on the compassionate side and ended up expelling them. Broke their mothers' hearts. But what could I do? I've got a whole town to take care of. Can't expect everyone to put up with their shenanigans.

'Now they've set up their ridiculous Toll outside. They think they've got one over on old stick-in-the-mud Aubrey. Think I'm a silly old fool, but I'd like to see them do my job, they'd wet their pants at the responsibility. Sorry, do forgive me. You don't want to hear me wittering on about my problems. It's a joyful occasion so let's have some fun. Can you stay for the day?'

CHAPTER THIRTY EIGHT

RILEY

The Mayor brings the cart to an impressive stop at a jaunty angle by the hedge and we climb out. By now the hubbub of voices is overwhelming and although I can't yet see anyone it sounds as if we've landed in the middle of a huge crowd.

We follow the Mayor through a wooden gate and he leads us down a steep grassy slope. We find ourselves on a wide avenue of leafy horse chestnuts, thronged with people, all chattering excitedly and heading in the same direction. They nod deferentially to the Mayor as he passes by and he tips his tall hat in acknowledgement, greeting each person by name.

Aubrey Rowbotham must be well into his seventies, but he walks like a much younger man, purposefully and upright, threading his way through the crowd. We have some difficulty keeping up with him, constantly distracted by all the sights and sounds, but we manage to keep sight of his peacock-blue hat bobbing along.

Everyone is sporting vividly-coloured, homemade clothes and equally outlandish headwear - it appears, in this town, the Mayor's coat and top hat are not considered an eccentricity. I wonder whether they dress like this every day, or whether it's just some kind of fancy dress for the fair. I feel drab and underdressed by comparison.

Most people are carrying baskets or woven picnic hampers and some have bright rugs slung over their arms. The heat of the day ensures a pervading smell of body odour, but this is offset by the scent of freshly cut grass - not too bad compared with the world-class stench of the Charminster Compound.

I realise all the townsfolk are staring curiously at us as we pass, gawking at our clothes, nudging each other, whispering or giggling in our wake. But they appear friendly enough and the girls especially, seem to be very taken with Luc. I feel a new sensation - a small spurt of green jealousy - as I see him smile at a particularly pretty blonde, who's shamelessly eying him up. She's pulled ahead by an older man who I guess is her father. He speaks sternly to her and she soon stops smiling.

Up ahead, I see another unexpected sight - a wonderful creamy-coloured castle perched on a low hill, with a dark grey wall around its base. The crowd suddenly comes to a stop and we finally manage to catch up with the Mayor. Without any warning, Mayor Aubrey Rowbotham takes hold of my arm and propels me forward as the crowd parts to let us through. I see what's caused our abrupt halt - a small red iron bridge which only allows two abreast. As we cross, I stare down at the dark green river below us, hiding beneath a mess of tangled reeds.

We step off the bridge into a huge field where the fair is being held. The stalls, rides and events are all set up here, in the shadow of the large storybook castle.

'I must dash off to resume my judgely duties,' says the

Mayor. 'I'll meet you in the tea tent at 4pm for afternoon tea. Enjoy yourselves. Any problems, find Marcia in the VIP tent by the show jumping arena. She knows you're here.'

And with that, he strides off into the crowd, until all we see is the iridescent tip of his top hat.

To our left is a fenced-off shooting range, but instead of guns, the competitors are wielding huge crossbows. The bright cloth targets are wrapped around large wooden discs propped up on stands, under five tall sycamore trees. Luc grins at me and we wander over to watch.

As far as I can tell, each competitor hands over a token - a piece of fruit, a small cake, or the like - as their entrance stake which goes into a large basket. Then they are handed a crossbow and half-a-dozen or so arrows, with which they have to try and hit the red inner ring. If they manage it, they go through to the next round, if not, they're out of the competition. Most entrants hit the blue or white outer rings, prompting good-natured jeers from the onlookers. I guess the competition winner will receive the basket of goodies. A young boy, helping his father man the stall, notices us and tries to get Luc to enter.

'Afraid of embarrassing yourself in front of the young lady,' says the boy's father.

'Something like that,' replies Luc.

'Come on in, I'll show you how it's done. Let you have a few practice goes.'

Luc climbs over the fence amidst a few rowdy cheers. He takes a silver bit out of his pocket and passes it to the man.

'Very generous. That'll get you a few goes.'

His first practice shots go wildly out and strike the grass, but as he gets a feel for the crossbow, he starts hitting the cloth. He looks disappointed that he hasn't hit the inner ring and his last shot lands a millimetre from the red. Everyone 'oohs' in sympathy and Luc clambers back over to join me.

'That's harder than it looks. Good fun though. Do you want a go?'

'Maybe later.' Normally it's the sort of thing I'd love to do, but we haven't had any lunch and I'm hungry. I just want to wander around and relax, after our adrenaline-filled morning. 'Have you got any silver left?' I ask. 'I'm starving.'

'Me too.' He pulls out a handful of silver bits from his pocket. 'We're loaded,' he grins. It's the first time he's smiled in a while and I feel my heart lighten. Maybe things will be okay.

'Brilliant,' I reply .'Let's go and find some food.'

We head towards an impressive striped marquee. There are wooden tables and chairs outside the tent, with a spit roast, a barbeque, a salad bar and a covered stall piled high with various wrapped sandwiches, cakes and fruit. Inside the marquee, are more tables and chairs but there isn't a spare seat to be had. In the corner, a long curved bar sells alcohol, juices and smoothies. In the opposite corner, an Irish fiddle band is pumping out energetic tunes and loads of people are dancing.

'Riley, do you know what I'm thinking?' Luc says. 'What if we spend the whole day here. Maybe even see if we can stay the night somewhere. I think we need a proper break before we head back on the road. What do you think?'

'That would be good.' I smile at the thought of not at having to venture outside straightaway. It's so exhausting and unpredictable out there. It would be good to not have to worry for a while. The only niggle of concern is that our parents will still be worrying about us, but I push it to the back of my mind. One more day won't make a difference. 'Shall we find that Marcia woman? See if she knows somewhere we can stay?'

'Yeah, let's go *now* then we can come back, eat and relax.'

We head off to find the show jumping arena, caught up in the festive mood and excited at the thought of an indulgent, relaxing afternoon, free from the worries of the road. We pass Shetland pony rides, craft stalls and a beautiful red and white striped helter skelter slide that I decide to have a go on later.

We stop for a few moments to watch the birds of prey and their handlers. There are falcons, hawks, buzzards and a magnificent eagle owl. They are fascinating, beautiful creatures and we both agree we could easily watch them all day, with their intelligent yellow eyes and haughty expressions. Finally, we spy the VIP tent with a couple of burly bouncers outside.

'Hello,' I say to one of them. 'Is Marcia here? The Mayor told us it would be okay for us to see her.'

'Wait there,' he says and disappears inside the tent. He returns moments later with a large round lady, dressed from head to toe in royal blue silk. She has an unflattering blue bonnet perched on her shiny bowl haircut and a row of green bangles jangle on her arm. She's drains the contents of her pint glass as she strides towards us.

'Hello. I'm Marcia Rowbotham. You must be our visitors. Care for a drink? I'm on the Old Ozzlehorn, it's a great tipple.'

She shakes our hands and we follow her into the tent. The interior sparkles like a glamorous five-star hotel in a scene from a movie. We have to take our footwear off at the entrance and put on a pair of silken embroidered Turkish slippers. I can see why, as I step from grass into deep cream shag-pile carpet.

Long sofas and ornate armchairs have been arranged in cosy groups around low dark wood tables. Dining tables are laid out in elegant rows. Crystal chandeliers glitter from the ceiling and a string quartet plays soothing sounds, blending with soft chatter and the clink of glasses and silver cutlery. You'd never guess we were in the middle of a field on a hot summer's day.

Next to the bar, a sumptuous buffet is laid out on white cloth-covered trestles and the VIPs are digging in with abandon, all as outlandishly dressed as Marcia Rowbotham. It's a strange sight and these eccentric people look completely at odds with their formal surroundings.

'What can I do for you young 'uns?' she says, handing us half pints of beer and motioning for us to sit on one of the sofas.

'We were wondering if we could stay here overnight and carry on with our journey in the morning?' I ask.

'Course it would. Not a problem. You can stay with us at the Lodge. Aubs and I will meet you for afternoon tea at four, we'll talk then. Now I must get back to meeting and greeting. You go off and enjoy yourselves. We'll see you later. Leave the glasses in the tent, when you've finished.'

She heaves her huge bulk off the soft armchair and is gone. My stomach rumbles with disappointment that she didn't offer us any of the delicious-looking food from the buffet, and the beer's making me light-headed. But on second thoughts, I'm relieved we won't have to make small talk with strangers.

We spend the next three-and-a-half hours, eating, drinking and dozing in the sunshine. We also have a good wander around the fair, exclaiming at the gorgeous farm animals - shaggy coated cattle, llamas, plumptious poultry, curly horned rams, comical ducks, spotted pigs, yellow-eyed goats and all their adorable offspring. We watch the show jumping, the pony and trap display and the tractor racing.

As much as I'm enjoying all the sights, my breath is shallow and my senses are heightened. Each time Luc touches my hand or my arm, it's like I'm on fire. I had told myself that nothing could ever happen between us, but my body is telling me otherwise. And every time I look away from him, I feel his eyes on my face. I don't think he's going to give up on me.

The highlight of the afternoon's entertainment is Penny Purvis, a drunken goose shepherdess, trying to herd her flock through a tricky course, in front of an amused audience. She's wearing a microphone and swearing like a trooper to her oblivious birds, prompting howls of laughter and outraged gasps, before being forcibly removed from the arena.

Time whizzes by in a contented blur and soon four o'clock rolls around - time for tea.

CHAPTER THIRTY NINE

Eleanor

Four months later, on an icy cold February morning, Johnny returned to Gloucestershire. The bombings had eased off now, but the borders stayed firmly closed. The military were frantically recruiting as nearly half their force was still trying to get back from overseas and there were rumours they would start compulsory drafting soon.

Petrol was non-existent and there'd been no food on the supermarket shelves for weeks. People hawked produce in the streets and goods were traded as British coin was currently worthless. People wanted food, alcohol, tobacco and medicine. Pharmacies and hospitals had been emptied of stocks. Supplies, supposed to be on their way, just weren't getting through to their destinations. Electricity, phones, gas and water were functioning, but only intermittently and people hoarded bottled water.

We were lucky to be in a small village and not a big town or city where there were riots and looting. It was a surreal time, where a person could be stabbed to death for a pack of cigarettes.

Johnny came round to call for me on a Saturday night. I was nervous about seeing him again as a lot had changed since we last met. He came in and chatted to my parents and my brothers. He'd brought a case of red wine and a caddy of loose-leaf tea with him as a gift for my parents and they were delighted to accept such a generous gift. He said not to worry, he had plenty at home and he would be offended if they didn't accept.

It was unsafe to go out at night now, due to the curfew and I wondered how Johnny had managed to avoid it. He wanted to take me out that evening, but my parents said no and he accepted their decision. We went and sat in the conservatory at the back of the house instead. My mum offered him a glass of the precious wine, but he declined and said he'd rather have a cup of tea. We had to drink it black, as we had no milk.

'You've got petrol,' I said.

'Yes, I've got good contacts.'

As I sat in the wicker armchair, next to him, I smoothed my hands over my stomach. His eyes followed my hands and I heard his sharp intake of breath. His eyes widened and then he composed himself, looking up into my defensive eyes.

'Is it his?' he asked.

'Yes.' I had the good grace to look down.

'How far gone are you?'

'Twenty six weeks.'

'Congratulations.' He didn't sound as if he meant it.

'Maybe this wasn't such a good idea,' I said. 'To meet up again after all this time.' I felt bad for him.

'You being pregnant doesn't change why I've come here. I've

got a proposition for you and I'd like you to hear me out before you say anything, or make any decision.' His voice sounded harsh and unfriendly, but I was curious to hear what he'd come to tell me.

'What is it, Johnny?'

'I went back home and ... well, Bournemouth's a virtual war zone now.

'What!'

'No one's safe, not even in their homes. I've had to hire armed guards to protect my place.'

I couldn't even begin to imagine what it must be like.

'My next-door-neighbours, the Donovans, they own a security firm and they've come up with a good idea. Eddie Donovan's a smart man and I trust him.'

'What's his idea?'

'We've sectioned off the area where we live and hired guards to protect it from the looters and all the nutcases. In our area, we've all clubbed together and put up an enclosure. We had to do it quickly, before they trashed everything. It's basic, but it's high and secure. And now we've got guards patrolling its perimeter 24 7. Some outsiders got mad because we've sealed-off quite a few roads. They asked the army to check it out, but the army's agreed we're within our rights to defend our properties.'

'I can't believe you've had to do all that.' My mind spun.

'The thing is, Ellie, we should do the same for your village. And we should do it quickly. Eddie will help me sort it.'

'Is it really necessary here? I mean, we don't really need protecting. We haven't had much trouble.'

'Unfortunately, it's just a matter of time. They could trash your village in an afternoon if they wanted to.'

'They?'

'The nutters. The people who don't give a rat's arse about decency or morality. The ones who never had anything to lose in the first place. They'll be in and out so quickly, you won't know what's hit you. They steal, destroy, rape and murder, and that's the friendly ones. I've seen a lot in the past four months.'

I was appalled. I hadn't come close to realising how bad the situation was. I had been too busy, grieving and then adjusting to my new condition, to pay full attention to the outside world. My parents were disappointed in me for getting pregnant. Dad was so cross that he hardly spoke a civil word to me for about a month. But they gradually came round to the idea and it soon became something positive, to take everyone's mind off the collapsing country.

'Come and speak to Dad,' I said to Johnny. 'I can't really say what to do for the best. He'll know the right people to talk to about this. Thank you.'

He paused, studying me, as if weighing something up in his mind.

'You know that wasn't really why I came back here. You being pregnant threw me off guard. I lost my bottle. I didn't want you to see me upset, so I just told you all that stuff about the perimeter fence to cover up my shock. But it doesn't matter anymore. I want to be truthful now.'

'You mean there is no fence?' I asked, confused. 'Did you make it up?'

'No, there is a perimeter fence, but that isn't why I came here.'

'So why did you?'

'What I meant to say to you was ...' He took a deep breath and continued. 'I love you, Eleanor.' His face flushed. 'Would you come and live with me in Bournemouth? I've got a beautiful house in a protected neighbourhood. We can bring your baby up together. I'd do anything for you, you must know that. I'd look after you.'

I was shocked and overwhelmed by his declaration.

'I don't know what to say. I don't love you, Johnny. I mean, I really like you and I respect you, but live with you in Bournemouth? I don't know. What about my family?'

'It's okay. Just think about it. Tell me when you've had a chance to take it in. You wouldn't regret it. We'd have a good life. Think about what's best for you and for the baby. If you want to, we can still do the perimeter fence here, whatever happens.'

I didn't sleep at all that night.

We married at my family home in Uley and then Johnny and I made a life together in Bournemouth, a place I had never seen before. As it turned out, I never did to get see the original town of Bournemouth, the way it used to be before the attacks. We mainly stayed confined to the safety of the Talbot Woods Perimeter.

When I arrived at his house, I found out just what a true visionary my husband was, because every single room was piled-high to the ceiling with boxes and crates. After the terror attacks, and during those first stages of social and economic decline, most of the population worried about their immediate safety and petrol for their cars or where they could buy a pint of milk. Johnny, however, was busy securing his future.

Before the shops sold out, he spent all his money and got store credit in as many places as he could. He stockpiled goods - from crates of whisky and chocolate, to batteries, generators and power tools. He figured if, by some miracle, the world pulled itself back-on-course, he could just return his purchases and there was no harm done. Anyway, the world did no such thing and Johnny ended up with an enviable stash of goods to put him in an incredible position of power. He bartered wisely and steadily increased his stores.

Our daughter, Riley, was born within the Talbot Woods Perimeter and we had a second child just two years later, another daughter, Skye. We were both fairly content considering what was going on around us. Johnny threw himself into building a safe and comfortable life for us all. He adored being a family man and couldn't do enough to ensure our well-being and happiness.

The outside world rarely touched our cosy existence. I knew Johnny probably had to face some tough challenges, but he refused to share all his experiences with me and I didn't push him to tell me. Young and naïve, I preferred not to dwell on what he might have had to do in the course of his business life. By the time, I matured enough to worry about his career, our roles had been set and it felt like it was too late to question the type of life we led.

I buried all the raw, unexplored feelings I had for Connor and kept my grief hidden deep where I couldn't find it. I immersed myself in my new role as the supporting wife and doting mother. If it sometimes felt like play-acting, I didn't mind. I would imagine myself as the lead character in a play - the glamorous mistress of the manor house. I cultivated lasting friendships with my neighbours and became more and more vivacious and outgoing - a great laugh, an absolute scream, a total head case - that was Ellie Culpepper. It was like this larger-than-life character had taken over the real me.

My two beautiful children were the centre of my life. I was enthralled by my little girls, falling more and more in love with them every day. I gazed at their sleeping forms in wonder and inhaled their sweet, sweaty scent. I didn't dare let myself think of Riley's connection to my lost love, Connor. I loved my girls equally as mine and Johnny's children - little people in their own right.

Johnny too, showed no favouritism, fiercely protective of them and this raised him even higher in my esteem. As the years whizzed by, I slid deeper into the easy contentment of privileged family life and the small, hidden stone of grief grew smaller.

My youngest brother, Tom, now one of Eddie Donovan's guards in the Uley Perimeter, got a site transfer and joined us in Bournemouth five years after I first arrived there. At first glance, it seemed a strange career choice for Tom the pacifist, vegetarian, champion of the underdog. But the changes to our country had a sobering effect on most citizens and much re-evaluating and shifting of morals took place. Tom said he still believed in his old values, but his previous lifestyle was irrelevant now that our lives were constantly under threat. He wanted to actively contribute to the protection of his family.

He did his guard training at Uley, along with my other two brothers who stayed on with my parents. I think Tom had itchy feet and was desperate for a change of scenery. He'd always been so used to flitting around the country on some crusade or another. Now it was a shock to find himself a virtual prisoner in his small home town. Much as he loved the rest of my family, it drove him mad having my parents constantly fussing around him.

I was thrilled to have him in Bournemouth with us. We'd always been close siblings and, although neither of us mentioned Connor, he was an unspoken bond between us. To my delight, Johnny suggested giving Tom the annexe to our house and he was very happy there in his bachelor pad.

One wintry November day, I lay upstairs on my bed, engrossed in a great book Johnny had got hold of for me - a scary thriller that had me speed-reading to find out what would happen in the end. Reading and drawing were my greatest passions and my husband loved to surprise me with battered paperbacks or rare art materials that had me jumping up and down in excitement and flinging my arms around his neck. He'd always tell me to stop overreacting, but I knew he loved to see me so happy.

At the end of a chapter, I decided to nip downstairs and make myself a cup of tea and grab a piece of the delicious flapjack Riley had made in her cookery class yesterday. Riley was fourteen now, and developing into a doe-eyed stunner. Skye was a twelve-year-old tomboy with enough cheeky character to get away with whatever she wanted.

Halfway down the stairs, the doorbell chimed. Dammit. It was too late to pretend I wasn't in. They would've seen me through the window already. The girls weren't due back from school for another two hours and I cherished my quiet time. Who would be interrupting me at this time of day? Johnny was out working. I sighed and went to open the door, yearning for my book and the piece of flapjack that would now have to wait.

It was Tom.

'Quick, Ellie, let me in. I'm on duty and I'm not supposed to be here.'

'What's up, Tom?' I asked, startled and intrigued.

'I think you better sit down.'

'The girls?' I had a moment of pure terror.

'Nothing like that, everyone's safe.'

'Tell me then. What is it?'

He guided me into the kitchen and we sat on the L-shaped sofa.

'I've got some incredible news.'

'Ye - es?' I waited for him to continue. 'For God's sake, Tom, you're doing my head in. Spit it out.'

'Connor's alive and he's in Bournemouth right now.'

I thought I'd misheard him.

'Did you hear me, Ellie? Connor's not dead.'

My stomach went into freefall. Why now? So many thoughts rushed through my brain. But I had to know one thing before I heard all the details.

'Does Johnny know?'

'No. Only Mum, Dad, Ollie and David. And you and me, of course.'

'Do me a favour and don't tell anyone else.'

'Of course, sis. Are you okay? This must be a massive shock.'

'Tell me everything.'

CHAPTER FORTY

RILEY

Luc and I sit at a long trestle table in the tea tent, opposite Aubrey and Marcia. A three-tiered silver tray is stacked high with freshly baked cakes and warm, crumbly scones. Ramekins contain mountains of clotted cream and homemade strawberry jam. It all looks incredible, but Luc and I are stuffed from our long lunch of local beer and barbeque.

'Dig in, m'dears,' says Marcia, dolloping a huge lump of jam onto her cream-smothered scone.

'Shall I be mother?' Aubrey's holding of a large brown teapot, which he's positioned over my cup. 'Nettle tea. Not too bad actually, although it is an acquired taste.'

'I'll give it a go,' I say. 'Thank you.'

He pours out a cup for us all, launching into a eulogy on the high standard of competition entrants this year. 'Della's Longhorns were outstanding. They absolutely deserved first prize. Did you two manage to see any of our rare breeds? Spectacular! I'll wager you've never seen finer.'

'It's a great fair,' I agree.

'It is, isn't it. Now Marcia tells me you want to stay.'

'Is there a guest house?' Luc asks. 'We can pay for our board.'

'I'm sure you can, but we wouldn't hear of it. Marcia's already said you're to stay at the lodge house. We have plenty of space. That's settled. Bit embarrassing, can't remember your names. Did I hear one of you say you were a Donovan? Eddie Donovan's relation perchance?'

'I'm Lucas, his son.'

'What did I tell you, Marcia!' The Mayor pounds the table with his fist and our tea jumps out of our cups.

'Aubrey! For goodness sake, watch what you're doing. You're making a terrible mess.' Marcia takes the linen napkin from her lap and starts blotting up the spilt tea.

'Yes, sorry, clumsy.' The Mayor looks chastened. 'But what a small world. He's due here in October in an advisory capacity. We have trading links with Melksham. Mayor Turnbull recommended the fellow. Wonderful, wonderful.'

'And you, m'dear?' asks Marcia. 'Your name? You must excuse our awful memories. So much going on today ...'

'Riley Culpepper.'

'Oh, my dear,' she says. 'Terrible, terrible business. I'm so sorry.'

'Eh? What's that?' the Mayor says.

'You know, Aubrey. Don't be dense.' She turns to him and unsubtly drops her voice. 'That terrible business about the girl from the Talbot Woods perimeter. We had a picture delivered from the Guards. Of the killer.'

My cheeks flush and for one terrible moment I think I'm going to cry. I've been coming to terms with everything, slowly.

But sometimes, when people take me unawares, it just sends me over the edge. I swallow hard, willing the tears to stay unshed, but I can't prevent one from running down my cheek. I'm horrified and embarrassed.

'Oh, my dear, your poor sister. I am so terribly sorry,' says the Mayor.

'Thank you,' I say.

'Would you like a hug?' asks Marcia, looking very awkward, but trying hard to be consoling. Her worried expression makes me smile and stems the unwelcome rush of emotion.

'I'm fine,' I say. Under the table, Luc takes my hand and I don't pull away.

'I don't suppose anyone fitting Ron Chambers' description has passed through here?' I ask, getting myself together.

'Not that we're aware of, I'm afraid,' says the Mayor. 'But he might have passed outside the walls. Those awful boys outside only set up their Toll this week, so he would have gone by unobstructed. Let me contact Luis, our Chief of Security. Do you know if this Chambers fellow was on foot or horseback?'

'Actually, he stole my Mother's AV, so I guess he would still have been in that,' I reply.

'A thief to boot. What a ghastly character,' says Marcia.

Twenty minutes later, a small, compact man in uniform is standing to attention next to us in the tea tent.

'Please do sit down, Luis,' says Marcia. He sits at the end of the table and opens a red hardback log book.

We all lean in to peer at the pages where they record all

vehicle and foot traffic that passes by their borders. Scanning down, Luis sees an entry that could well relate to Chambers. It states that a dark-coloured AV skirted the walls at 02.10 on the fifteenth of July. The vehicle could easily have been Ma's stolen AV. Unfortunately, it had been too dark to see who was driving, but there weren't any passengers noted.

'Do your parents know where you are?' says Marcia suddenly, looking from me to Luc with a piercing stare.

Our hesitation gives us away.

'You silly children! They must be out of their minds with worry. If my two had done anything like that ... Come with me, we're going to contact them right this minute.'

Luc and I stare at each other in a panic. I'm not mentally prepared to speak to my father just yet and guess from Luc's expression, neither is he.

'Could we contact them later?' I ask. 'Pa will be at work, and Ma isn't very well.'

'I hope you don't expect me to believe your parents would rather be working or sleeping, than hearing their child is in fact safe and sound and not dead in a ditch!' Marcia's voice becomes shrill and people are beginning to stare.

'Shall I ...' Luis makes an exiting motion with his hands.

'I should if I were you,' Aubrey replies. 'Thank you, dear fellow. Now, Marcia, let's all calm down. We'll contact the parents after the fair. You two run along for a bit and we'll meet by the bridge at six, if it's alright with you.'

'But, Aubs ...'

'Now, Marcia, a couple of hours won't make any difference.' He winks at us as we hastily leave the tea tent.

Aubrey and Marcia Rowbotham live in Lowstone Castle Lodge House, a beautiful dwelling, constructed from the same creamy stone of the nearby Castle. Like a mini castle itself, it's circular with four turrets and a tiny drawbridge.

We are now in The Rowbothams' well-used study, sitting in front of Chippenham's only radio communications device, listening to Luc's mother crying through the static. It's terrible and Luc is really shaken up. Marcia Rowbotham stands next to us, arms folded across her massive chest. I hate her for making us do it, but part of me is a little bit grateful because, without her, our parents would still be in their hellish limbo.

Guilty doesn't even begin to cover how I feel. Our initial reason for making the trip, now seems flimsy and feeble - a stupid thing to have done, especially as we've gained nothing in the way of information.

Luc's father and my Uncle Tom are on Security business in Southampton with the two choppers and will be with us within an hour. Pa is on his way back from Hook Island and doesn't even know Luc and I have been located. Luc's mother is waiting at our house in the Talbot Woods Perimeter, so she can tell Pa as soon as he returns.

It's a shock to realise we're going home and I can't believe we've been on the road for just nine days. It feels like a lifetime between now and that first early morning when we left the Perimeter.

CHAPTER FORTY ONE

Riley

Luc and I stand shivering on the Rowbothams' terrace. They've tactfully left us alone while we contemplate just how bad our imminent family reunion will be. We hear the helicopters before we see them. And now there's no escaping the serious trouble we're in.

'Jesus Christ, Luc!' Eddie shouts in his deep baritone, as he descends from one of the helicopters. They've set down in the litter-strewn field where the Autumn Fair was held only hours ago. He looks like an angry giant as he strides across the grass towards us. We walk hesitantly to meet him.

'What the bloody hell have you two idiots been playing at?' He hooks Luc's head in his arm and pulls him towards his body in a bone-crushing embrace. Then he draws me to his chest with his other arm. 'You're a pair of bloody nightmares. Don't you ever, ever put us through anything like that ever again.'

I catch sight of Uncle Tom behind him and he steps forward, sweeps me up in his arms and kisses the top of my head.

'What've you done, Riley?' He tips up my head and stares at me with disappointment in his eyes.

I lower my gaze.

'Your mother is hysterical and your Pa is angry like you

wouldn't believe. We've been worried sick about the two of you. I honestly thought you were more sensible than this. It was a thoughtless thing to do.'

'I'm sorry, Uncle Tom, but I was so angry about Skye. No one was doing anything.'

'That's because there was nothing anyone *could* do. Don't you think we explored every avenue? Tried everything we possibly could to find the killer?'

'It didn't feel that way,' I replied.

'Come on,' he said. 'I don't want to argue. I'm just glad you're safe. Let's take you to your Ma; she's dying to see you.'

Eddie has finished bear-hugging Luc and has reverted to angry-mode.

'Right, Luc, I want you in that copter now. Your mother needs to see you pronto. Richard!' he calls to one of his guards. 'You and Marco drive my wife's AV back to Bournemouth. Jerry, take Luc in the copter and hover back over the AV - make sure they don't run into any trouble.' He turns to look at me. 'Riley, you're coming with me to your grandparents' house. Your mother's having a nervous breakdown over you.'

'Dad,' Luc says. 'I need to say goodbye to Riley. There's something I have to ...'

'I don't even want to hear it, Luc. Now get in that copter and I'll see you later at home. Tom, can you get Riley settled in the other one? I've got to see the Mayor and thank him for dealing with these two. Let's hope Bonnie and Clyde here, haven't completely ballsed-up my meeting next month. I'll be two minutes.'

I realise I'm not even going to get the chance to say goodbye to Luc and I don't know how long it will be until I next see him. I'm going to Gloucestershire and he's going back down to Dorset. And I also realise that I don't want him to go. That I can't bear the thought of us being apart.

I catch his eye and smile, trying to convey what's in my heart. I smile a promise that I hug to myself and he gives me a look I can't decipher. Then he is taken off and away into the summer night sky.

On the short flight, I contemplate my situation. I started this trip with the clear intention of avenging Skye's murder, but I haven't even made a dent into locating Chambers. My reasons for leaving the Perimeter now sound feeble, even to my ears, so I know my parents won't be impressed with my explanations. I've had the adventure of my life, but the conclusion is missing and out there in the English countryside Ron Chambers has escaped justice and is probably laughing at his good fortune.

Despite the deafening whirr of blades and judder of the engine, I fall asleep on Uncle Tom's shoulder and now he's gently shaking me awake.

'Riley, darling, wake up. We're here.'

I open my eyes, disorientated. When the helicopter door opens, I feel the cold north wind hit me like a slap in the face. It feels as though it's turned from an Indian summer to an early winter, missing out autumn altogether, and I start to shiver.

Eddie places a blanket around my shoulders and leads me along a narrow lane bordered with hedgerows and tall trees. It opens up onto a small cul-de-sac with a turning circle in front of five medium-sized detached houses.

My grandparents live in the Uley Perimeter, established by Pa and Eddie at around the same time ours was built. There's nothing strange in the fact I've never visited them here before. Even helicopter travel holds its dangers and, as I said before, Pa has never been happy to let Skye or me travel outside the perimeter fence.

Our grandparents usually visit us once a year, when they use either Pa's or Eddie Donovan's chopper for the journey. If not for the copters, they wouldn't be able to visit at all, because road-safety has a whole new meaning these days, as I can now testify.

I stand in front of Grandma and Grandpa's house; an ordinary-looking Cotswold stone building with a sloping roof and a small chimney. Its wide front lawn runs straight on to the pavement with no fence or hedge to screen it from the road or the other properties. They are all there in the doorway, waiting. My uncles - Oliver and David, my grandparents and Ma, who now runs across the grass towards me.

She squeezes me so tightly and kisses me all over my face and hair, white-faced and crying.

'I thought I'd lost you too,' she weeps. 'I couldn't have borne it. I love you so much, my darling, darling girl. My baby.' Then I'm completely enveloped, as my uncles and grandparents come to greet me.

'I'm sorry. I'm so sorry,' I sob.

'Hush, you're safe now, that's all that matters,' Grandpa soothes.

Eddie Donovan stands to one side of us, tactfully waiting until the initial emotion of our reunion has simmered down.

'I'll be heading back now, Eleanor. You take care.'

'Eddie, thank you for bringing my baby back safe.' Ma kisses his cheek and they hug briefly.

We wave goodbye to him as the copter spins upwards and away.

Uncle Tom, Ma and I follow everybody else into the brightly lit house. Ma looks meaningfully at her brother and he stares back at her with an unreadable expression. Then Ma leads me through to the cramped sitting room where I get the biggest shock of my life. For there, sitting on the edge of a faded terracotta sofa, in my grandparents' house, sits a person I have never met, but whose face is tangled up in my brain like a tumour. He gazes up at me with a nervous smile.

It is Ron Chambers.

'You,' is all I can whisper.

'I think it's about time you found out the truth,' says Ma.

CHAPTER FORTY TWO

Eleanor

Tom and I sat in the kitchen while he told me Connor's story. It broke my heart to hear it. I cast my mind back all those years ago, to when Connor had been taken by the soldiers from my parents' house. I remembered the heartbreaking terror of it all. The not knowing. And now, after all this time, I was finally going to find out what had happened to him.

The soldiers had put him into one of the convoy vehicles along with several other prisoners. They were taken to Portsmouth. Once there, Connor had been briefly interrogated, thrown into jail and left to stew for almost six months, without charge.

During a spitefully cold February, they released him with no explanation. His camper van had disappeared, he had no money and he had no means of contacting anybody for help.

Weak and disorientated, his first thought was to get home to Ripon to see his parents and build some long-overdue bridges. But Ripon was miles away and he didn't know how he would get there, other than walk. Another option was to try to make his way up to Gloucestershire, back to me.

After four months of struggling on foot in freezing conditions through newly hostile territories, he reached Uley in rags, starving and barely alive. It may have been June when he arrived, but summer was slow to arrive that year.

By the time Connor reached his destination, Eddie Donovan had been hard at work and the Uley Perimeter had been sealed off from the outside world. Guards patrolled constantly and a large impenetrable set of iron gates kept the undesirables out. Connor was understandably wary of approaching the guards and lacked the energy for any sort of confrontation in his present state. The possibility of being arrested again was one he couldn't face.

He decided to pay a visit to Abigail Robbins' mansion, set a couple of miles outside the Perimeter fence. He didn't particularly relish the thought of seeing her, as he was fairly sure she was partially responsible for what happened to him. But he was out of other options. Anyway, maybe she could shed some light on why Uley and its inhabitants were now behind bars.

Abigail herself opened the door and Connor hardly recognised her. She was plastered in make-up, wearing next-to-nothing and she shook uncontrollably.

'Connor? What are you doing here? You were arrested. You look awful, skinnier than ever.'

'They let me go. What happened to you?' He didn't wait for a reply. 'How can I get into Uley?'

She laughed, a dry, hollow sound. 'You won't get in there. No one can. It's only for the privileged few. They've barricaded themselves in and left the rest of us to rot.'

'Where's Eleanor?'

'You mean you haven't heard?' She smiled a mean smile. 'She married Johnny Culpepper. She didn't hang around after you left. Legged it down to sunny Bournemouth. Now she's lording it up with her rich husband.' She paused to gauge his reaction and was disappointed to see none. 'Poor baby. Did you think she'd wait for you?'

Connor felt sick. He didn't know whether to believe her or not.

'Now I, on the other hand, am much better suited to you,' she said. 'I've got a new profession - I'm a tart, a hooker, a prostitute, whatever you want to call it. I can do you a really good deal, Connor.' She put a hand up to his cheek and stroked it wistfully.

'Where are your parents, Abi?' he asked, holding her wrist and pushing her hand away.

'Shot. They are quite dead. I live here now while my darling friend Eleanor gets to live a wonderful new life with her wonderful family. If it wasn't for me, she'd never even have met Johnny Culpepper. Now tell me, is that fair?'

'No,' said Connor as he backed away from her pathetic figure. She was crying now, slumped in the doorway. Another girl came to try and help her up. The girl shouted at him.

'What've you done to her?' Then she yelled, 'Earl! There's a tramp at the door. I think he's done something to Abi.'

Connor ran.

He spent the next six years drifting, from town to town and

from job to job. He didn't have the energy to return to Ripon. After Uley, he was too afraid of what he might find there. He put all thoughts of people he once knew, out of his tired mind and concentrated on surviving.

One day, he had the good fortune to be kicked in the leg by a beautiful black horse with a white star on its nose. He lay in the dirt on the compound floor, willing the horse to finish him off, but instead he looked up to see the concerned face of a grey-haired man.

'You alright, son? I think Cleo got you good and proper. Let's 'ave a look at that leg. Mmmm, nasty. We'll get you to the doc.'

'I can't afford ...'

'Tut, I'll sort you out. If it wasn't for this temperamental mare, you wouldn't be bleeding all over the ground would you.'

Connor gratefully let the kind man place him on the horse and lead him across the compound to the surgery. He was seen within the hour and accepted the offer of temporary lodgings with the man, by way of compensation.

Corby Chambers and his wife Irene were a kindly couple in their mid-sixties. As a qualified electrician, Corby was desperately busy. Luck and natural progression led to Connor becoming his apprentice.

And so, over the next four years, he settled contentedly in the newly walled compound of Bath, where he worked as an electrician's mate, soon becoming proficient enough to branch out on his own. He eventually left the Bath Compound with many fond memories and having made several good friends, but it was now time to move on.

After only a matter of years, Connor ended up in Dorset. More specifically, in the Charminster Compound, where he successfully applied for the position of electrician. The job came with a very nice apartment and some very interesting gossip on the lives of the rich Perimeter inhabitants.

No coincidence then, that Connor found himself in this part of the country. He had no illusions that he and I would ever regain any of our past connection, but was perversely curious as to why I'd been so quick to abandon hope he would return to me and why I'd gone back to my ex-boyfriend again. He felt angry and betrayed by me and he needed to exorcise the demons of the past.

Prior to arriving in Dorset, he decided to change his name to something that would give him more anonymity. He didn't want me to hear his name and feel uncomfortable that he was there or, even worse, feel sorry for him. Being a highly- sought-after tradesman, it was likely his name would become well-known, in whatever area he settled in and he wanted to observe me from afar, at his own pace without fear of discovery. Maybe he'd contact me in the future, but he wanted it to be on his own terms, in his own time.

He experimented with a few different names, before settling on Ron. He didn't particularly like the name, but it was the end of his first name, spelled backwards, so he felt a certain affinity with it. He chose his new surname after his two saviours - Corby and Irene Chambers who had felt like family to him. And so he became Ron Chambers.

He heard many people talk about the wealthy Culpeppers, Johnny Culpepper in particular. But after hearing all the talk, he only knew me now as a beautiful, rich lady with two pretty daughters. Then, almost fourteen years after they had last seen each other, he ran into my brother, Tom.

Tom was at the compound visiting his new girlfriend, a gardener who did a lot of work at our Perimeter. She and Tom had been a sort-of item for the past few months. It was a tricky business, trying to have a relationship with someone who didn't live within the same walls, but I think that was part of its charm - the difficulties and the dangers.

'Connor?' Tom exclaimed, as he made his way to his girlfriend's bedsit. 'It is you, isn't it? We thought you were dead, man.' He clasped Connor's arms.

'Tom? What are you doing here?'

'I live in Bournemouth now, near my sister. God, Ellie's gonna freak.'

'I heard she got married.'

'It's a long story, mate. Do you live here? Is there somewhere we can go and chat?'

CHAPTER FORTY THREE

Eleanor

Tom drove me to the compound and dropped me outside a large seventies style apartment block.

'I'll pick you up at ten, okay?'

I looked at my watch. That would give me three hours. I worried three hours would be too long. Then I worried it wouldn't be long enough.

'See you later,' I replied. 'Thanks, Tom.'

I started walking up the entrance steps, stopped and turned to watch as Tom drove out of view. I could hardly feel the ground beneath my feet and I clutched the metal handrail. I was scared and excited, but I didn't let myself think about what this reunion would mean. Was I mad to be doing this?

The apartment numbers blurred on the foyer wall. Eventually 26B came into focus and I pressed the button.

'Hello?' came a tinny voice. That familiar northern accent which made my stomach flip.

'It's me. Eleanor.'

A buzzer sounded and I pushed the heavy glass door. I walked up the stairs, almost dizzy with anticipation and nerves, stale cooking smells assaulting my nostrils. Finally I reached his floor and, as I emerged from the stairwell, I saw him standing there in his half-open doorway. He grinned. I smiled nervously back. As we gazed at each other, the years disappeared and I realised, on one level at least, nothing had changed.

'Ellie.'

'Hi, Connor.' He looked the same but different. He had filled out, turned into a man. His shoulders were broader and his face had lost its youthfulness. Thick stubble grazed his chin and his hair had flecks of grey. I wondered what he thought of me.

He put his hand on the small of my back to guide me into the apartment. His touch lit up all my nerve endings.

We sat opposite each other in a large airy lounge.

'You look good, Ellie. I missed you. All these years ...'

'I know. I thought you were ... Did Tom tell you, we thought you were dead?'

'Yeah. Abi and Sam did a good job didn't they?'

'She lied to my face. She told me you'd been shot. Killed.'

'Nice.'

'I knew she could get a bit jealous, but I'd never have thought she could be so spiteful. Vindictive. Why? What was the point?'

'Oh, she was unhappy. She wanted to spread it around; make us as miserable as she was. I saw her after they let me out. She enjoyed telling me you were happily married to Johnny.'

I coloured. What must Connor think of me ... running back to my ex?

'It's all history now though.' He stood up. 'D'you want a drink? I've got elderberry wine. It's pretty horrible ...'

I laughed. 'Thanks. I'll give it a go.' I stood up to follow him.

'Sit down. I'll bring it in.'

As I sat there, nerves assailed me. I felt sixteen again. Uncertain. Unconfident.

Connor came back into the room with two glasses. He sat next to me this time. His thigh brushing mine. The wine glasses on the coffee table, the scent of my lover returned from the dead.

'You're so beautiful, Ellie. More beautiful now. I missed you so much.' He took one of my curls and twirled it through his calloused fingers.

I couldn't speak. He kissed my eyelid, my cheek, my mouth.

Connor and I began a desperate, hungry affair. Compulsive. I had my security and comfort at home with a loving family and I had my childhood sweetheart returned to me. My pale skinned, dark-eyed lover. It was exhilarating, but uncomfortable. I hadn't realised how much I'd missed him and we did our best to try to make up for all the stolen years. We inhabited a bubble, completely separate from normal life, like stepping out of time. Our meetings had their own illicit flavour, their own shape and colour.

We chatted in his little kitchen, as a pan of risotto bubbled on the stove. He sat at the table sipping a beer.

'Remind me. How did we manage to let Bletchley and Abigail wreck this?' I asked him.

'I never liked that bitch,' he replied, stretching out his legs onto the other kitchen chair. 'You sure you don't want any help?' he asked.

'No, I want to cook you a meal. Just sit and talk to me. I really don't know how I had her as a friend for so long.' I shook out a tablecloth and watched it billow down over the table. Then I put a cream candle on the centre of the cloth and took Johnny's lighter out of my pocket to light it with. A yellow flame flared to life.

'We could've been together all those years,' Connor said, staring at the candle. 'And now we're hiding away in my apartment like criminals. We could've had a family of our own. I'd have loved to have had kids with you, Ellie.'

Another secret.

I took a sip of my beer. I hadn't meant to speak of it, and I knew it would be yet another betrayal of Johnny and his years of love and kindness, but I hated to see the sadness in Connor's eyes. And I felt he deserved to know why I'd married Johnny so quickly after his disappearance.

'Connor,' I began.

'Mmm?'

'You need to know something ... Riley. Well ... She's yours.' I hadn't meant to blurt it out like that.

'What?'

'Riley's yours. Your daughter.'

'What do you mean? She's ... Riley's my daughter? I've got a daughter?'

'After you were taken away, I found out I was pregnant. I

didn't know what to do.'

His face bleached white. He stood up, frowned, balled his fists and pressed his lips together.

'Connor? Are you okay?'

'So Johnny had her too? He had you ... and he had my child.'

'I know. I'm so, so sorry. But I really thought you had died. If I'd had any idea you were out there somewhere, alive, I would've searched for you ... I would've ...'

'I've got a daughter.' He exhaled and sat back down. The candle flickered.

'Connor ... Are you okay?'

'I don't know.' He chewed his thumb nail and stared at a point on the wall.

I felt nervous. I thought he was going to do something. Smash something up or shout or ... something. I turned off the heat on the stove and came and sat opposite him.

'Connor ...'

'What?' he snapped, then immediately looked contrite, reached across and took my hands. 'Sorry. I know it's not your fault. But I feel cheated. Like my life was stolen ...'

'I know.'

'When can I meet her?'

'I really don't think that's ... That's not going to be possible. Riley thinks Johnny is her father and ...'

'Does *he* know? Does Johnny know she's not his?'

'Yes. He knew from the start.'

'Does she look like me?'

'Yes. Very much like you.'

'I have to meet her.'

'No. She wouldn't understand. It would hurt her too much.'

'But ...'

'No.'

Eventually, he accepted they would never be able to meet. He didn't like it, but reluctantly agreed that such a revelation would not be good for Riley. We had no appetite for anything that evening. The risotto went cold, congealed and I threw it in the bin.

Connor and I continued to see each other whenever we could. Tom knew about it and, while he disapproved, he also understood the depth of our feelings and knew about the injustice that originally doomed our lives together.

A few months later, Connor secured a short-term, but well-paid job within our Perimeter. It was a word-of-mouth thing and I felt very nervous about him getting the contract with my good friends and neighbours, the Donovans. I warned him to keep his head down and be careful. I dreaded to think what would happen if Johnny recognised him.

I loved Johnny and I adored my girls, but Connor was like a drug that made me high. I could think of nothing else but my overwhelming need to be with him. It almost drove me insane to know he was working next door, but I couldn't see him.

One night, Johnny was out at Hook, the girls were asleep and I'd left the Perimeter to drive over to Connor's apartment.

We lay entwined on his bed and I still wondered at the effect he had on me, even after all these years. I felt like a teenager again, nervous and in awe. I'd been there several hours and knew I'd have to leave in a few minutes. I couldn't chance being away from the Perimeter for too long.

I stretched and sat up, but he pulled me back down towards him. I didn't resist and we lay there together for a while longer.

'You're a bit serious tonight, Ellie.'

'Just thinking.' I traced a pattern with my finger on his chest.

'Thinking about what?'

'You know what you could do ...'

'I can think of plenty of things I could do,' Connor smirked.

'Not *that*,' I laughed. 'No honestly, I've had an idea.'

He raised an eyebrow.

'If you cut a small entrance hole in the perimeter fence, somewhere out of the way, it would be easy for us to meet up.'

'You want me to vandalise your beloved perimeter fence?'

'I know it's a bit radical, but it would be worth it. It's getting really tricky for me to get out and see you. The guards are going to start gossiping and I'm worried someone here will recognise me.'

'Hmmm.'

'Oh I know!' As we lay there talking, my idea took on more shape. 'You could make the hole next door ... at Eddie and Rita's. The Perimeter backs onto their garden. You're working there anyway. It would be easy and they're away all the time ...'

'Hang on,' he laughed. 'Slow down. Do you know what would happen if they found me doing that? They'd put a rope round my neck.'

'How would they ever find out? You could make it right at the back of the garden, behind the poolhouse, behind all the bushes. No one would ever see it.'

'I don't know, Ellie.'

'It could be an entrance you could crawl through to meet up with me. It would be romantic, exciting.' I flashed him a pleading smile. 'The poolhouse is the perfect place to meet.'

'God, okay, okay.'

'Really?' I squealed.

'Yes. But on one condition.'

'What?'

'Stay here tonight. For at least a couple more hours.'

'I can't, Connor. You know I've got to ...'

'Oh well. Deal's off.

'Grrr. Okay. But they might notice I'm ...'

'Stop being so paranoid, woman.'

'Can't help it.' But I shivered in anticipation of another two hours in the company of my lover.

'Now come here and kiss me.' His rough fingertips softly tilted my chin up towards him and all thoughts of home were obliterated.

I am ashamed and horrified at my selfishness, but I was in a blind whirlwind of rekindled passion. That's what I keep telling myself anyway.

CHAPTER FORTY FOUR
Eleanor

'Here, look,' I whispered. 'This is perfect.' I picked up a large stone and placed it just inside the fence, next to the hole.

Connor had managed to disable the electricity and cut out a small section of fence at the back of my neighbours' garden.

'I'll be able to leave a note for you under the stone, with a date and a time. And then you can crawl through to meet me.'

'I might not always be able to make it though,' Connor said.

'Well same here. But we can try.'

'Can we try now?'

'Eddie and Rita are away, Luc's training today ...'

'Anyone else?' he asked.

'Nope. The poolhouse is always unlocked. There's a nice comfy sofa ...'

He grabbed my hand and led me through the trees towards the poolhouse.

The Donovans always let me know when they would be away, so it was easy for me and Connor to meet up. Sometimes he'd be there and sometimes he wouldn't. Sometimes I would be so desperate to see him, I'd get Tom to cover for me and I would drive over to the compound. But it was dangerous on all sorts of levels, and the risk of being discovered increased.

One summer evening, Johnny was out working as usual. He wouldn't be back until early morning. I felt bored, restless. I couldn't settle to anything. The girls were in their rooms. I felt caged in. I didn't feel like an adult with responsibilities. I didn't feel like a parent. I had a yearning to do something fun and reckless, like going out partying or getting drunk, or ...

I went down to the annexe to see Tom.

'Hi, Sis. What's up?'

'Bored.'

'What are you? Twelve?'

'Ha, very funny. I'm serious. I might go and see Connor.' I walked past him, into the kitchen and sat at the table.

'Don't.' He closed the front door and followed me in.

'Johnny's out. The girls are in their rooms. It won't hurt.'

'You need to end it, Ellie. It's going to wreck everything. End it or come clean.'

'I know, I know. It's just ... It's complicated. It's Connor. Oh, it's not fair.'

'You're right, it's not fair. But what about Johnny? What about the girls?'

'I know. I'll end it.'

'You said that before.'

'No. I mean it. I'll end it tonight.' He raised his eyebrows and I felt scepticism radiating out of him.

'I will.'

'You should.'

I stood up and headed back towards the front door. My heart

beat excitedly at the thought of seeing him. How could I possibly end it? I'd think about it. I ran back home and shouted up to the girls that I'd be at Tom's if they needed me. Then I jumped into my AV and started up the engine.

Charlie Duke's disapproving stare followed me out, as I drove through the Perimeter gate.

'Miserable old git,' I muttered. I turned left and was immediately blinded by the full glare of the dying evening sun. I quickly flicked on the windscreen filter, muting the sharp rays. A muffled thud startled me and my heart sank as I saw a dark figure lying by the side of the fence. I didn't stop, but slowed down and glanced in my wing mirror.

'A man.' I breathed out and realised I'd been holding my breath for quite a time. I sucked in a lungful of air and made brief eye contact with him in the mirror as he lifted his head. I must have hit him and I felt a lip-biting pang of concern. But everybody knew you didn't stop for anything outside the Perimeter. People had been killed before, doing just that. In fact it was a common trick used by muggers to get people out of their vehicles – they'd pretend to be hit and then attack the concerned driver.

I'm sure he'll be okay. I reasoned, convinced and then banished my already stretched conscience.

I suppose I should have turned back and asked one of the guards to check him to see if he was okay, but I didn't. I drove to see Connor and left my girls home alone. I returned, safe and sound, to Tom's annexe by five am. By the time I got home,

Skye was already dead.

My baby was dead and it was my fault. Mine.

A knock at my bedroom door. *Go away*, I thought. *Leave me alone.*

'Ellie,' a whisper. 'Ellie, it's me. Tom.' I heard the door brush across the carpet. Johnny and Riley were downstairs somewhere, living their own personal hells. I was curled up in my bed living mine.

'Ellie, I'm so sorry,' Tom cried. 'I can't believe it ... Skye ...'

'It's my fault.'

'Don't be ridiculous.'

'It is. If I hadn't gone out ...'

'If you hadn't gone out, Skye would still have left the house. You'd have been asleep. You wouldn't have heard her.'

'Luc found her,' I said. 'They're saying it might have been Luc.'

'Well that's crazy. But things have changed ...'

'What? What's changed?'

'Connor's been arrested. They're saying it was him who killed her. They found a hole in the fence and ...'

'Oh my God,' I hissed. 'No! That was nothing to do with ...'

'Ellie!' Tom bent down and grabbed my arm. I was sobbing again. 'Ellie! That hole?'

'Yes!' I said. 'Yes!' I almost shouted.

'Shhh! For God sake keep your voice down.'

'Yes, we made that entrance so he could come and see me.'

'You idiot! What were you thinking?'

'I know. It's a mess. I've made a mess of everything.'

'Too late for all that. They're going to execute Connor.'

'No! We have to get him out. You have to get him out, Tom.'

'I know,' he sighed. 'Give me the keys to your AV. I'll sort it.'

We sent Connor to lie low at my parents' place in Uley. They had always been fond of Connor and were overjoyed to see him alive and well. They didn't know he was also Ron Chambers, wanted for murder. They didn't know he was my lover. They didn't know anything.

But I eventually had to tell Johnny everything and this betrayal, on top of Skye's death, was more than he could take. He said he thought it would be a good idea if I left for a while. He said I should go away and think about what I wanted - meaning Connor or him.

I couldn't believe he was still prepared to accept me after all I'd put him through. I sobered up quickly and went home to see my parents and Connor in Uley. To decide what to do next. The worst part was leaving Riley behind. I knew she was disgusted with me – first for the drinking and then for abandoning her.

When I got to Uley, I did a lot of thinking. And although I now lived in the same house as Connor, I hardly saw or spoke to him. Everything had changed. I had changed. I realised what I'd done and I felt ashamed, disgusted. I will always blame myself for Skye's death, and the guilt now constantly plucks away at me, like a warped discordant guitar. But I welcome it.

The guilt is something I deserve to live with.

CHAPTER FORTY FIVE

RILEY

My world shifts and spins. My life shatters into a million lies. Ma has just told me the truth. The ugly, unadulterated truth. A truth which makes me want to vomit or scream or cry or fall into a mind-numbing sleep for a century. I stare from her, to Chambers, to my lap. And then I raise my eyes back to her with disbelief and something bordering on hate. She sits next to me on the sofa. Chambers sits opposite. I feel his stare.

'It can't be true.' A tear drips onto the back of my hand and I wipe my cheek angrily. 'Why would you ... How could you be so deceitful? What about Pa? Poor Pa ...'

Ma stands up, her face drawn. I see her look desperately into Chambers' eyes and I want to slap her. 'Connor,' she says. 'Would you mind ... leaving me and Riley for a few minutes?'

'Yeah. Sure.' A soft voice with the trace of an accent. He stands up and leaves the room without looking at me.

Coward, I think. *My biological father* ... I get up and walk away from Ma, over to the sofa that Chambers has just vacated. I don't sit down. I turn and stare across at my mother. Who is this woman? I don't even know her anymore.

'How could you do that to Pa? I thought you loved him. He adores you.'

'I know.' She's crying now. 'I know. I've got no excuses. I was wrong and I've paid the price for it.'

'We've all paid the price for it,' I snarl. 'For your *affair*. Oh my God! I can't believe it!' I feel my emotions spiralling out of control. 'How could you let me go on thinking it was Chambers who killed Skye, when you knew …' My voice cracks and breaks. I try to steady it. '… When you knew it wasn't him. You should've confessed to everybody there and then. You should've told everyone you're a … you're a …' But no matter how disgusted and hurt and angry I feel, I can't call Ma any of the vile words that are crashing around my head. I just can't.

'I'm sorry,' she sobs. 'I'm so, so sorry, my darling girl.'

'Does Pa even know?'

'Yes, yes. I told him everything. And I still love him. He's my life, Riley. You and he are *everything* to me.'

'Well, obviously not.'

She flinches. 'What can I do?' she asks. 'How can I make this right? For you.'

'You can't,' I say. I don't want to be so harsh, but I can't help it. I want to inflict hurt. To make her pay. Even though I see she's devastated. Repentant. Broken. 'So what are you going to do?' I ask.

'I'm coming back home.'

'Does Pa want you back?' I'm outraged and hurt on his behalf.

'Yes.'

'You know I don't want anything to do with that man.

Chambers or Connor or whatever the hell his name is. I don't even want to see him. He's nothing to me.'

'He's your biological father, Riley.'

'I have a father and it's not him.'

'Okay,' she says. 'God, I've really messed this up. I shouldn't have told you. It's just, I didn't want to have any more secrets.'

'I wish you hadn't told me. That's a secret you should've kept to yourself. I'm going out.' I leave the room.

'It's late! It's dark out there! You don't know the area ...' Ma's voice follows me into the hallway.

I hear other voices coming from another room, but I ignore them. Ma follows me into the hall, but I open the front door and slam it behind me. The night air hits me like a freezing slap, but I like it. I want to feel cold and uncomfortable. To shiver. I run down the road, away from the cul-de-sac of houses. I cross the wide road at the bottom of the hill and see a large deserted playing field in front of me. The kissing gate squeaks as I push it open and sidestep through.

I sit on the wet grass, my arms wrapped around my knees, too exhausted to think. I stay there until I can no longer feel my fingers and toes and can't stop my teeth from chattering.

Uncle Tom finds me before sleep does. He drapes my shoulders with a blanket and helps me up. 'Come on, you,' he says. 'It'll be okay. Come back to the house. Connor's gone. You need to sleep. It'll be okay, I promise.'

I let him soothe me and together we walk back up to the house.

CHAPTER FORTY SIX

RILEY

Luc's waiting for me down at Coy Pond. Pa told him I'd be back this afternoon. Only four days have passed since I last saw him back at the Chippenham Compound, but it may as well be four years, what with everything that's happened.

I now realise that I may never find out who killed my sister. That Luc and I were chasing a lie. A dead end. Someone out there knows who did it, but I will probably never know the truth. I'll have to learn to accept that.

It's a crisp autumn morning and the colours are bright and heavy – dying leaves against a deep blue sky. The sun's power has diminished, like it's here but wants to leave.

I'm nearly at Coy Pond and I'm nervous. Will Luc still feel the same way about me? Will it be okay? Or will things be awkward and weird? I've had too much sadness and anger and uncertainty in my life recently. I need something good. I need to see if I can be kind to myself.

I walk down the crumbling stone steps and crunch my way along the gravel path. After only a few seconds, I see a figure up ahead – Luc. He's sitting on a mossy wooden bench, wearing jeans and that grey hoodie he looks so good in. My heart lifts and flips. As I draw closer, he glances up and grins, getting to his feet, and I forget my earlier doubts. I know instantly that everything's going to be alright.

I smile as we walk towards each other. My heart is pounding. After everything that's happened, at least I still have this ... I have Luc.

'Hey,' he says.

'Hey.'

Somewhere close by a blackbird sings. Luc takes my hand and as we walk along the gravel path together I feel the faint sparks of hope.

* * * * *

EPILOGUE

He was in his early thirties, but had the look of someone far older. His clothes were dirty and worn, his once fair hair was thick and darkly matted and he was limping quite badly. Holding onto his left shoulder as he hobbled along, you could clearly see the overgrown, filthy nails on his right hand, the back of which was a mass of scratches.

But more distressing than his overall appearance, was the fact he was a grown man sobbing out loud in unashamed misery. Snot and tears collected in a wretched glob on the side of his chin and he angrily wiped his grimy sleeve across his face, adding a clump of black dirt and grit to the mixture. *How did I get here?* he asked himself. *Once upon a time I was happy, loved, on top of the world and I'm, starving, aching and bloody miserable. Nobody even knows I exist.*

Jamie had been on his way to the compound in Boscombe. The girl at the Poole Shanty had told him about it. 'They're looking for cheap labour,' she'd said, 'and they're taking on outsiders.'

The girl was gorgeous in a short-haired pseudo-soldier sort of way. He didn't think she'd be living on the outside for long. She was about nineteen he reckoned; not yet worn down by the grinding harshness of life on the outside. Feisty and tough - he knew it was a necessary armour and he also knew through all that spikiness, she liked him.

This was just the spark he needed to gee him up a bit. Most people he came across were horrible and it was a relief to have a laugh, pretend things weren't as bleak as they actually were.

He'd tried to act disinterested, but all the time, he was contriving to meet up with her accidentally on purpose at the Boscombe Compound, which was where she was now headed with her pig-ugly friends. To avoid appearing too keen, he watched her leave the shanty, waited a day and then left to make his own way there.

Then that stupid rich bitch had smacked into him with her AV. She'd looked at him in the wing mirror and he'd instantly known she wouldn't give him a second thought - *would never stop for a nobody like me.* He supposed he should be grateful she didn't have shock plates, but she'd really banged up his leg and his shoulder didn't feel too good either.

How was he supposed to make it to Boscombe now? He'd never catch up with the girl again either. She'd said she was going to see what Boscombe had to offer and then she thought she might head up to London.

Yeah right, he'd thought, but had been strangely buoyed up by her optimism. Okay, well more buoyed up by her tongue ring and what she'd said she could do with it. And now that opportunity was gone and he was injured badly and why couldn't anything ever just go right for him just once? More tears escaped. *I'm just a low-life, no-hoper, snivelling loser*, he raged silently to himself.

To rub salt in the wound, Jamie was currently limping outside one of Bournemouth's most prestigious areas, The Talbot Woods Perimeter. He took care not to get spotted by the guards who patrolled the inner fences. There was no way for him to get inside anyway so they'd probably just ignore him, but he couldn't face any sort of confrontation tonight.

Through the humming electrified wire, he glimpsed the mansions which sat grandly in gardens landscaped to the max. Each one had its own distinctive style and its own fancy security system, no doubt.

'Tossers!' he shouted ineffectually. It was more of a strangled sob and it kick-started a bout of coughing. *God, I'd kill for a well-brewed beer*, he thought.

It was a warm evening and he sweated in his filthy sludge-coloured T shirt. He'd tied his grubby stained jacket around his waist and his feet sweltered in worn out leather boots. He wished he had sandals, but these boots were the only pair of footwear he owned, and they were ready for the scrap heap.

It was getting dark now and he realised he'd have to find somewhere to sleep soon. He didn't allow himself to look in at the lighted windows with their scenes of rich domesticity. He used to lose himself in fantasies of this nature, but it was way too painful and completely pointless; he was no masochist.

Jamie was hungry, starving in fact. Then he remembered the homemade berry bar the old lady had given him yesterday at the shanty. She said he reminded her of her dead son (morbid old cow) but that he looked like he could do with a decent meal. Predictably, she invited him to eat lunch with her family and he accepted immediately. This was nothing new; he often aroused motherly instincts in women. It was a natural gift, like having a good singing voice or being a good kisser.

The food she'd prepared had been bloody awful, but it had filled a hole. The only thing on the menu that tasted any good was her berry cake, which he had raved about, in the hope she would give him some more. When he had said his goodbyes, she slipped a wrapped berry bar into his jacket pocket and told him to take good care of himself. Now, when he reached into his pocket for the bar, it wasn't there.

'What?' He had been saving it. Building himself up to enjoying its moist oaty sweetness. Now finding it gone was just another kick in the teeth. He checked his other pockets. *Maybe I put it in my bundle*, he thought, knowing full well he hadn't, but deciding to check anyway. He untied the piece of thin canvas material he used to carry around his few possessions. Every day, he meticulously checked it for holes as he'd lost items before, where some creature had nibbled through the material. He spread it out on the uneven dried earth and sifted through his belongings, but the bar wasn't there either.

It was in my pocket, I know it was. This was rapidly turning into a disastrous night. Then, it dawned on him he had probably lost it when the AV had knocked him flying. He wasn't too far from where it happened and so he decided to turn back and search for it. If he didn't, he knew he would end up dreaming about the damn thing.

He limped back with his eyes glued to the ground. It was almost dark now and he cursed the woman who'd knocked him down. Finally, he saw tyre marks, not far from the gates, where the vehicle had skidded to a halt earlier this evening.

'Right, where are you?' He scanned the track and the surrounding area, but he couldn't find it. It could have gone flying in any direction. He combed the area, straining his eyes, but the bar had been wrapped in a large green leaf, tied with twine and, if it wasn't out in the open, it would be nicely camouflaged in its leafy surroundings.

Jamie pulled back a small bush, crossly, not expecting to find what he was looking for, when suddenly, he spied it lying in a clump of weeds, right by the fence.

'Yes!' He laughed out loud, feeling ridiculously happy at this small triumph. Then he frowned, as he noticed a gaping hole in the electric fence, right next to his berry bar. He snatched up the bar and put it back into his pocket, ensuring he buttoned it closed this time. Then he examined the hole. It was big enough for a person to climb through, as long as they were careful not to touch the electrified sides. Should he? Shouldn't he?

* * *

Fourteen year old Skye lived next door to the gorgeous Luc Donovan. She thought his house was the nicest on the Perimeter. During the last few weeks, she'd occasionally snuck out of her house late at night, to meet up for a laugh.

He always started off annoyed, but he never told her to go home straight away. He'd have a game of cards with her or a swim, before saying her Pa would kill him if she kept coming over at night without permission. She ignored his protests and just laughed at him, calling him a chicken and a wimp, although this was miles away from what she really thought.

Skye had decided to meet him again tonight, and this time she'd make it crystal clear how she really felt about him. He'd have to be blind not to realise anyway, she'd dropped enough hints for God's sake.

Pa had been out working on Hook Island all night and had gone to bed, tired out, at about one thirty. Ma was next door at Uncle Tom's. She must've crashed there for the night. Riley had gone to bed ages ago and she always slept like a log.

Skye had her own rooms in the warren-like attic on the second floor and she loved the higgledy piggledyness of them. She'd also started to appreciate the bonus of having her own separate staircase which led almost directly to the back door. The only thing she had to be careful of was Woolly making too much noise. She knew he wouldn't bark at her arrival, but his claws made an awful clattering racket on the old wooden floors as he twirled around and around in a mad frenzy of greeting.

Luc was delicious - seventeen, dark haired and popular in an 'I don't care' sort of way. Even her parents loved him. Both sets of parents were really buddy-buddy and they were always going on group family picnics together or visiting each other's houses for barbeques, parties, Christmas drinks and stuff. However, Skye knew their parents would go ballistic if she and Luc started seeing each other, not least because Skye was only fourteen.

Skye guessed Luc had a bit of a thing for Riley, but he hadn't a hope of getting anywhere with her, as Riley always set her sights on older, harder to obtain boyfriends. Skye thought she was mad. Luc was the fittest bloke in the Perimeter, if not the whole of the country.

* * *

Jamie chewed his lip as he looked at the hole. He'd get drafted, beaten up or shot if he got caught, but this was too good an opportunity to pass up. It was fate. What treasures might he find on the other side? At the very least, he might find more food, or a comfy place to sleep. That decided him. He would sleep in relative safety tonight, away from the scavs and muggers and he'd set off for Boscombe in the morning.

Taking off his coat, he maneouvered it and his bundle through the hole first. Then he made himself as small as possible and squeezed his way inside, ignoring the sharp pain in his injured shoulder and tensing his body, fearful of getting a shock from the fence.

Safely through, he shrugged his jacket back on and found himself surrounded by fruit trees and manicured shrubs and bushes. He yanked a small golden apple from a low bough and

put it into his pocket. Then he picked a tiny under-ripe plum and took a bite, spitting it out in disgust at the sour taste.

He was obviously in someone's garden, some rich person's garden by the look of it. He saw a large white timber summerhouse in front of him. It was octagonal in shape and he crept closer to investigate. The summerhouse, or poolhouse, sat about twenty feet away from an Olympic-sized swimming pool, its underwater lights casting a dancing glow around the area. He could see the main house the garden belonged to. It was more mansion than house and was miles away from where Jamie stood staring. No lights were on.

He turned back to look at the poolhouse. It had round blue glass windows, set into each of the eight sides, like portholes. The door had a white wooden frame with a stained glass window depicting scenes of picture-book sailing boats on stylised waves under a blue sky. A generator hummed and Jamie deliberated over whether or not to break the glass to gain entry. But he hesitated, worried about alerting the guards and strangely reluctant to destroy the tranquil scene.

It stirred a distant memory of his childhood that made him feel oddly nostalgic. He rolled his eyes at his own sentimentality and half-heartedly tried the wooden door knob, before preparing to smash his elbow through the door. But to his surprise, he turned the knob and the door opened.

Jamie smiled in disbelief and gave a low whistle. 'Yeah, I could cope with a bit of this,' he said out loud.

It was a poolhouse, but most people would have been proud

to have it as their main residence. The door opened onto a lounge with comfy looking furniture. Next to the lounge, was a luxury shower room, sauna and a small kitchenette. Jamie did a little dance over to the fridge, forgetting the pain in his leg for a moment and, oh my God, ice cold beers.

He was sure now that he'd died when the AV had hit him and he had been transported to a heaven invented just for him. He pinched himself hard. It wasn't even cheap home-brewed beer, it was the almost-extinct foreign stuff.

He popped the cap, using his fist and the hardwood coffee table, then he downed half the bottle in one greedy slurp. Nectar, ambrosia, liquid paradise. His head fizzed and his body relaxed. He lay on one of the striped sofas, sighing as he took the weight off his injured leg. Draining the bottle, he opened a second and began tucking into a party-sized packet of crisps that lay on the table. He hadn't eaten crisps for half a lifetime. He tasted artificial flavourings, combined with excessive salt and his taste buds went crazy.

Sod the berry bar, he thought, beer and crisps are the way to go. I'll just finish these and then I'm going to try out the shower, get some hot water on my poor neglected skin. He smiled to himself and wriggled comfortably into the sofa. Before long, he was asleep.

* * *

Skye was most definitely upset. Luc had as good as rejected her and she felt stupid and humiliated. He had unconvincingly faked tiredness and gone back to bed, but she could tell he wasn't really tired, tired of her more like. She allowed a few tears to fall and kicked her legs half-heartedly against the side of the pool. She knew she should probably go back to bed, but a small spark of hope within her thought maybe Luc would change his mind and come back out to her.

She sat there for ages, dangling her legs in the water, until she realised she was shivering. She was freezing cold in fact. She swung her legs out of the pool and stood up stiffly, deciding to warm herself up with a hot shower in the poolhouse.

She'd have to pretend tonight hadn't happened. She couldn't have borne it if she and Luc were no longer friends and so she decided she'd have to wait a while before she made a move on him. It was probably her age putting him off. Once she hit sixteen, he would declare his undying love for her, she was sure of it.

Skye opened the poolhouse door and walked through the darkened lounge, to the large, tiled shower room. A strange, stale smell permeated the air, but she only noticed it on the edge of her consciousness, she was too preoccupied with her thoughts. She pulled the shower room light switch, stripped off her bikini and stepped into the large glass octagonal shower unit. The hot water felt amazing on her cold, clammy, prune-like skin and she stood there for ages, letting the water heal her tender heart and her bruised ego.

Reluctantly, she turned off the jets and reached for a towel, feeling suddenly exhausted and longing for her bed. Then she froze. What was that? She heard a thud, like something falling on the floor, followed by ... a snore?

'Hello?' she tentatively called out. Who would be sleeping in the poolhouse?

She tiptoed into the main room in her bare feet. It was dark, but light shone into the lounge from the shower room. She made out the form of someone unfamiliar lying on one of the sofas. Before she could stop herself, she gave a scream, instantly waking the person from their illegal slumber. It was a man, an outsider from the look of him. Wild-looking, filthy, with matted hair and now she had unwittingly woken him up.

* * *

Jamie must have fallen asleep, because the next thing he knew, he was awoken by a high-pitched scream. He jumped up, quickly realising where he was. Years of travelling around strange, inhospitable places, had meant his mind was always finely tuned to his surroundings, whether awake or asleep.

He saw a young, naked girl backing away from him, groping around for her towel, which lay on the floor. The light from the shower room made him blink and he tried to refocus. He felt oddly fuzzy and strange, realising he must be slightly drunk.

'Listen!' He tried to think how he could stop this girl from landing him in trouble. 'I won't hurt you.' But his voice sounded gruff and hoarse, even to his own ears. The girl started to scream again. She wrapped the towel around her and tried to run past the sofa, where Jamie stood. He grabbed at her, to stop her from leaving.

'Calm down,' he said, catching hold of her wrists, so her towel dropped onto the floor again. His damaged shoulder burned with the effort of holding her. She had a great body, but he wished she'd shut up. He was thankful the main house was set so far back from here, but any of the guards could walk past at any moment and hear her screams. He finally managed to get a hand over her mouth which she promptly bit, pushing him away from her with her one free hand.

'Jesus, you bitch,' he gasped, as her teeth sank into his flesh and a searing pain flashed through his already throbbing shoulder. She ran towards the door, picking up his bundle of possessions to try to cover her nakedness. At least she'd stopped screaming for a second.

'My stuff!' he shouted and lunged towards her to try and grab his bundle back. She yelped and dropped the bundle. While he was reaching down to retrieve it, the girl grabbed an empty beer bottle from the floor and smashed the bottom of it against the wall, holding it in front of her, like a weapon.

'Don't come any closer,' she trembled, 'or I'll slash you.'

'Look,' said Jamie, raising his hands, but still holding onto his possessions. 'I was just sleeping here, but I'll go. I don't want any trouble. Just let me go. I won't hurt you.'

But the girl was backing towards the closed door and, if he didn't stop her escaping, she'd alert the whole perimeter and then he'd be done for. He calculated the distance, dropped his bundle and lunged towards her, finding his hands around her slim, white throat. She slashed up at his chin and he felt a stinging pain as he saw his blood drip down onto the wooden floor. But he pushed her back at arm's length, so she couldn't reach his face with the bottle.

The problem was he was doing her some serious damage - she was choking. Finally she was forced to drop the bottle, to try and prise his hands from around her neck, and so at last he could release her, shoving her away from him. But the force of this push sent her flying backwards into the door, crashing through the stained glass window and clutching at her throat, her eyes bulging in her head.

The noise was terrific and Jamie expected half the Perimeter to come running at any moment. She sat there, inside the empty door-frame, in shock, covered in splintered wood and coloured glass. They stared, dazed, at one another.

'I'm sorry,' Jamie looked down at the naked, gasping figure. She was bleeding all over from hundreds of tiny glass cuts and, with the fragments of stained glass, her white skin looked like it was encrusted with sparkling precious jewels.

'I didn't mean to hurt you. Are you okay? Stupid question. I have to go. I can't get caught here, they'll kill me. You'll be alright.' He was panicking. She seemed okay to him, just a bit shocked and messed up.

He heard a small creaking sound and looked up to where it emanated from the top of the door frame. She followed his line of vision upwards, tipping her head back, just in time to see a large shard of blue glass sky fall out of the frame and drop, with deadly accuracy, into her throat.

Her eyes moved downwards and locked onto Jamie's, they widened momentarily. She opened her mouth and tried to speak but, instead, warm blood frothed from her lips. She fell backwards and lay awkwardly across the door frame, half in and half out of the poolhouse. The glass shard still protruded grotesquely from her throat and blood pumped from the wound, quickly pooling around her lifeless body.

'No,' he exhaled as he realised she was past saving and he had better get as far away from there as he could. He gathered up his blood-soaked bundle and the remaining contents of the fridge, scanning for anything else that may be of use to him.

He decided to break the habit of a lifetime and travel by night. He would aim to reach the Boscombe Compound as soon as he could, hopefully before dawn, although it would be tough going with his banged up leg. If anyone asked, he would say he spent the night outside Boscombe's walls.

Hopefully, the girl from the Poole Shanty would already be inside the Boscombe Compound and he'd charm her into accompanying him to London. He'd make something up - the promise of a great job once they got there, or something. He didn't plan on ever coming back.

* * * * *

THE CLEARING

Book Two in the Outside Series

Is coming January 15th 2013

Other titles by Shalini Boland:

HIDDEN (Marchwood Vampire Series #1)

THICKER THAN BLOOD (Marchwood Vampire Series #2)

A SHIRTFUL OF FROGS

~

ABOUT THE AUTHOR

Shalini Boland grew up in Gloucestershire but now lives in Dorset with her husband and two young sons.

www.shaliniboland.co.uk

CPSIA information can be obtained at www.ICGtesting.com
Printed in the USA
LVOW12s0126141113

361095LV00002B/106/P